M000011607

LION'S LEGACY

LION'S LEGACY

L. C. ROSEN

**UNION
SQUARE
&CO.**

NEW YORK

**UNION
SQUARE
&CO.**

NEW YORK

UNION SQUARE & CO. and the distinctive Union Square & Co. logo are registered trademarks of Sterling Publishing Co., Inc.

Union Square & Co., LLC, is a subsidiary of Sterling Publishing Co., Inc.

Text © 2023 L. C. Rosen
Art © 2023 Colin Verdi

All rights reserved. No part of this publication may be reproduced, stored in a retrieval system, or transmitted in any form or by any means (including electronic, mechanical, photocopying, recording, or otherwise) without prior written permission from the publisher.

ISBN 978-1-4549-4805-6 (hardcover)
ISBN 978-1-4549-4806-3 (e-book)

For information about custom editions, special sales, and premium purchases, please contact specialsales@unionsquareandco.com.

Printed in the United States of America

Lot #:
2 4 6 8 10 9 7 5 3 1
unionsquareandco.com

Cover and interior design by Marcie Lawrence

For every queer kid out there who feels like they have no history and no legacy.

And for Tom and Jo, for teaching me that we do.

The skeletons stare at me from across the moat, waiting. If you'd asked me, even two days ago, if I believed that reanimated skeletons, their joints tied together with ribbon, were possible, I would have said no. Even with everything I've seen—the pit traps and rolling boulders, the ancient mechanisms that somehow still functioned, the scepter that controlled fire—I would have drawn the line there. But now I have to say, I'm a believer. You sort of have to believe in a thing after it spends hours trying to kill you.

"Dad . . . the bridge is getting lower," I say, trying not to sound too panicked, and failing. We're currently on a man-made square of an island. On one side, across the water, is the rest of the lost temple we've come through to get there—and the skeletons. They make strange hollow clanking noises as they bang together, teeth chattering, their hands reaching out for me. I have a gash on my shoulder where one got too close. They can tear us apart. The ribbons waver along with their movements, making them blurry, as if they're covered in rags. They don't go in the water, though. The water dissolves their ribbons, and the skeletons fall apart.

We came out here via a big wooden bridge that drops down from a device in the ceiling. It lowers for a few minutes, then rises for a few minutes, back and forth, like a pendulum. And right now, it's not swinging in our direction: it's lowering. We just made it across last time it came down, but the skeletons were far enough behind they didn't make it. But this time there's nothing stopping them.

"Dad . . . ," I say again. I turn around, focusing the camera I'm holding to film him instead of the skeletons. He's kneeling in front of an altar, a brightly colored lacquer box on top of it.

The box has a puzzle wheel for a lock—a complex image broken into different rings he needs to rotate into place to make the image line up and open the box. But he doesn't know what the picture is supposed to be.

"Almost, Tenny . . . ," Dad says, carefully turning one of the rings into place. "Almost . . ."

There's a small click, and he pulls the top of the box open. Inside, laid in an indentation, is a katana. It gleams in the dim light of the torches. It has a white enamel sheath and an intricate hilt, but we don't have time to admire it as the bridge has now reached arm height and the skeletons are clamoring onto it and toward us.

"We have to go," I say to Dad.

Dad looks behind us and sees the skeletons and nods. He grabs the katana and unsheathes it, tossing me the scabbard. "Let's hope the legends are true," he says. On the side of the small island opposite the bridge are stairs that lead down into the water. We don't know how deep the water is, but it's nearly black, and if there's a shore on the other side, we can't see it.

Dad runs down the stairs and holds the katana in front of him, then cuts into the water with a few quick strokes. There's no splashing, though. Instead, the blade carves, like a knife into soft wood. The water freezes like cut glass where the katana has sliced it. Pieces of it go flying and hover in the air, crystals rotating. And in front of us, a small valley through the water. It's clear, but too dark to see to the bottom. It must go very far down. Dad has made a path in the water. Carefully, he puts a foot on it.

Behind us, the bridge falls into place. I hear the hollow beats of the skeletons' footsteps charging us.

"Come on," Dad says, now stepping fully onto the path he's carved through the water. It holds him. It shouldn't be possible, but then, neither should the skeletons. I run forward and step onto the water with him. It feels like walking on Jell-O that bounces under my boots. Dad slices through the water again, carving us a path farther and farther forward, away from the skeletons. I film it all, then turn around to film our pursuers. They've stopped at the water's edge. They don't know if they can use the path. Neither do I. But I don't want to find out.

"Faster," I hiss.

We keep walking forward as Dad carves the water. Around us, the room is made of old brick, covered in moss, low enough to see the ceiling but with the walls far enough out they're hidden in darkness. Carefully, I reach into the water on either side of us, the parts Dad hasn't carved. Still liquid. Still deep. And freezing cold.

I look behind us. A skeleton is mimicking me, carefully placing its hand on the carved water. It doesn't go through. It doesn't dissolve the little ribbons holding its bones together. "Dad," I say.

The skeleton steps onto the path. It holds him.

"Dad, they can walk on it, too. Faster!"

3

Dad glances back and sees the skeletons on the water. He starts carving faster. The strange, crystalized bits of water fly out as he keeps running forward. We don't know where we're going, but we know what we have to get away from.

Dad keeps slicing and I stay close, sometimes turning back to check how near to us the skeletons are. Closer every time. This could be it. Our last adventure.

"Dad!" I scream.

"I see land," Dad says, and points. In the distance is another stone shore, stairs leading out of the water onto an island like the one we were on. He starts carving faster, heading toward it. Behind us, the hollow clanking of bones is closer.

"We need to jump," I say.

"What?" Dad says.

"We'll swim. They can't follow."

"Tenny, how can I swim with this katana? It'll cut the water up. You know physics well enough to tell me what'll happen?"

He knows I don't. I'm a high school freshman. I haven't even had physics yet. "Then carve faster!"

"I am!"

The skeletons are quicker, though. I look behind us. They're a swarm of bone and ribbon nearly on us. But then I hear something. The sound is growing quiet. I tilt, looking behind the pursuing skeletons. There should be dozens of them, but there are only ten now. Enough to tear us apart, but where did the others . . . behind them, the path is gone. Water again. Okay, that's something. We have options now:

4

1.   Hope Dad carves fast enough that we reach the end and can climb up those stairs, then push the skeletons back into the water. Hope they don't kill us before or during that particular battle.

2.   Swim to shore. Sword might cut the water, Dad might sink lower on one side, lower and lower as he keeps swimming, cutting, until he's at the bottom and the water above him turns liquid again.

3.   Turn and fight the skeletons now. Not my favorite.

4.   Something that uses the best of everything.

I shrug my backpack off, put the camera around my neck, and dive into the water.

"Tenny!" Dad shouts. "What are you doing?"

"Keep carving!"

Dad keeps slicing into the water as I swim. I can hear the skeletons rushing closer and closer to him. Shore isn't far now, though. I'm a good swimmer, I made sure of that after that water trap in the Mayan temple. I reach the stairs and turn around. The skeletons are practically on top of Dad.

"Throw the katana!" I shout.

"What? We'll lose it!"

"Throw it! At the water! Then dive in!"

Dad looks behind him as a skeleton grabs at him and pulls his backpack off. He shrugs out of it before it can pull him back. Then, his face grim, he throws the katana at me and dives into the water in one motion. The katana spirals through the air like a comet, coming closer, closer . . . Finally, it lands in the water near me, the blade hardening the water as it hits, the hilt clinking as it reaches the surface. It stays. I reach forward and pull it out, like King Arthur.

Dad is swimming for me, and the skeletons are standing confused on their little crystal island. I film it as the carved water gradually turns back to liquid, and the skeletons silently fall into it.

Dad walks up the stairs, sighing, drenched. He cocks an eyebrow at me.

"If you knew the katana would hold in the water like that and not sink, why'd you dive in first?" he asks. "I could have thrown it and we could have dived in together."

"So I could film it," I say.

Dad grins, then starts laughing. He puts his arm around me and hugs me close. "I love you, Tenny," he says. "You're a genius."

I laugh. "I love you too, Dad."

Relief floods over me. We have the katana. We are out of immediate danger. We did it! We found the legendary Misumune katana, the water-carver. We navigated a lost temple filled with traps, riddles, and supernatural monsters. And we had a damn good time doing it. I keep laughing, and so does Dad. I know it's a release for both of us, all the anxiety flying out of us in the sound of joy. He keeps hugging me. I keep hugging him.

"We gotta find a way out of here, though," Dad says.

"I just hope there are no more skeletons," I say. "That's all I want."

"Same here, Tenny." He takes the flashlight that hangs from his belt and shines it forward. "Hopefully this isn't long. Our rations were in my bag."

"And the extra flash drives were in mine," I say. "We only have, like, an hour of time to film left."

"Camera okay?" Dad asks.

"Yeah," I say, holding it up. It's small, waterproof, shockproof. Good quality. There were a few more in my backpack just in case, but this one seems to have held up.

"Lose any footage?" he asks.

I check my jacket pocket. The memory card is still there, enclosed in a watertight plastic case.

"Nope," I say.

"Okay, then let's see where this leads."

He shines his flashlight ahead of us. The stone platform we're on narrows into a hallway leading forward. Only one way. We march ahead.

It's a short walk, only twenty minutes, and no traps or skeletons on the way. We're wet, and shivering, but I don't mind it because I can feel we've reached the end. We found the sword. We just need to follow this path to the exit. But at the end of the tunnel, the hallway is blocked by a waterfall. A waterfall with an odd smell.

Dad stops before walking through it, holding out a hand to block me. "Acidic," he says. "We walk through that, our skin melts off."

"Great," I say.

"It is," Dad says, holding up the katana with a grin.

I smile and lift the camera. Dad poses, showing off, before slicing a door through the waterfall. The water—greenish now, I see—solidifies under the sword's touch, creating an arc of solid water. Dad kicks it down and it shatters like glass. In front of us is a way out.

"Quick, before it goes liquid again," I say. We rush through the open space and find ourselves in a large circular chamber, the walls carved with beautiful patterns. Above us is a slatted roof that lets in fresh air and moonlight. I look back at the waterfall, which comes out of a slit in the wall. Where the water was carved it just stops, the flowing water curving around it into the rest of the liquid parts. The waterfall ends at the floor and then seeps into two metal drains on either side. It's beautiful. I make sure to get a slow shot of it. Then I turn around and get the whole room. The producers are going to love this.

At the far end of the room is a ladder, bolted to the wall, leading to freedom.

"We could have just come in this way?" I ask.

"Well, we would have had to get through that acid bath somehow," Dad says. "I guess with modern technology, we could have . . . but what would be the fun in that?"

He turns and winks at me—well, at the camera—then heads for the ladder. We climb. It's pretty high, and at the top is a grate. But, of course, it's locked. There's a wide opening, too large for a key, in the wall. I carefully film, clinging to the ladder.

"I know this one," Dad says. He takes the katana and inserts it hilt first into the opening.

There's a click, and the grate above us pops open.

And then we're out. We climb up and into fresh air. The breeze smells so much better than the stale air of the temple below us. I look out over the tiny island we're on. It's so small it doesn't have a name, barely five miles in any direction. No one has lived here in centuries. No one wants it, either. It's mostly rock and some wild sheep. It's miles west of Nemuro, just outside Japan's borders. International waters. Dad had liked that for some reason.

"Let's go find Toma," Dad says. "I feel like we're south of where we went in."

"That feels right," I say.

We start walking. The ceiling of the room below us is underfoot, but it's covered with grass and leaves. I would never have noticed the holes in it until we were on top of it. And besides, all the clues led to the entrance of the temple. No shame going in the front door, I guess, since we made it out. But it feels a little silly that we probably could have avoided the skeletons if only we'd done a full survey of the island when we landed this morning.

We walk for about twenty minutes before we spot Toma and his boat, right where we left them. Toma is sitting in a folding chair on the shore, his small yacht parked out in the deeper water, an inflatable motor raft next to him onshore. He has a fire going and a portable speaker out, smooth jazz playing from it. When he hears our footsteps, he looks up and grins when he sees us.

"You got wet," he says.

"But we found it," Dad says, holding the katana aloft.

Toma whistles. "I didn't think it was actually real," he says. He stands up and walks over to Dad, staring at the katana. I step forward and look too, filming it. I hadn't really had a chance before, but now I can see it up close. The Misumune family crest is on the sheath, and the handle is carved bone or ivory, made to look like waves. It's beautiful. Mrs. Misumune is going to be so happy when we give it to her. She's this nice old lady whose ancestor owned the sword, and she helped us find it by letting us go through all her stuff while she brought us cookies and tea. She told us stories too, about her ancestor, and how supposedly he held off an entire flood that would have destroyed their village. Now we know how.

Though that part won't make it onto TV. Dad always says no one would believe the magic we've found, and if they don't believe the show, then they won't believe the history. I mean, we leave some of it in— the cut waterfall will probably stay. Stuff that people might think is weird old mechanisms or tricks. People believe in that. Not so much the magic. He'll probably say the skeletons were mechanical, and only show their shadows. He's good at that, been doing it for years. He started out with just a little handheld camera and videos uploaded to YouTube, but his know-how propelled it bigger—now we're on a streaming service with fancy network producers. Dad is careful about what he sends them, though. Always at the edge of believable. And he makes sure not to bring a crew along—they can't be trusted. Plus, the unpolished handheld style is the show's trademark.

"It sliced through water, too," Dad says to Toma, rotating the blade in the light. "Just like the legends."

Toma laughs. "No way," he says.

"Tenny's got the footage," Dad says, walking past him to the raft. "We were chased by living skeletons." That's Dad testing, seeing what people will believe, what to put in the show, what to keep just for us.

Toma turns to me, his face skeptical.

"They weren't very welcoming," I say. Later, Dad will probably leak some of the real footage online, get people talking, theorizing. "Keep the truth illusive," he says, "and people will watch to find it."

I don't love that part, but I think he's right about the magic being too unbelievable. Even if it is real, it never feels it. Like right now, I feel like I'm in on a joke. Skeletons held together with magic paper. It's absurd. But the katana is real. Its history is real. And I want people to see that more than I care about whether they believe in magic skeletons.

We load the chair and boom box onto the raft and take it out to the yacht, where Dad and I shower off and change into the clean clothes we'd left there with our regular phones and wallets, while Toma pilots us back to Nemuro. I use a satellite uplink to set up my computer and upload all the footage from the camera into the cloud. Dad can cut stuff later and organize it to send to the producers. They have editors who will turn it into a good show.

And then I lie down. I'm so tired I can feel it in my bones . . . no, no, I don't want to think about bones now. I just want to . . .

I wake up when Dad shakes me. We're docked in Nemuro city. I rub my eyes as we step off the boat. The sun is just rising and the fish markets along the docks are all opening up, men bringing in their haul. It smells like the sea.

It's not a big city, not by my native New Yorker standards, but it's got the vibe that small coastal cities have. Big sky, ocean everywhere, people who look gruff but are actually friendly. We spent a day here before we left. There are some beautiful views and this cool arch sculpture. But I'm glad to be going home. I miss New York. I miss Mom.

Dad pays and thanks Toma and then we start walking back to the hotel. As we walk, Dad takes out his phone and calls someone. Probably one of the producers.

"Yeah, we got it. Oh yeah, it's a beauty. People are going to want to study this, draw it, absolutely worth a whole touring exhibition, like last time. Same deal, I go where it goes, talk about the find."

I frown. It sounds like he's talking to his broker. I'm never involved in this part of it, but I know Dad has a guy who reaches out to collectors and funders who will buy the stuff he finds for museums and helps set up exhibitions. Dad never talks to me about all that, it just sort of . . . happens? But this sword belongs to the Misumune family. We met them. They helped us find the temple by showing us some old scrolls and one gorgeous kimono that had a secret message in the pattern. We shouldn't be selling it through a broker. We should be giving it back to them.

"Dad," I say. He ignores me, keeps talking.

"Well, yeah, whoever is willing to pay the most," he says into the phone, holding up a finger at me, telling me to wait.

It's not like with the scepter we found in the treasure cave outside Paris. There was no family there. I mean . . . it should have stayed in France. And it did. The Louvre found an investor who bought it.

I stop walking. Dad keeps going.

I've never thought about it before. What we find. I've always just loved the adventures, the thrill, being with Dad. And yeah, it's kind of fun being on TV. It's not a big show, but it has fans. I get fan mail. Hate mail since I came out, too, but more fan mail.

But . . . the stuff we find. I stare at the katana. Dad has it slung over his shoulder. The Misumune family crest gleams on the sheath. The mask we found in the Mayan temple in Guatemala—our first adventure—where did that end up? I take out my phone and search.

It's in the Smithsonian, in DC. That isn't right. It should be in Guatemala, shouldn't it? It's their mask, after all, their culture. Did they sell it to the Smithsonian? Is it on loan? I check the website, but there's no information.

I look up. Dad is way ahead of me, still on the phone, and I hurry to catch up.

"That much?" Dad is saying. "Wow. Yeah, that's a nice profit."

"Dad," I say. He holds up a finger again. "Dad!"

"Hold on." Dad sighs into the phone. "Tenny, you're fifteen, you ought to have better manners."

"Why are you talking about selling the katana?" I ask. "You told Mrs. Misumune we'd bring it back."

Dad raises his eyebrows. "Well, sure, back to the world. Back into the light. This way she can see it. I'm sure whomever ends up with it will want to talk to her, maybe borrow that kimono, have her talk—"

"But it's hers," I say. "It belongs to her family."

Dad scrunches his eyes like he's going to laugh. "Maybe hundreds of years ago, but you can't expect me to give it back to her because she has, like, a few genes in common with the guy who originally wielded it."

"But—" I say. Dad holds up his finger again and goes back to the phone.

Mrs. Misumune was nice. She was old but loved talking to us through the translator Dad had hired. Told us all the family stories. About her ancestor, but also about her grandkids' art projects, too. About how her daughter had recently told her she was a lesbian and it had taken time, but family was important to her, and she'd learned about queer people, and now she marched in pride parades. She gave us tea and let us poke through her things. I took hours of footage with her, and she signed the release forms without asking for a thing, except that we bring back the sword. She said she wanted to see it. See her family legacy. And now we're just . . .

"Okay, talk later," Dad says into the phone, and hangs up.

"Dad, we promised."

"Tenny, come on, she didn't really think she was going to just bury this in the back of her closet like her old photos and kimono," he says. "She just wanted to see it."

"I don't think that's what she meant."

"Tenny, listen, this is a museum piece."

"Isn't that her decision?" I ask. I can feel myself getting hot, like I do when I'm angry. Usually, it's with Mom, though. I never fight with Dad. We're too busy in temples, on adventures.

"And what about the mask we found in Guatemala?" I ask.

"What?" Dad asks, confused.

"The mask we found. Why is it in DC? It's not American."

"Well, no," Dad says. He stops walking. We're outside the hotel now. "But they paid the most through a patron who bought it to donate to them so they could put on a real exhibition. No museum in Guatemala was going to do that."

"But it's a Guatemalan artifact," I say. "It's part of their history."

"It's Mayan," Dad says. "What is this even about?"

"We should give the katana to Mrs. Misumune," I say, crossing my arms. "That's the right thing to do. If she wants to donate it to a museum, it's her choice. Or we should at least ask her."

"Uh-uh, if the Japanese government finds out we brought it to Japan, there'll be all kinds of legal holdups, UNESCO might get involved."

"UNESCO are the good guys," I say. I'm sure of that. I've visited plenty of heritage sites with Mom.

"There are no good guys or bad guys here," Dad says, his voice rising. "I'm doing what's best."

"Best for who? You?" I'm shouting now. People on the street are politely trying not to stare.

"Best for history, Tenny. These objects need to be protected, put places people can see them. The people with the most money can do that."

"But how can people get money if you keep stealing what should be theirs from them?"

Dad's face goes cold as stone.

"Stealing?" he asks. "You think I'm stealing?"

"Well," I say, swallowing. "If we go into another country and find some historically significant object and then just leave with it . . . or if we have something"—I gesture at the katana—"and we know who it belongs to but sell it to someone else . . ."

"It belongs to us now," Dad says. "We just spent weeks looking for a temple—years if you count all the research *I* did before that—and then we went to it, made our way through traps and killer skeletons to bring it back. Who else could this possibly belong to? If Mrs. Misumune wanted her family sword back so badly, she should have gone and done that herself."

"But, Dad," I say. He's really angry now. I've never seen him like this. I can feel myself starting to cry. "It's . . . not right."

Dad rolls his eyes. "I knew I shouldn't have brought a child with me. If you don't want to be a part of this, Tennessee, you can just find your own way home."

And then he turns and walks away. I know I'm not supposed to go after him, so I don't. Instead, I go into the hotel. I still have our keys. I walk up to my room and wait for him to come back. The sun goes up, then down. I keep waiting.

TWO YEARS LATER

❧ ONE ❧

What I love about Fridays is my first period is free, so I can come in late. And yes, that means sleeping in, which is nice, but better than that, it means when I walk to school, Greenwich Village is already awake. Most days it's people in suits on their way to work, or other teenagers going to school like me, but everyone is still groggy, things are still getting set up.

But on Fridays, the city is fully awake by the time I walk to school. And one of the best things about New York is that you can vanish just by turning a corner. Walking to school, I'm not Tennessee Russo anymore. It's the thing I've loved the most since I left Dad's TV show two years ago. If anyone recognizes me, they don't say anything. I'm just some kid.

Well, some queer kid. The pride button on my backpack at least labels me that much. Which I love too, because as I walk through the Village, I see other queer people and there's like this link between us when we recognize each other. Two butches nod at me like we're friends. A twink with a group of college kids, two of whom are fighting loudly, gives me an eye roll, and I know exactly what he means: straight people, oy. I'm glad to be gay, glad to be part of whatever weird little network I'm in, glad to have a family, even if I don't know them.

I have Mom, sure, and I love her and she's great, but it's not the same. And Dad . . . well, when your dad walks away from you in Japan and you find your own way back to the hotel and then he doesn't call for a day or answer his phone and you're completely alone in a foreign country so you have to call your mom to buy you a plane ticket home and you still haven't heard from him, and maybe he's dead or maybe you're dead to him and you don't know until a month later when he emails you with "Want to join me at the unveiling of this katana?"—after something like that, your dad doesn't really count as family anymore. Especially when you haven't spoken since then. Sure, there was the apology email when I didn't respond to the invitation—"I know things got a little heated and you had to make your own way home, but that's nothing compared to the ruins we've explored, right? I knew you'd be fine, but I'm sorry if you were worried"—but I didn't respond to that, either. Even if I wanted to. Still want to. But I have this family now that's better than Dad. This weird family of neighborhood queers I've never spoken to, and then at school, I have my friends, and David. David, whom I've dated for a year and a half. David, who saw me alone in the cafeteria and didn't just stare and whisper, talking about me on TV, talking about how I came out on TV. He came over and said hi. And he asked me out. And he gave me my first kiss a week later, tilting my chin up to his with just his finger. He introduced me to all his friends—the Good Upstanding Queers, they call themselves, because they all want to be lawyers and politicians and stuff, so they always behave themselves. As opposed to the other queer table in the lunch-room, who can sometimes be a bit much.

And a month ago David told me he loved me, and I said it back, and we had sex for the first time.

David and all his friends—our friends—they took me in when Dad abandoned me, when I hadn't even been at school in a few years because of the show and didn't know anyone. I could have been that freak ex–child star, but they made me part of their family. Way more than Dad is.

Which is why I'm glad to see David standing by my locker when I get to school. I smile and walk up to him. He's so handsome— tall, sandy blond hair, bright blue eyes, wide shoulders, and a broad stomach, which I think is so hot. He's wearing a polo and cardigan. It's December, and the school never feels warm enough, so we have to layer up. And he always dresses like he's an adult already, which I like. Nothing casual or lazy, he says. He helped me pick out my entire wardrobe.

But he's not smiling when I smile at him. And when I go to give him a kiss, he pulls back. I can feel myself immediately break out in a sweat, and not just because I still have my peacoat on. Something is wrong.

"Ten," he says in a heavy voice that tells me it's about me, too. About us.

"David?" I ask.

"Can we talk?" Those aren't good words, either. My brain tries to figure out what it could be. We're breaking up because of something I did? I haven't done anything, though. And he loves me, right? Maybe he's sick. Dying.

I nod, and he pulls me into the bathroom down the hall.

"What is it?" I ask, and the words tremble a little, which I hate. I've faced off against the reanimated dead, but my boyfriend wanting to talk to me makes me so scared I can't even get a word out right.

"So . . ." He swallows. "Two weeks ago, Brandon and I met up at his place for the science project we're paired up on, you know? The bio thing?"

He pauses and I realize I'm supposed to respond, even though I don't like this already. Brandon is another of the Good Upstanding Queers. He's red-haired and pretty and wants to be a reporter. David is still looking at me, so I nod.

"Well . . . one thing led to another. And we kissed."

There it is. There was one time my dad and I, in a treasure cave in France, had to run from a rolling boulder down this long hallway. Those words are like a boulder dropping and coming toward me. All I want to do is run. But he reaches out and grabs my wrist.

"I'm sorry," he says.

I take a deep breath. I can forgive this. This is nothing, right? "Well, if it was just a kiss—"

"It wasn't," he interrupts. "It was at first, I mean. But then . . . it was more."

"Oh." The boulder is closer and closer.

"And . . . the thing is, Ten. I really like him. I think . . . I'm so sorry, but . . . I want to be with him. I have been with him. We've kind of been dating since then . . ."

22

And now the boulder has hit me. It never did in that temple. Dad saw an alcove and pulled me into it, and the huge rock rolled by us and we laughed with relief. It looked great on the show, too. But this is what it would have felt like to get hit by it, I know. This is what it's like to be thoroughly crushed, every breath pushed out of you, every muscle popped, every bone shattered by more weight than you were ever meant to handle.

"So . . . sorry," he says. He lets go of my wrist. "I'm breaking up with you."

I nod. "I got that." I feel myself starting to cry but hold it back.

"Just . . . don't make a big thing of it, okay. We should stay friends, right? We are friends. And you're friends with Brandon, too. It's just . . . a little shifting, right? We're the Good Upstanding Queers. We're not drama queens. We're not going to make a big deal of it, right?"

I nod again, just so he'll leave.

"Good. So, still friends. I'm glad you're handling this so well . . ." He pauses, and I feel like I'm supposed to say something again, but this time I don't. "Okay, well. See you at lunch."

He leaves and I finally let myself cry for real. Just bawl for a moment, my face collapsing like a landslide. I take out my phone and text Daniela. She's my best friend aside from David, another of the Good Upstanding Queers.

TEN

> David dumped me
> He cheated on me with Brandon and now he's leaving me for him

I wait a minute. She's probably still in class, but Daniela is an expert at under table texting.

DANIELA

Oh thank god he finally told you

It's like being hit with a second boulder. You'd think there'd be nothing left to crush, but . . .

TEN

You knew?

DANIELA

We all did
I'm sorry Ten ♥
But it's better this way
Now we can all just go back to normal

They all did? "All" must mean every one of our friends. Not the whole school, right? And no one told me. They all just . . . watched. Laughed, maybe?

TEN

Everyone knew?

DANIELA

Don't worry about it

> We all think it was tacky of David to cheat
> But they'll make a cute couple, and we'll find you
> someone new
> No drama, or people won't take us seriously,
> right? That's our motto 😮

I stare at the messages for a minute without responding. So many people want me to respond and all I can give them is silence. Normally I'm good at decisions. I see options in front of me like lists, and I can choose one quickly, and once I'm in, I'm in. But I don't see options here. What options are there? Respond with "sure thing, no drama"? I'm supposed to what . . . just smile when David drapes his arm around Brandon at lunch the way he always did to me?

They've always been like this. They don't want to be seen as bad gays—too dramatic, too slutty. The other queer table at the lunchroom is loud and messy. Everyone is always sleeping with everyone, they make out in hallways instead of just exchanging kisses. They dress loud. They *are* loud. Teachers don't love them. But they love us. No drama from us.

Not even, apparently, when it's warranted.

The bell rings. I rinse my face off and make my way to class. Thankfully, I don't have classes with any of our Good Upstanding Queer friends today. I'm in the AP History class, a double period, which none of our friends is in. They thought that was so cool. That my wanting to be an archaeologist, like both my parents, was cool. They never asked about my dad, about the show, though they knew. Everyone was so nice. So classy. So polite. But I guess that's not the same as being kind.

I manage not to cry, but I barely take anything in, either. We're talking about ancient India and I want to say something about the century-old queer sculptures at Khajuraho that I learned about during my internship at the museum, but I can't bring myself to raise my hand. Same in math class. And then it's time for lunch.

I walk into the cafeteria and immediately realize it was a mistake. It's like looking at a pool of water and thinking it's not going to be that cold but then you dive in and it's freezing. I can't do this. I can't just sit with everyone and pretend I'm cool, that it's normal. I don't want to be the one to cause drama. I know that'll just make it worse. I know if I start something, make people choose sides, then they'll all side with David, because I'll be the one causing the drama, and that immediately makes me the loser. Even if this is all because of what he did. All because of his choices. But I don't want to lose my friends.

So I walk in and grab a tray and some lunch, like I always do. Then I turn and start walking toward our usual table, also just like I always do. They're all sitting there, talking, laughing—just like they always do.

Except David is next to Brandon. He has his arm around him, just like I knew he would. But I can do this, right? I can be the bigger person.

David looks up. Our eyes meet.

He smirks.

And suddenly, I realize, I have options.

1. Turn around, walk out. David sees this and feels like he's won, something, somehow. That he's the mature one and I'm the one being a drama queen about this.

2. Go sit down with them, act like nothing is wrong. Everyone will be happy, but David and Brandon will think what they've done is okay. That I'm okay with it. I'm not.

3. Go make a scene at the table. No one will ever talk to me again. I still have half of junior and all of senior year to get through.

4. Something totally unexpected.

I don't smile, but I make it seem like I don't even see them. I walk right past the table, then down the aisle two tables and sit down next to Gabe. He's cute, with dark skin that's almost blue where the light hits it. He's also kind of the opposite of David, with a pink fro-hawk that's grown out a few inches, and pierced everything, including holes in his ears you can put a finger through. He's wearing a tank top even though it's December. The tank top has a naked man riding a gun on it.

"Um, hi," Gabe says. The rest of the table turn to look at me. The Bad Queers. Some look confused. Some look happy I've joined them. They're not actually bad. I'm kind of friends with some of them, or think I am? Wish I was more. When did I become such a snob? When did I accept that my table at lunch was "good" and this one was "bad" just because David said so?

"Hi," I say, smiling at the table. Then I turn to Gabe. "Wanna make out?" I ask. I know the answer is yes. Gabe has been flirting with me for over a year. He knew I was with David, but that never seemed to bother him.

"Sure." Gabe grins. "When?"

"Now," I say. "David cheated on me. You don't mind being used, do you?"

"Not at all," Gabe says, lunging for my face.

It's weird kissing someone who isn't David. David's kisses were always forceful, demanding, but Gabe's kisses feel more searching. Curious. I guess that's because we've never kissed before. His tongue darts softly between my lips and I open my mouth more, accepting. He wraps his arms around me then, holding me tight, one hand sliding down my lower back. I wrap my arms around him, too, and squeeze his ass. I can feel him grin when our mouths meet again. After what feels like enough time, I pull back.

"Well, you definitely got his attention," says Lexi, one of the other Bad Queers. "He's staring bullets at you."

I don't turn and look. I can feel my heart go a little faster. I don't care what David or Brandon thinks, but I hope Daniela and the rest of them aren't going to make a thing of it. I hope I haven't just gotten myself kicked out of the only queer community I really know.

Maybe option four was a bad choice. That's the thing. I know my options—doesn't mean I always pick the good one.

"You okay?" Gabe asks. He puts his hand on mine and it feels so much more intimate than what we just did. I pull my hand away and make myself smile.

"Absolutely. And thanks," I say to Gabe, "for letting me use you."

"Anytime," Gabe says. "Maybe you'll be around over break?"

"Maybe," I say, giving him a look I hope is coy. At least he likes me. Someone does. I look around the table, and people are smiling at me, not glaring, not rolling their eyes, the way they would be at my usual table. Maybe I'm a Bad Queer, too.

Okay, probably not. I'm literally dressed in a blue blazer. But . . . "Can I eat with all of you?" I ask.

"Sure," Gabe says. The others nod. I take my lunch out and we all eat and talk, and sometimes Gabe runs his hand up and down my spine, which makes me shiver but in a good way. I don't look back even once, but when lunch is over and I'm sitting down in English class, I glance at my phone. I have one new message from David:

DAVID
Real mature.

I delete it, block him, and smile.

❧ TWO ❧

The rest of the day, I see some people staring. Lingering looks of pity, some of confusion, a few guys checking me out. Mr. Robertson, the chem teacher, gives me a look of sympathy, which is super embarrassing for both of us. It all makes it worse, honestly. Maybe sitting with the others, kissing Gabe—maybe that was all stupid. Burning a bridge. Who am I friends with now?

Walking to my internship after school usually fills me with the same kind of feeling as Friday mornings. That feeling of queers all around me, of feeling like I'm part of something bigger. But today, it's like I can't quite connect. And that makes me even sadder.

David never got that feeling, which I still don't understand. We argued about it. He always said there was no difference between being gay and straight, aside from who got us horny. But there is. It's why the grumpy drag queen outside the place that sells sunglasses winks at me, it's why I feel a little less alone when he does, and it's why when I get to the Museum of History and Culture, in the East Village, and check at the desk who I'm assigned to today, I'm not surprised to see the name Anika Phan. She's the only queer curator—visiting for a year from the Schwules

31

Museum in Berlin, a museum devoted entirely to queer culture. She latched on to me the moment she saw my pin. It's like a secret handshake.

I check my phone in the elevator as I ride up to the top floor where Anika is working. Texts from Daniela:

DANIELA

> So, you're with Gabe now?
> That's so great!
> I'm glad you rebounded so quickly and we can all go back to normal
> I mean, he's not who I would have picked for you but he's great for a rebound
> It's okay he's a little slutty

I raise an eyebrow and type back:

TEN

> Turns out David was a little slutty, too.

DANIELA

> Oh, this is like a revenge thing?
> Well, good thing we're about to go on break
> You can get it out of your system, and everything can go back to normal by New Year's

I roll my eyes and put my phone back in my bag as I step off the elevator. The top floor is divided into one large gallery and a big staff room where people do research and prepare shows. I swipe my card to get into the staff room. Anika's big show before she leaves is going to be May through July, and it's called *Pride Before Stonewall: Queer Art from Around the World before the 1960s*, which is both an idea and a title she told me she immediately regretted. I didn't understand why at the time, but now I know: it's just too much history. Too many pieces. Too much context. I'm thrilled to be learning it all, but it's also a lot of work. Good work, though. Kind of reminds me of research with Dad, but then I remember Dad so I try not to think about it.

"Good, you're here," she says, looking up from her computer.

She has this faint German accent that makes her sound kind of mean, but she's actually extremely cool and part of me turns sad working on this show because it's going to be the last thing she does before she leaves. "Bertholet agreed to lend us the Utamaro, but I am not sure where to put it."

"That's great," I say, throwing my bag down. The Utamaro in question is an eighteenth-century Japanese print she's wanted since she started putting the show together with a title I can't bring myself to say aloud in front of my mom. I hadn't even known stuff like that existed before I started working on this show. And, yes, the print absolutely makes me blush to look at, but knowing that this was art from across the world and literally hundreds of years ago makes it important to look at. Makes me proud of it, I guess? So much of my own history as a queer person, and I just didn't know it. Even me, with two archaeologist parents. When I told Anika that, a month after we started working together, she nodded and looked kind of sad.

"Queer history is always being erased," she said. "That's why it is so important for queer historians to demand it is kept alive. Like through this exhibition. I want all the queer kids like you to see how vast your history is. How you're part of something just as old and epic as any other kind of history. Far older than American. Not your Indigenous peoples, of course, but the country. Queer people have been around much longer than the United States. And you spend how many years learning that in school? And none on queer history." She shook her head and looked at me. I was crying. I'm kind of too much sometimes. Then she hugged me.

"It's okay," she said. "I had to learn it all myself, too."

Getting assigned to Anika might be one of the best things that's ever happened to me. "You don't want to put it with the Asian section?" I ask, leaning over her desk to look at the computer screen. There's a blueprint of the gallery and little images of the art she moves around on it.

"I keep thinking it should be with the erotica for . . . well, obvious reasons."

"Yeah," I say, trying not to blush. "Maybe a transitional piece? Do the sections connect?"

"The erotica section is here, remember?"

I nod. She's putting it in an alcove with a curtain to account for "puritanical American morals."

"So it can't really transition," I say. "You have to go through the curtain."

"Yes!" she says, suddenly realizing something and quickly moving the pieces around on-screen. "We put it opposite the curtain. The first thing you see as you walk in. And we put the Asian section here, around the curtain on the other side. Perfect. Thanks, Ten."

"I didn't do anything," I say.

"No?" She looks confused. "I suppose not. But thank you anyway."

I roll my eyes. "What am I working on today?"

"You're helping me write up some of the plaques for the pieces," she says.

"Helping?"

"Fact-checking and proofreading."

"Ah, the boring parts," I say, half-joking.

"That is what it is going to be for a while, kid." She raises an eyebrow at me. She wears big square glass frames and a severe black bob. She's also wearing a scarf, a navy one today with a pattern of gold stars. I gave her a trans pride pin and a pride pin like mine to wear, but she never does. I think if they were like nice enamel or something instead of plastic she might? But maybe pins in general just aren't her thing. She keeps them on her desk, though.

She hands me some printouts of plaques—the kind that say the name of the piece, artist, date, and some of them have nice little paragraphs Anika has written about them, and why they're important. There are only a few typos, but checking the official names and dates is the boring part as it means cross-referencing with the official logs in the computer and then double-checking with other official databases. And it's always right anyway. I don't think Anika has ever made a real mistake. I check as she sends emails following up with other museums, asking them to loan her pieces for the show. We work quietly, contentedly. It's boring, but it takes up all my brain. David is gone.

Well, almost gone, I guess.

"So," she asks suddenly, after about a half hour. "Any plans for the holidays?"

"Just Hanukkah at home," I say.

"With your mother?" she asks, her voice going up oddly at the end. She's met my mom. She's come for dinner, and they talk on the phone. I flinch as I realize it. She's figured it out.

"Yes."

"Not doing anything with your father, though?"

I sigh. May as well get it over with. "Who told?

"I'm deeply ashamed I didn't figure it out sooner. I just thought Tennessee was a more common American name."

"It's not." I sigh. "Mom just loves Tennessee Williams." One of the big advantages of puberty is that I look pretty different at seventeen than I did at fifteen. On the show, I'm like a stick figure, still baby-faced. And since I have Mom's last name, I can sometimes get away with people not recognizing me. It means people at the museum haven't asked about it, which was great. Here I was doing archaeology, sort of, but real work, and it was like I could do it without Dad. Like I wasn't haunted by him.

"I watched the show, you know," Anika says. "My friends and I in Berlin, we would get together every week."

For some reason, hearing that is like a jolt of electricity in my veins.

"Why?" I ask.

"It was exciting!" she says, turning and grinning at me.

"But . . . you're a real historian, a museum curator. You should know—what he does . . . it's . . ."

"Yes." Anika nods. "Your father is a thief. I hope you don't mind me saying that."

"Not one bit. That's exactly what he is. That's why I left."

"When you left, they said it was just because of school."

I shrug. "I know." I'd let them use that lie because I didn't want more drama, more emails. I just wanted to remove myself from it.

"But it was still fun to watch! You and him, hunting artifacts!"

"Yeah, but—"

"My favorite was season two, 'The Treasure Cave of Amaro Pargo.' I thought you were going to die. Honestly. The fact that your mother let you go with him amazes me."

I'm used to people saying that. It amazes me, too, sometimes. But I have a prepared answer, back from when I did the occasional interview. "The first time I went without her permission, so from then on she just made me promise to be careful and carry a satellite phone," I say quickly. Everyone is always most surprised by that. Not my father's knack for finding trap-filled tombs to raid, or how we kept surviving. Just that Mom let me go starting right after my bar mitzvah.

"Still. All those traps, the one with the pit especially. And those old technologies you found, amazing that they held up, but what if one day they didn't and exploded?"

I nod. I don't want to get into how some of them were even more terrifying than just old tech.

"I don't know why you kept doing it."

"Because it was fun," I say. I'm grinning, I realize. I stop. This is the problem with talking about the past: I remember how much I loved it. Then I miss it. "I know it's danger and chaos and rooms filling with water until we solve a puzzle, but . . . it was fun, too. Adrenaline, I guess."

And when I miss it, I miss Dad, too. Despite everything, I miss him, and I feel guilty for missing a thief who just left me and vanished. Then I feel angry at him for everything he did. Then I get angry at myself for missing all of it anyway. It churns in me, all these feelings. It always makes me cry, too, which is so stupid. I don't want to cry. It just . . . happens.

"Fun?" She shakes her head. "Well . . . it was fun to watch. So I guess that makes sense."

"And then I realized he wasn't giving these artifacts back to the people they belonged to and instead selling them to whichever museum paid the most. That was . . . not cool." I can feel the emotions pressing out from inside me now. My face feels warm, my hands are clenching.

She frowns. "I'm sorry, should I not have said anything?"

"It's okay," I say. "I haven't seen my dad since the end of season four." I do the math in my head—season four was actually my third season, when I was fifteen. "Two years ago. A little more. Apparently once I started questioning the ethics of what he was doing, he didn't want me to be his cameraman and co-star anymore."

"Well, you did the right thing," she says. "And you got to have adventures most of us only dream of."

"Yeah," I say. I'm grinning again. I make myself stop, again. "Still. I wish he was, like, a good person."

"He seemed like a good person on the show. Aside from the stealing, I mean."

LION'S LEGACY

"He is," I say. "No, that's not right. He's a good dad. But a bad person. Does that make sense?"

"When you came out to him . . . that was a really special moment, you know."

I do know. I remember it, remember the emails I got after, the message boards, the outpouring of love. Hate, too, but so much love.

"Yeah. He said we could cut it from the footage we sent the producers to turn into a show, but"—I pause, trying to figure out how to say it—"he did it right, so I kept it."

"'Thank you for telling me,'" Anika quotes my dad's speech. "'And I love you, never doubt that. Queer people have been around for centuries, since the beginning of history—in every culture in the world, no matter how much they try to hide it. In many cultures, you would be considered special, a god, even. Don't ever doubt that, okay?'"

I force a laugh to keep from tearing up as the emotions boil in me. I remember exactly how it smelled when he said that, like rotting leaves and hot stone. Exactly how his words echoed. He'd said that to me when we were trapped in a Mayan tomb. We'd been trying to escape for hours. I was hot, dehydrated enough I could feel it, could feel my body starting to fade. I thought we were going to die, so I'd just told him. And . . . he'd been amazing.

"You must be a really big fan," I say.

"Well," she says, tilting her head. "I remember that part. It was important to a lot of people."

"Yeah," I say. I can feel my eyes watering.

"I'm sorry," she says, laying a hand on my arm. "I shouldn't have said anything."

"It's okay . . . I just . . . don't want you to think I'm okay with what he does, that I understood when I was a kid . . ."

"I don't think that for a moment," she says, pulling me in for one of those awkward sitting hugs.

"Sorry," I say.

"That's okay," she says, letting me go.

I pull back and wipe my face with the backs of my hands. "Can we go back to work, though?"

"Of course."

"We can talk about it more later if you want. You probably have questions."

"Well." She smiles. "Later, sure."

Everyone always has questions. We just covered a few of the big ones: Why did I leave? Why did Mom let me go? Was it fun? The only other big one is: "Was it real?" Dad works hard at that, making sure it's all on the edge of believable, and people always want to know. How can there be traps that a thirteen-year-old and his dad avoided, undiscovered ruins, plus all that other stuff he leaves illusive—why weren't there good shots of those "mechanical" skeletons? Have we replicated that "chemical" the scepter sprayed? But between what we don't get on camera and the shaky footage, we had to narrate a lot of missing stuff sometimes, and that makes it harder to believe. For the history, we always showed our proof, our research. The other stuff . . .

But none of that was important to me then. What I loved wasn't being on TV, it was the adventure, the discovery, and, well . . . the fun. More than fun. Excitement. It was the only thing I looked forward to, those trips, those ruins, all that near-death experience and strange treasures.

Season five just ended. I try not to watch it, but sometimes, late at night, I can't help it and binge. Never with Mom, I don't want her to see how much I miss it. This time he found an undiscovered Egyptian temple. Recovered a sacred headdress. It was a good season. Not as good as when I was on it—all the reviews say so—but still fun. Still watchable. You could almost smell the old stones, and there was one trap, with a hidden pit, that I would have caught a mile away but Dad just . . .

It's not just me. No one can turn away from it, even when the whole world can see he's a thief. UNESCO has sanctioned him. People call him out online and in articles sometimes. Tunisia even sued him, but he just hasn't gone back to Tunisia and no one is making him. It doesn't matter much, though. Same as it doesn't matter about the stolen stuff at any other museum. Dad's famous, a hero. He gives archaeology lectures at Yale. Professionals like Anika seem to love him even as they hate him. I can tell. That's how I feel, too.

I don't know where the headdress ended up, of course. I'm sure he gave a great lecture at the exhibition opening. But I don't look that part up. The katana we fought over ended up in Japan.

I sigh and force myself to go back to fact-checking the plaques. It empties my mind again. I feel better by the time I need to get home.

"See you Monday?" Anika asks when I turn all my day's work over to her.

"Yeah. Email me if anyone else agrees to lend us stuff, though. I want to keep track."

"I will. Have a good weekend, Ten. And sorry again, if I shouldn't have—"

"It's okay, really," I say, smiling to reassure her. "And I will tell you all about it next week if you want. Just need to mentally prepare myself and it's been a long week."

"You okay?"

"My boyfriend cheated on me," I say. "Has been for weeks. I just found out, but everyone knew."

She shakes her head. "I'm sorry, if I knew I wouldn't have said anything about your dad."

"It's okay. I mean, it sucks, but, like, you can't fix it. I can't fix it. It's just like Dad. I'll get used to it."

"That makes me sad. You're only seventeen. You should be more hopeful."

"I'm very hopeful for this exhibit to be amazing," I say.

She laughs. "No pressure on me."

"You brought it on yourself," I say, wiggling my eyebrows.

"I guess so. Good night. Say hello to your mother for me."

"Will do. Bye."

I shrug on my backpack and head back home. It's already pitch-black outside. Or as pitch-black as it gets in New York. Sometimes I think the sun sets faster in the city, and everyone keeps the lights on to fight it off together. Futile, maybe, but walking home through dim light is better than walking home through complete darkness. I've been in total darkness. It's not fun.

But everyone in New York keeps a light on, not just for themselves, maybe.

I walk west and then up to Chelsea, back home. I take the elevator up to our floor and walk down the hall to our apartment and when I open the door, the house smells warm, like cooked dinner and wine. I shut my eyes. Mom's not a good cook.

"Hey, Tenny," Dad says, poking his head out of the kitchen into the hall. "I'm back."

✹ THREE ✹

I silently take off my backpack, choices running through my head:

1. Go to my room without saying anything, wait for him to come to me, to knock, to beg to apologize. He probably won't do that, though. He'll send Mom, who will remind me he's my dad and tell me to try with him, just a little, and then I'll come out and he'll act like nothing has changed, like the two years he's been gone never happened.

2. Sarcasm. "Oh, what brings His Highness for a visit?" No, that's not funny. "Here to steal something?" Too mean.

3. Scream. Just pick up right where we left off. Then he'll scream and we'll keep screaming until Mom makes us settle down and then Dad will leave, maybe for more than two years this time.

4. Hug him. I really, really want to hug him.

"Oh," I say, "and what brings His Highness for a visit?" Option two. Stupid. He raises an eyebrow at me. He knows it's stupid, too.

"C'mon, Tenny, I was a jerk, you can do better than that."

I smile, make myself stop. "So you're here to steal the nice silver then?"

He flinches, and it feels good. He steps out of the kitchen. He's wearing an apron and holding a glass of wine and leans against the wall. "Well, that's better. And . . . I'm sorry for the fight we had. I'm the grown-up, I shouldn't have yelled and then not shown up for a little while."

"Two years," I say, rage boiling inside me. Of course he chooses today to waltz back into my life. As if today wasn't awful enough already.

"Yeah . . . I'm sorry," he says, looking down. "I'm really sorry." It sounds like he means it.

I sigh and go up to him and give him a hug. He smells like sand. He always smells like sand. He hugs me back tight. I'm still angry, but also, I missed him, and I'm angry that I'm glad to be hugging him again now. That knot inside me. Or is it me? I'm a knot, and it's because of him. And here I am hugging him, glad to be hugging him. I make it so easy for him.

"That better?" he asks. "All forgiven?"

"No," I say, pulling back. "Absolutely not. But I missed you."

"I guess that'll do." He smiles. "Man, you got tall."

I roll my eyes and take my jacket off and put it on the coatrack. I look a lot like Dad. Which is probably a good thing; he's not just on TV because of the archaeology. We're both tall even if I'm not quite as tall as him, and I'm broader—wider shoulders, and the six-pack is gone since I stopped running from giant boulders, but we both have the strong jaw, the high cheekbones, and even though I'm only seventeen I have what feels like perpetual stubble and a hairy chest and stomach.

He's got light brown hair and blue eyes, but I have Mom's dark brown hair and eyes, and I'm paler like her, maybe a little pinker underneath, rather than tan like Dad.

"Where's Mom?" I ask, looking around. I don't see her.

"Oh, she's—" Dad starts, but then I hear the key in the lock behind me. She wasn't even home yet. Dad comes up to me and puts his arm around my shoulder, turns us to face the door as Mom walks in. She looks up and pauses, then takes her key out of the door. She looks at me first. I don't know what expression I should make. I don't know what I should say.

"Henry." Mom turns her eyes to Dad. "How the hell did you get in?"

"Picked the lock," Dad says, wiggling his eyebrows. "But I brought wine." He holds up his glass. "And I bought everything to make dinner, and I'm cooking, so you shouldn't kick me out now."

He grins and Mom tries not to, I can see it, but she smiles back. Then she forces her eyes serious again and turns back to me. Dad's charm always works on Mom.

"There's always delivery," she says, then turns her eyes to me. "You okay?" she asks.

"We're great," Dad says, squeezing my shoulder.

"So you made up?" She takes off her coat, hangs it up, and walks into the kitchen. There's another glass of wine there, waiting, and she takes it.

"I think we're good," Dad says.

Mom turns to look at me. I know she'll kick him out if I ask her to. But I also know she doesn't want to. And neither do I. As much as I hate him, having him back, all smiles and happy to see me, like we're not fighting—it's what I've wanted. I realize what I feel in that moment: relieved. Relieved that he's back. Relieved that he's not gone forever. And if I squint, I can almost imagine that this is the apology I've waited for, and that things can go back to normal. So I nod at Mom. I want to squint.

Mom smiles and takes a long drink of the wine. She's happy to see him, too. Mom met Dad when she was a young archaeologist on a dig he was investigating. He wasn't as famous as he is now, but he was still well-known—the young bad boy of archaeology. He brought her into the ruins with him and they walked a hundred-year-old rope bridge over a chasm, figured out the trick to an ancient mechanical door, and recovered the Merseburg Tome (which a wealthy German patron could afford and so is on display in Nuremberg). And somewhere amid all that, they had time to conceive me (gross to think about, I know). Mom found out after he was gone, off to the next adventure, but she called him and he became a sporadic presence in my life until I was about ten, and then he was here every winter, and every summer, to tell me about his adventures. I was his ideal audience. And then, when I was thirteen, he realized he could have a bigger audience and he brought me along to film it. Three adventures. Three seasons. And then the fight and . . .

Mom knows he's never going to settle down and suddenly propose or anything, but when he visits, he doesn't always stay on the sofa or in a hotel. I try not to think about it.

"Dinner is almost done," Dad says. "Why don't you set the table, Tenny?"

Mom comes over and ruffles my hair as Dad goes back into the kitchen. "Are you really good?" she asks in a near-whisper.

I shrug. I'm not. I got dumped, my friends aren't my friends, and Dad is the least awful of all that. At least today. Because what he did wrong was years ago. And what he did right was coming back.

"I'm still angry, but he is your dad," she says as Dad steps behind the oven. "Trying to change someone is always futile. You get to decide if you forgive him. But he's a good cook. And he has great taste in wine. So let's just try to enjoy this before we deal with the rest of it, that okay?"

"Yeah," I say.

"But if you ask me to kick him out, I will."

I nod. "Thanks."

She kisses me on the cheek and walks back into the kitchen, and I follow. The kitchen opens onto the dining room, which is actually just part of the living room. It's a big apartment for New York, especially on the salary of an archaeology professor, like Mom. But Dad sends child support, and I still earn residuals from the three seasons I was on the show, which have more than filled up my college fund, so I was okay with Mom and I using the leftover money to buy us a little more space. Mom decorated the place, of course, with pretty pale-yellow shades and framed rubbings she's taken of ancient carvings she's found on digs, mostly in Germany. My favorite, though, is a reprint that hangs by itself next to one of the windows, a reproduction of Albrecht Dürer's rhinoceros woodcut. It's Mom's favorite, too. Based on just a description and quick sketch done by someone else, it's sort of right, and sort of wonky, probably because Dürer never saw an actual rhino. The man who described the rhino was from Portugal, and he'd seen it because an Indian man had brought it to Portugal as a gift. Like a game of telephone. That's history sometimes, Mom says.

I take out plates and placemats and set the round wooden table. Dad is making some kind of curry, by the look and smell of it, and he keeps doing this thing where he shimmies as he cooks, like he's dancing, which Mom keeps laughing at. It makes me smile, too. I hate that it feels so easy to forgive him. That maybe he thinks it's over, like the only thing he needed to apologize for was the fight, and not what caused it.

I set the table and give myself a wineglass, hoping Mom is tipsy enough to let me have a little. I think I deserve it. Dad comes over and dishes out the curry, which smells fragrant and reminds me of something he and I ate once but I don't remember what. I just remember sitting in some small restaurant with a blue tiled floor and laughing at something with him. I shake my head to make the memory go away.

"So," Dad says, sitting down. "Your mom says you have a boyfriend? Tell me about him."

As though today weren't terrible enough. "Actually, we broke up." I stare at the food in front of me. "Today."

"Oh, honey," Mom says, reaching out and putting her hand on mine. "I'm so sorry."

"He was cheating," I say, my face feeling warm. I can't do this in front of Dad. He doesn't deserve to see me at my worst. I pull my hand away from Mom and make myself eat, blinking the tears away. "It's fine. It's over."

"I'm sorry, Tenny," Dad says. "You want me to get someone to curse him? I know several people who can do that."

I roll my eyes. "No, thanks. I'm just . . . dealing with it."

"Well"—he pauses dramatically—"maybe it would help you if you got away for a little while?"

I take a bite of food. It's warm, good, with plenty of cumin, which he knows I love. So this is why he's back. A new adventure. I can feel the word *yes* struggling to pop out of my mouth. Leaving my ruin of a social life to explore some real ruins? The adrenaline, the discovery, the traps—I miss all that. I miss knowing I'm the first person to lay eyes on something in over hundreds of years. I miss reading lost stories and recording them for people. I miss finding out something new. The only thing I've found out about lately is David's cheating.

"Away where?" I ask finally. This is why he's back. Maybe. But I'll say no when he asks me. If he asks me. He hasn't earned me coming with him again.

"Greece," Dad says.

"For the show?" Mom asks.

"For the rings of the Sacred Band of Thebes."

I drop my fork and look up at him. He grins. He knew what this would do. He knows I can't say no now. I almost want to hit him, I'm so angry and excited all at once.

"You have a lead?" I ask, trying to keep cool, but it comes out too loud. He smiles. He knows he's won already, that I'm going, but how could I not? We'd looked for so long. Even when we weren't adventuring, we spent time in libraries looking for any evidence about the rings of the Sacred Band of Thebes, or just the sacred bands, as we called them.

"I know a woman whose dig just uncovered the Temple of Iolaus."

I lean back in my chair. I want this so bad. This was *my* treasure. *My* idea. After I came out, when I was fourteen, Dad tried to do what Anika's been doing—teach me some queer history. He loved the Sacred Band of Thebes. An army of three-hundred men, one-hundred-and-fifty queer couples, that formed around 379 BCE. They had a ceremony pledging themselves to each other at the Temple of Iolaus. And there were a few fragments of texts that said they exchanged rings. Gay weddings, maybe. Gay warrior weddings, thousands of years ago. Gay history. My history.

They existed for years, new couples coming in, men of all social classes. The idea was that they'd fight harder to protect their lovers than just brothers-in-arms. And that seemed to be right: the Sacred Band was fearsome—they fought off armies far larger than they were, the Spartans included, and won. Some people claim they weren't really all gay lovers, or gay at all, that the translations about love and partnership mean fraternal love, brotherhood. And some people say they didn't exist, or at least that all the stories about them are exaggerated, maybe that it was stories about different armies all attributed to one. But when Dad told me about them, I just knew they were real. That this was a part of my history I wanted to know more about: an army of gay men, all married—maybe not in the modern sense, but at least committed, bound, in love—that was maybe the most powerful army in the world at the time. It would upend all the ways people thought about gay people. It would show how strong queer love is. Real queer love, not whatever David and I had, which clearly wasn't going to help us fight in any army. I wonder what that even looks like. It's pretty clear that none of the Good Upstanding Queers would have fought alongside me. For me. I'd like to see what those kinds of queer friends are like. Or just evidence of them.

"So it's real?" I ask, and I know I sound too excited. But I spent years dreaming about the sacred bands.

Dad shrugs. "It seems to be real. The rings . . . I don't know. But I want to find out. And I want you to do it with me."

I've wanted to find some evidence of the sacred bands and their queerness so badly for years. And those rings they exchanged at the Temple of Iolaus seemed like the best part of them, their bond. And maybe, depending on how you read some of the fragments, the rings were magic? I know that since I'm someone who's run from animated skeletons and touched a scepter that can control flames, I should be a true believer in magic and stuff, but it's rare. I know it's rare. I've only encountered it twice, and Dad only a few times more. And it's not even clear what the rings are supposed to do—"make two minds one" is one of the translations. "Make two fight as one" is another. So I don't know about that part. But magic or not, the rings are special. And they had to have come from somewhere for the ceremonies. There had to still be some out there to find. That's what I told Dad. And he said we should try.

So we researched, buried ourselves in books. Mom helped, too, but we never found anything. Until now.

I take a deep breath. I want this so badly. I don't even need to consider my options, since there's only one: yes. Except—

"What do we do with the bands if we find them?" I ask. I don't want him just selling them off to the highest bidder. I want them out in the world somehow. I want everyone to see them, to be able to look at them and know the history of the Sacred Bands of Thebes. And if we find them, we can do that—provided Dad doesn't just sell them off like he has everything else, ever. I clench my fist, anticipating a fight.

Dad nods. "I knew you'd ask that." For a moment, his face is cloudy, and I think he's going to start yelling again, like in Japan, but he looks down and when he looks back up, he's smiling. "So, because these are something you wanted to find, and it's more important to me that you come along than how much we make off this, I will let you decide what we do with them. If they exist and we find them, of course." He pauses. "And survive."

"I . . ." I stop. Did he really just say that? I want to hug him. I want to forgive him all at once. I hold back. It's not enough. It could be a lie. A trick. Dad doesn't usually do that, but some things sound too good to be true. "I get to decide what to do with them?"

He nods. "Completely up to you. The footage goes to our usual producers, though. I'm under contract."

"That's . . ." I nod. I look at Mom. She looks at me expectantly. I turn back to Dad. "And we'll do it all by the book, right? We're not going to disturb any graves or knock over any walls or destroy these historical ruins, right?"

"I never mean to do that," Dad says quickly. "I'm just trying to figure out the ruins, and sometimes that means stuff collapses or explodes. That's why we film it all."

"The Treasure Cave—"

"That was one time," he says, sighing. "And if I hadn't knocked the wall down, we would have been drowned when the room filled up." He looks annoyed but takes a breath and makes himself smile again. "But yes, it's all going to be aboveboard this time. My friend running the dig, Jean, says we're welcome to investigate. But we should head there soon."

"How soon?" I ask.

"Tomorrow," he says.

"Henry," Mom says. "You didn't mention that. He still has a week of school before break."

"Sarah, you can take him out of school for a week. Tell them it's for a special educational trip. They know who he is."

Mom leans back, considering. "Fine, but you're buying me a plane ticket, too. I'll stay in Athens. We'll have a day there. I haven't had a vacation in ages." She smiles sweetly, then turns on Dad, her tone changing dramatically. "And this way, if you decide to abandon my son in a foreign country with no idea how to get home, I'll be there to clean up after you."

"A fair deal," Dad says, almost looking ashamed for a moment, but then grinning again, all charm.

"I haven't agreed yet," I point out. And I mean it. I'm still so angry, and none of his apologies are right yet.

"Right," Dad says, turning back to me. "You going to say no?"

I look at Mom again.

"You want to talk privately?" Mom asks.

"Oh, come on," Dad says, rolling his eyes again. He's getting annoyed now. Part of me likes that. Let him get annoyed. He deserves worse.

"I just want to ask her something," I say, standing and walking to my room. Mom follows.

"You can ask me," Dad calls after us. I turn to look at him but he hasn't moved, he's just sipping wine. "And your food will get cold."

In my bedroom, I don't even turn on the lights. It's a mess anyway and Mom will start cleaning it up. I just sit on my bed.

"What's the matter?" Mom asks, sitting next to me. "Isn't this exactly what you wanted?"

"Yes," I say. "That's the problem."

"What?" Mom laughs.

"Can I trust him? To do what he promises?"

Mom sighs. "Look," she says. "Your dad is a lot of things."

"A thief," I say.

"Yes, by my way of thinking, and yours. But he's also an excellent archaeologist, believe it or not. He tracks these treasures down with real research."

"I know."

"He's smart, and charming, and funny . . ."

"Mom."

"And he's also an adrenaline junkie, a womanizer, a glory hog, just to name a few."

"So . . ."

"But I've never known him to be a liar. By omission maybe, but never a blatant lie."

"Oh," I say, and I feel relief spread through me like honey, making pins and needles as it runs down my arms. "So I should say yes?"

"You should do what you want to do. But I wouldn't mind a trip to Athens, if that's what you're asking. We can see the Jewish Museum! My grandmother, her father was from Greece. Not a great place to be a Jew, though, so she went to Italy, and married your great-grandfather. My dad's dad. But she was from Athens, so maybe we can find something about our family there."

"Okay," I say. "But Dad—"

"I'm not making that choice for you, Tennessee. Do you want to do this? Adventure with your dad again? Do you trust him? That's what you need to ask yourself."

"Yeah," I say, not meaning I trust him, but that I need to decide. "What about my work at the museum? I can't just leave Anika."

"I'm sure she'd understand," Mom says, patting my knee. "You should email her."

"Yeah," I say, "yeah, okay." I take out my phone and send a quick email to Anika.

Hey, Anika, would it be okay if I took until the New Year off from the museum? My dad is back in town and he wants me to go find the rings of the Sacred Band of Thebes with him, for the show. I don't think I should go, though—you need my help, right? Thanks, Ten

I hit send and Mom smiles at me. "If she says it's a problem, I'll talk to her."

"Mom, no, if she says it's a problem, I'm not going. I'm not a kid, I don't need you to fix things for me. And I don't know if I want to go. Dad is still Dad, and I don't know if I can trust him—"

My phone starts to ring in my hand. I look down; it's Anika. Calling. Weird. Mom sees it and gets up. "I'll leave you to talk to your boss then. I shouldn't interfere with a work thing."

"Thanks," I say, as she leaves the room. Then I hit answer. "Anika? Are you butt-dialing me or something?"

"You should go, Ten."

"What?" I ask.

"The Sacred Band of Thebes, the show. I can handle everything with the museum, you'll still get full credit, a pristine record, you should go."

She sounds so serious.

"But my dad, he—"

"Forget about him. He is . . . incidental. What you'd be doing is important. Finding queer history. And putting it on TV in a way that no one can deny its queerness."

"Deny?"

"Of course. The stuff in the exhibit we're putting together—its queerness is often questioned. History always questions queerness and always assumes it's heterosexuality. How many men found buried together are assumed to be just friends? Or look at trans people like James Barry, who, after his postmortem, people said had only disguised himself as a man to be a doctor, not even entertaining the idea that he could be trans until recently. Even the Sacred Band—called an army of lovers—is said by some to be about brotherly love, platonic ideals, not sex. Our history is forever being overwritten. If you do this—find these rings, do the show, put it all on TV—then you get to control the story. You get to fight back against that erasure."

I swallow and nod. She's right. Queer history, especially from before Stonewall, is always being erased. I didn't even know the stuff in the exhibit we're putting together existed until I started helping Anika.

"Ten," she says again into the silence of the phone. "I know there's a lot going through your mind. But you asked for my permission, and I'm giving it. If you don't want to go because of your father, I would understand, of course. I do not pretend to know what your relationship is like. But this is an opportunity, not just for you, but for all of us. So you have my permission, and I hope you go, and I hope you take back our history."

I nod, even though she can't see me. "Okay," I say. "I'll . . . email what I decide, okay?"

"Of course. And I do not mean to pressure you. I just want you to know you have my support. And it could be important."

"Thanks," I say.

"Good night, Ten."

"Good night, Anika."

I hang up.

So I have permission to go. Encouragement, even. There are so many reasons to go—and I want to, I so want to—but then, on the other hand, there's Dad.

Go, trust Dad to do the right thing. Or go and *make* him do the right thing. Save queer history, even if he tries to auction it off. Somehow.

Don't go. Regret it forever. Go back to school Monday and see David with his arm around Brandon again. Deal with Daniela telling me to get over it. Wonder if they were ever really my friends.

I stand up and go to the dining room where Dad is still eating, checking something on his phone.

"I'll go," I say.

He looks up at me and smiles so broadly that I wonder if I've fallen for a trick somehow. But then he gets up and hugs me again. "I'm so glad, Tenny. I've missed doing this with you. It's just not the same."

"Me too, Dad."

I hug him back and close my eyes. I can trust him. I'll make sure the bands go to the right people. I'll make sure Dad does the right thing. And then, maybe he'll do the right thing on his own next time. Maybe if he just sees me do it . . .

❦ FOUR ❧

When we can turn on our phones on the plane, I check mine for messages. I'd emailed Anika last night to tell her I'd decided to go and she'd just sent me back a bunch of heart emojis, then a crying emoji and *Will miss you. Have fun. Can't wait to watch next season.*

I email her back an eye-roll emoji, but she can absolutely tease me about this. Then, before I hit send, I add:

Maybe I can get these bands for your exhibit.

A text from an unknown number comes through suddenly.

UNKNOWN

So want to hang out this weekend?

PROBABLY GABE

It's Gabe
I got your number from the student directory
Pretty sad now that I've typed that ☺☹

I laugh and text back:

TEN

> On a plane to Athens, actually
> Random, I know
> but my dad dropped in
> He's kinda chaotic

I watch the little "..." appear for a few seconds.

PROBABLY GABE

> Like you

I laugh again.

PROBABLY GABE

> Randomly making out with strangers. That's
> cool though
> When will you be back?

I frown a little.

TEN

> Not until the New Year
> sorry :(
> Can we chill then?

I feel bad, leaving him hanging like this. But it's not like we're boy-friends. We haven't even had a date. Was what he wanted to do over break a date? I don't know.

PROBABLY GABE

> For sure
> Take photos of hot Greek dudes for me
> Naked if possible

I snort. Definitely not dating. Or at least not exclusively.

TEN

> I'll see what I can do
> See you when I'm back

I turn off my phone before he can text back. I don't need to be thinking about him. Or about David. Or my friends—his friends—and how they didn't care how much he'd hurt me. I can leave all that behind. A serious bonus to this trip. Like walking in New York, I can cast off who people thought I was—not the guy who was cheated on, not David's boyfriend, not the guy who used to be on his dad's show, like I was before David . . . well, maybe that again. But this time it's different. It's my show, too. It's my search, my history.

Dad talked the producers into springing for first-class, so our seats are more like pods that can turn into beds. Mom told me to sleep—we're landing Sunday morning—but I feel too hyped up. I look at Mom through the window between our pods. She's in the window seat and Dad is across the aisle from me. Dad is out like a light, but Mom is watching a movie. I tap on her knee and she leans forward to talk through the window.

"You okay?" she asks. "You should try to sleep."

"I will," I say. "But . . . this is okay, right? Just jetting off like this?"

She smiles. "Sure. Your finals are done and school doesn't mind, my classes are covered. It's exciting. And I haven't been to Athens in ages."

"But I mean, me going with Dad. Ruins."

She shrugs. "You know it makes me worry, but I also don't ever want to keep you from anything. And I've done it, too, don't forget. When your father and I met."

"Yeah."

"Are you having second thoughts? We can ditch him in Athens. Forget the bands."

"No," I say quickly. "I guess I just want to make sure it's all okay. Like you weren't just saying it was okay because you want Dad and me to get along again."

She smiles, and glances behind her out the window, then back at me. "No. I'm not going to let you put your life in danger in some old ruin, just because I want you and your dad to get along. Therapy is much cheaper. I want you to do what you want. I know how much the bands mean to you. I was with you all those nights doing research. And then after you and Dad fought . . . it was like you gave up not just on them, but on all archaeology. All history. So this makes me happy. You following your dreams. Nervous, sure, but . . . happy."

I nod. I guess she's right. After Dad and I fought I stopped researching the bands. Stopped researching anything outside of what I needed to for papers. It wasn't until the museum that I got interested again.

"Thanks for making me apply for the internship," I say, realizing now what she was doing.

She puts a hand through the window and strokes my cheek. "You don't have to be an archaeologist, of course. You can be whatever you want, but . . . you loved it, and when you stopped you seemed sad, so . . ."

"Yeah," I say. "Well . . . thanks."

"Sure. Now try to get some sleep." She leans back.

"Wait, Mom?"

"Mmmm." She leans forward again.

"If the bands are real, and we find them . . . what are the laws about what we're supposed to do with them?"

"Oh, well, Greece is very specific about that, honey. They were the first country to declare all antiquities found in Greece to be property of the state, back in the seventies. You need to report anything you find to one of the local archaeology authorities within . . . what is it?" She looks across the aisle at my dad, who's awake now.

"Fifteen days," Dad says. "But we might not find the bands in Greece. And even if we do, those laws are notoriously easy to get around."

"Of course you'd say that," I say to Dad, a dull anger throbbing awake in me. He hasn't changed at all.

"I'm just saying." Dad puts up his hands like I'm striking at him. I realize I'm glaring.

"You just want to do whatever makes you rich and famous," I say. My voice is a little loud, and the person the row ahead of us stares at me. I try to lean back, relax.

"I want whatever makes the stuff we find famous," Dad says, his voice not loud, but flat. He's annoyed, too. "What's the point of finding these treasures if they then just get buried in someone's boxes in the attic? These don't belong to one person. They belong to the world."

"They're someone's history," I say, almost hiss.

"Boys," Mom says. "You both know your positions. There's no point arguing. Henry, you said Tennessee can choose what to do with the bands if you find them, right?"

"Yeah," Dad says.

"So . . . let's leave it at that," Mom says.

"Okay." I turn back to Mom. "But how do we follow the law then, and what happens if we do?"

"Well, you'd give the bands to the local archaeology authorities within fifteen days. Which is what you should do—I'd really rather not have my son on some UNESCO warning list before he can vote. You're not"—she searches for a word—"let's say 'established' like your dad is. It could affect your career."

"Sarah, don't worry him. I'll take the blame for whatever you choose," Dad says to me. "You can keep them if you want."

"Not in our apartment," Mom says to him. "They'd need insurance we can't afford for a start, not to mention we don't have much more security than a deadbolt and a chain lock." She turns back to me. "These laws were made so Greece can protect its history. You have some Greek blood, but you're not a Greek citizen. You'd be stealing their history from them, legally speaking."

"Okay, but what happens after I give it to Greece?"

"They sell it," Dad says.

"To a museum," Mom says. "A local one, probably. Or, if it's considered important enough, they give it to one of the national museums. And then it's put on display."

"See?" I say to Dad. "You said you want them to be on display, right?"

"Sure," Dad says. "But they should pay you, too."

"That's the job of whomever is sponsoring the dig," Mom says. "Then you write a paper about it."

Dad sighs. "The boring part." He settles back in his seat, almost vertical. "And now ask her what kind of display they'll be put on: exhibition hall H, item one hundred and seventy-two."

I ignore him. "What about the people it belongs to? Ancestors—" I stop. "I guess there won't be any in this case."

"The government won't give it to them, no," Mom says. "But these are also thousands of years old. Tracking ancestors would be nearly impossible."

"It's a museum piece, not an heirloom," Dad says. "Just go with the museum that's offering the most money. That's how you know it'll end up getting the best treatment in the museum. If they pay top dollar, they're showing it off—probably building a whole exhibit around it, maybe use some of our video, bring us in to give speeches, our photos in the exhibit. Then maybe the exhibit travels. Good money and good for the show."

I glare at him. He's right, which annoys me. If they pay more money, it means they want it more, and they probably have the money to really show the rings off. Which is what I want. Queer history. And there aren't any ancestors anymore. Unless you count all Greek people. Or all queer people.

"So if you're asking what I'd do with them," Dad says, "that's my answer. It's the smart one. Why give up a relic to someone who's going to throw it in storage and never show it off? The right thing to do is make sure it tours the world."

My brain feels fuzzy with all these ideas. I know Dad is wrong, ethically. I've seen him sell off things he should have given to people, countries, because of the money and fame. But Mom's version doesn't sound much better. They'd probably display the bands if I gave them to Greece, right? But would they get the attention they deserve? These are special. Not just to Greece.

"Would Greece celebrate the bands' queer history, too?" I ask. But Dad's asleep again and Mom has already leaned back with her headphones in. I close my eyes. We might not even find them anyway. They might not exist. This could be a dead end. Or we could die horribly in some trap. I'm getting ahead of myself.

But as I'm drifting off, I imagine Dad's scenario, too. Me, talking about the rings at a museum, an exhibit about the queerness of the Sacred Band of Thebes touring the world. People seeing my history—not Greek, but queer history—that no one ever talks about, no one teaches in high school. David maybe finally understanding why I cared about it, maybe seeing me at my best, missing me . . . no. Not that. That's pathetic.

But maybe if I got to talk about the rings, about history, maybe the whole community would come—the butches and college twinks and drag queens from the Village. All of us together, knowing not just that we're not alone when we walk through the Village, but that we're not alone ever. That our history is always with us. That would be something special.

I wake up from the not-really-sleeping I always do on planes as we land at the Athens airport, and wince against the sun as we exit the airport and climb into a cab.

As we approach Athens, I get the impression of the city as a white and orange ocean of buildings with islands rising out of it— green mountains topped with ancient ruins. One mountain rises above the rest: the Acropolis. Cities have different energies, like New York, where you're all together and all alone at the same time. Here it feels different, both like a big family estate divided into a bunch of apartments at different angles, and like the weird stillness of a church. The mountains and ocean, I decide, are two different cities. Athens roiling loudly below, Athens towering silently above.

Athens also has one of my favorite things about cities—the way the new just shoehorns itself in. A small villa, three hundred years old, right next to a twenty-story building made of glass. They shouldn't go together, but they do. That's how cities grow. If they all stayed the same, we wouldn't have history or archaeology, and watching them shift, seeing the change in the street, makes me feel like I'm part of history.

At the hotel, after checking in and dropping our bags in our rooms, Dad pops on a pair of aviators and smiles at Mom and me.

"You two have fun. I gotta find a translator. Ours bailed to teach in Cyprus, and the only Greek I know is a few thousand years old. Meet in the lobby tomorrow, Tenny? Nine sharp?"

"Yeah," I say, then turn to Mom. "You should come with us."

Mom looks up at Dad and they exchange a look I can't read. "That's kind of you, but no. This is a you and Dad thing. I've had my adventure. One was enough for me."

Dad shrugs, like he tried to convince her, even though he didn't. It's what I expected, but I'd sort of hoped she'd say yes. I feel anxious about going on another adventure with Dad like nothing has changed. He still hasn't even apologized—though I don't know how that would work. Some filmed statement saying he wishes he'd given the artifacts to the right people? That he'd been wrong?

I take a breath and think about the bands. That's what's really important.

Dad has already walked off, so Mom tousles my hair and looks down the street. "Breakfast first, I think. Then the Acropolis, the Jewish Museum, and . . . anything you want to do?"

"Is there a queer museum?"

Mom raises her eyebrows and checks her phone. "Yes, actually. Want to do that?"

"Sure," I say. "And maybe some Hanukkah shopping?"

"Perfect. I'll pick the most expensive thing on Ermou Street in case you're not back by the first night."

I laugh. "Sure."

It's still cool enough that the wind bites, but the sun is bright enough to cancel it out. It doesn't smell like I thought it would; it's almost nutty, the air, like the roasted peanut vendors in New York, and it smells like herbs and flowers, too, like oregano and honeysuckle.

At the Acropolis, we skip the guided tour and instead Mom gives me one, showing me the Parthenon and various sanctuaries and temples as we munch on egg-filled *tiropitakia*.

After so many years surrounded by history and people talking about history, I know it's impossible to absorb it all at once. But I try. I ask Mom questions, tell her what I know. It's how we operate—building on each other, a real-time essay. Dad and I are more back-and-forth, like a debate. I think that's because with Dad, exploring ruins, we're usually trying to translate or solve a puzzle—to interpret. With Mom, I simply get to enjoy the history around me.

Some stuff I know: how the Acropolis is actually one of many, how it was built and rebuilt over the centuries, what all the gods were gods of. But it's different in real life. I stare at columns sprouting up like bamboo, sun-bleached stones walked on by people hundreds of years before even Rome. And it's still here! *Still here!* I'm walking on stones some other guy like me walked on thousands of years ago. I don't know his story. He probably doesn't know mine. But here, we have the same footprint. We have something connecting us. History is community. The bands need to be celebrated the way the Acropolis is. They can't live in the dark forever.

It really is kind of the center of the world, I realize, looking out over Athens when we stand at the edge of the mountain. I look north, to where Thiva—modern-day Thebes—is. I can't see it or anything, but I picture it. A temple, long-lost. Some dark corridors. Rings glinting in the dark.

"You ready to head back down?" Mom asks.

"Yeah," I say. "I feel like maybe there's too much history here."

"Definitely too much for one day."

At the Jewish Museum, housed in a small synagogue, I look at old outfits the Greek Jews wore, and artifacts the Nazis stole. Did anyone try to give those back, I wonder. Does everyone really think like my dad? Mom asks the docents about our family, her mother's maiden name, but they don't have anything for us. Missing history.

After lunch we wander Ermou Street, where Mom not-so-subtly points out a pair of earrings I not-so-subtly buy. Then we head to the Athens Museum of Queer History and Culture.

It takes a while to find it because the door is barely marked and the building is so small. I make a face at Mom. She shrugs.

"Maybe it goes underground?" she says, opening the door.

Inside is a small desk where a gray-haired woman is typing and a few chairs around a table. It doesn't look like a museum. It looks like a waiting room. The woman looks up, smiling but narrowing her eyes.

"*Kalispera*," she says.

"*Kalispera*," Mom responds.

"American?" the woman asks before Mom can say anything else. Mom nods.

"Leo!" the woman calls. Mom and I look at each other, confused. Then a door at the back of the room opens and a guy my age comes out. And he's cute. Like, very cute. Tight white T-shirt showing off a broad body with slight love handles and a belly, skin like polished bronze, and the most perfect thick black eyebrows I've ever seen. He has a square face, and his black hair falls forward, which should be too much, but somehow works for him. He beams at us, and I involuntarily smile back. Like, way too big smile back.

The woman says something to him in Greek, and he nods.

"Ah, hello," he says, in slightly accented English. "Mrs. Adamos doesn't speak English. She'd like to know what you want?"

"Oh." Mom turns to me. I open my mouth, but I've completely forgotten why we're here. Mom continues, "This is the Athens Museum of Queer History and Culture, right?"

"Yes," Leo says.

"I'm queer," I say, and then immediately look at the ground because now I'm also deeply embarrassed. I feel like I need to tug on Mom's sleeve and back slowly out of the room.

"Good!" Leo says. "So am I."

Mom waits, so I make myself look up and talk. "So, we were hoping to see the museum."

"Ah," Leo says, nodding. "I see. This isn't that kind of museum. Not yet. It's just the name so far. The founder, Mr. Xiphias, wants to make it a museum someday, but . . ." He gestures around, arms wide, shirt even tighter on his chest. "No space. We organize events around the city. Sometimes we have lectures . . ." He opens the door he's come out of and nods for us to follow. Inside is just a small, carpeted room with a bunch of chairs set up and a podium.

"I'm Leo. I help here sometimes," he says. "But it's not a museum museum. I'm sorry." He smiles again and I realize we're standing very close. He smells like figs and rosemary.

"Oh," I say, then swallow. "That's too bad. And I'm Ten, by the way. That's my mom, Sarah. I was just hoping to see some queer history."

"Good to meet you." He thinks for a moment. "Well, the Archaeological Museum has a few vases . . . but nothing you'd want to see with your mother," he says in a low voice.

I laugh. "She's an archaeologist, she's seen it all. But is that it? No other queer history?"

"There will be a lecture here in the New Year, if you're staying that long, but with Christmas coming up, we don't have anything planned. I'm sorry."

"That's all right," I say, slumping—from the lack of history or from knowing I'm about to leave Leo, I don't know. I turn to Mom. "I guess we'd better find something else."

"Well," Leo says, "if you want, I can show you around. It's not queer history, but there are bars and a club, though it's a little early."

"And I'm only seventeen, so I can't drink."

"Me too," he says. "No one will check, though. Anyone can drink here."

"Not him," Mom says. She pauses, looking us over. "But I was just thinking of heading back to the hotel. Do you think you can make your way back on your own?"

Is Mom really leaving to let me hang out with this cute boy? Is she letting me decide?

1. Hang out with cute boy, maybe make out with said cute boy?
2. Go back to the hotel, fall asleep watching Greek TV, and throw off my sleep cycle.

Clearly number one is the healthier option. If only for my internal clock.

"Yes," I answer quickly. "I'll be fine."

✼ FIVE ✼

"You have your phone?" Mom asks. I nod. "Then call if you get lost, and don't do anything where I have to bail you out of a Greek prison."

"Really?" I ask.

"Sure," she says. "You're seventeen, and after David—"

"Okay." I do *not* need her talking about David in front of this cute boy. "Thanks." Mom shakes her head at us and leaves. Suddenly I'm very aware of how alone we are.

How empty the room is.

"Thanks for doing this," I say.

"It is my pleasure," he says. He grins at me. I grin back.

On the way out he chats with Mrs. Adamos; she hands him some money.

Outside, I look around, expecting to see Mom, but she's gone. The city feels different all of a sudden. Like before I was just on a ride, something on rails, and now I get to explore behind the scenes. I'm a little nervous and it makes me shiver. I put my hands in my pockets, but then Leo drapes his arm over my shoulder.

"Cold?" he asks.

"No, no," I say. "Just the wind."

"It's nice you visited now. Not many tourists in winter. It's emptier. We can see more."

"What are we going to see?" I ask.

"Well, your mother said no drinking . . ." He looks over, to see if I'm game anyway.

1. Drink? It's not like I've never drunk before. Worst-case scenarios range from waking up dead to waking up in my hotel room hungover.

2. Don't drink.

I choose option two. I don't want to risk it. And I don't want to go to some loud bar with Leo, anyway.

"I think I'd better not," I say. "I have to be up early tomorrow."

"What for?"

"Oh." I shrug. "My dad and I are going to Thiva. He's an archaeologist and there's a dig we're going to look at."

"Wait." Leo smiles and I turn away. The thing with being on an international show is it's shown internationally. "Ten. Tennessee! Tennessee Johnson, from the show!"

"Tennessee Russo," I say. "I have my mom's last name."

"Russo." He nods. "Sounds nicer. My mother and I watched your show! It helped me learn English."

I laugh at that. "No it didn't."

"And now here I am talking English to Tenny!"

"Oh, please don't call me that. Only my dad calls me that. Tennessee or just Ten."

"I think you're more than just Ten," he says. "One hundred, easily."

I look away to hide my blush. Up the street, the sun is setting, and the white buildings are turning as pink as I am.

"Should I not have said that?"

"No, I liked it," I say, turning back to him and smiling. I made out with a boy I barely knew like two days ago and now I'm flirting with this guy. What is going on? It's like without David keeping me in the boyfriend mold, I've gone liquid, moldable. And I'm doing the molding. I'm giving myself a new head. A dozen new heads. A thousand.

"Do you want to see some sights, then?" he asks.

"Besides you?"

He laughs. "There, that's better." He links his arm through mine and starts down the street, but when another pedestrian passes by, he drops his arm. "It's not like America here," he says in a low voice. "Sorry. We don't have marriage. Athens is the best place to be queer now. But . . ."

"I get it," I say. "We'll be careful."

"Not too careful, I hope. Come on, let's go to Gazi."

We take the metro, talking about ourselves. Stupid questions: when we came out (me on TV; him at fifteen, but just to friends), what we want to do (me, archaeology; him, unsure, but maybe something with museums), the holidays (I might miss Hanukkah; he'll celebrate Christmas with his sister). When we get off the train, we're walking close, even if our arms aren't linked. I keep glancing at him. His profile is striking, with a strong chin and nose, and a long neck that would be perfect to kiss.

"This is Gazi," he says, and I look away from him at the buildings around us. They're new, but blend in—white walls, orange roofs. But around them, rising higher, are what look like tall stone chimneys. "The old gas . . . um . . ."—he pauses, searching for a word—"where they took the gas up from the ground and made it usable. That's what that is."

"It's kind of cool," I say, staring at the stone towers, old but not Athens's usual kind of old, standing over the street like giants approaching a temple. But the street itself is very modern, with glass-walled buildings and bright lights. Leo pulls me down a street and points at a giant mural of what looks like a Frankenstein monster head, a wind-up gear coming out of its forehead. There are murals all over—eyes, robots, strange brightly colored people. I can't tell if it's graffiti or city art or something in between, but it's colorful and weird and alive.

"This is the gayest place in Athens," Leo tells me. And when I look around, I get it—the same feeling of walking down the street in the Village with my pride pin. Being seen, being part of a place.

"I love it," I say. He links our arms again and leads me to a small park where the cypress trees are covered in haphazard fairy lights, like sparkling cobwebs. At a small café where twentysomethings sit inside and out, smoking and laughing, we sit down at the only free table outside. Even here it smells like coffee—not like Starbucks, like real, dark, bitter coffee. Before I can even look at a menu, Leo says something to the waiter in Greek, and he takes them back.

"What did you order?" I ask.

"You'll see," he says.

"So . . . is there history here?" I ask.

He shrugs. "There's history everywhere in Greece. Queer history . . . that's harder. It's not like America, like I said. We all know that there were gay people, but it's not something we talk about much. The church here is still . . . well. They call it the Greek Orthodox Church, right?"

"That's too bad," I say. "So nothing?"

"Well, Alexander the Great, he warred with Athens," Leo says. "And he had men as lovers. And of course if you've seen the statues at the Acropolis, you can tell some of those sculptors appreciated the male body."

I laugh, but I'm disappointed, too.

"You wanted more," Leo says, frowning.

"I wanted a museum, I guess? Someone putting it in one place so people can see all that history, y'know?"

"Yes." He nods. "I wish I had that, too. My parents—they didn't know. And now they're dead."

"They're dead?" I ask. "I'm so sorry."

"My father died when I was young. My mother just a few years ago. Car accident."

"I'm so sorry," I say again. I don't know what else to say.

"I've brought the mood down," he says. "I'm sorry."

"No, don't apologize. Do you stay with relatives?"

He sighs. "My sister. She was eighteen when our mother died. But it's been very hard. She's a waitress. That's why I work shifts at the museum—to help with rent, with expenses. I'm a delivery boy, too. She does so much for me and I . . . feel useless."

"I'm sure she just wants you to do well."

"She barely sees me she works so much. We almost got kicked out last year. The shelters are overcrowded. We'd be on the street. I just want to help."

"You have a job," I say, reaching over and putting my hand on his. "You are helping."

"Not enough," he says. He sighs, then shakes his head and pulls his hand back. "I brought down the mood again," he says, and forces a laugh. "Tell me something else. Are you here for the show? Are you looking for something?"

I nod.

"What?"

"Do you know about the Sacred Band of Thebes?" I ask. Leo shakes his head. "They were an army, one-hundred-and-fifty gay couples who fought off armies much larger."

"Was there a movie?" he asks. "With elephants?"

"A different three-hundred warriors. Spartans. Sacred Band's enemies. The Sacred Band had commitment ceremonies at the Temple of Iolaus, and some fragments of ancient texts say they exchanged rings."

"Like a wedding?" he asks.

I nod. "A gay wedding. Of warriors. Thousands of years ago."

"That . . ." He grins. "That's very cool. The church would be so upset if they became real Greek heroes. Gay warriors who got married." He laughs.

"I want the world to see them," I say, nodding. "I want everyone to know that we've been around forever, we've been married forever, and our love was so strong it fought off armies. And I want other young queer people to see it and know that they're like . . . descendants of legends. There's a lion statue, the Lion of Chaeronea, that's supposedly where they were all buried, after they finally lost a battle. It's northwest, near Parnassus. Have you ever been?"

Leo shakes his head.

"Dad took me after I came out. It wasn't on the show. But he took me there and told me the story of the Sacred Band, and also about the Hwarang, a queer army in ancient Korea, and the Mahu, sacred queer people in Hawaii, about queer people in Norway, India, the pre-colonial Americas . . . so many histories all over the world, in almost every culture where we existed, and we were warriors, sages, heroes. How could there be all this history and even I—a TV historian—didn't know it?" I remember looking up at the lion that day, carved white stone tinted pink by the setting sun. He was regal, quiet for a lion. But still strong. He reminded me of a grandfather.

"You care about all this, don't you?" Leo says. "It wasn't just for your father, or for TV."

"Yeah." I nod. "I genuinely love it. And I want to find those bands. Especially now, with what you've told me. I want Greece to see them." The couples buried under the lion, hands clasped, might have been the band. Some wore rings, but not the special ones the fragments described. They could have been taken from them when they were buried, though, or by the soldiers who slew them. Passed down. Lost."

"Well, like those vases, I'm not sure how much attention the bands would get."

"Really? Millennia-old rings signifying queer warriors' commitment to each other?"

"History is the people who tell it, right?" he says.

"I guess."

"Is it scary? The adventures? It always looks scary. Tunnels filled with traps. I hid under the pillows sometimes. I had nightmares."

"Oh, I'm sorry," I say.

"Don't apologize. But it must be terrifying," he says, and looks away from me. "Going into those old temples, knowing how dangerous it is, getting hurt, not being sure anyone will find you if a door closes."

"I guess. But it's exciting," I say. "Like, I'm always scared, but it's always worth it, too."

"How?"

"Seeing things no one else has seen in centuries. Finding secrets. Like a mystery, maybe."

"I like mysteries," Leo says, looking back at me. "I liked watching your show. I don't know if I could do it, though. When I was little, my grandmother told me this story of when she was stuck in an elevator with a woman she didn't know. And the elevator phone didn't work, so they were screaming and kicking, but no one came. And the other woman started to cry. 'They're never coming. We'll die here.' Over and over and over. I had nightmares about that for months after she told me that story. Trapped in the dark, screaming and knowing no one is coming for me."

"Someone did come for her eventually, though."

"It took almost a whole day. I think what you do is like getting into an elevator, closing the door, knowing it will shut down, and hoping you can get out later. I don't think I could do it."

"I bet you could," I say. "I bet you'd have fun."

Leo shrugs. "I still have the nightmares." He looks around the café, willing whatever he ordered to appear. "Your passion is exciting, though." He pauses. "I hope that they do give the rings a show.

That they let you speak at the museums about their importance. It's very inspiring."

I blush. "No, it isn't."

"Yes, it is," he insists. "I'm not sure what I want. What would I even study at university?"

"You're very good at English," I say.

"From watching TV. Maybe I should go into TV," he says, looking up at the stars. "You're lucky you know what you want, Tennessee. All I want is not to get kicked out on the street."

I don't know what to say to that, but then the waiter sets down a plate of sticky-looking oval cookies, covered in ground nuts. They steam in the chilly air and smell of honey and cloves.

"*Melomakarona*," Leo says. "They're a Christmas treat." He picks one up and takes a bite, a crumb getting stuck on his lip. I grab one and bite into it. It tastes like Christmas—cloves, cinnamon, but also nuts and honey, and some citrus. I lick my fingers when I finish it. When I look up and see Leo watching, I smile.

"So why did you leave the show?" he asks suddenly.

"Well, I had to focus on school," I say, looking out at the street. I don't feel like dragging Dad into this maybe-date. The baggage of what actually happened. The knot and boil of emotions.

"Really?" he asks. "You gave up all that for school?"

His eyes are dark, and in the fairy lights they seem darker somehow. Endless. I don't feel the knot of emotions that I've been dealing with so much lately when thinking of Dad. Not the way I usually do. It's like they're faint, in the background. His eyes push it away.

"My dad and I had a fight," I say after a moment. "About what to do with the stuff we found." I grab another of the *melomakarona* and bite into it.

"But you made up?"

"He says this time, with the bands, if we find them—" I stop. I don't know if I want to tell him yet. "That we'll do the right thing."

"Give them to Greece?" He shrugs, taking another cookie. "I don't know how much that will help you spread the word about them. About queer history."

"I don't know," I say. "I have to figure out what the right thing is."

"Sometimes it's hard to figure out. But I think you can do it," he says, and licks some honey from his thumb.

I suddenly wish there wasn't a table between us so I could kiss him. Not make out, just taste the honey on his lips. I try to remember if it was ever this way with David, but how could it have been? It was David asking me out, on a nice date, then another nice date, and another and another. It was always nice. I wanted so badly not to be alone, to know I had a place. David offered me that. A table at lunch and a feeling of a new family. But it never smelled like dark coffee. I never considered if it was a place I wanted.

I look down at the plate, which is now just crumbs and a pool of honey. The sun has sunk low, and the sky is purple. It's chilly sitting outside.

"That way is a gay sauna, if you want to see some gay culture," Leo says.

I laugh. "I don't have my bathing suit."

He raises one perfect eyebrow. "Not needed."

I laugh again. "Not sure I'm a public skinny-dipping person. Why don't we just go for a walk?"

The waiter brings the bill and I pay it, not letting Leo put any money down.

"A thank-you for the tour," I say.

"Fine, but I'm going to buy you something sweet later."

We walk around some more, enjoying murals and an art gallery with photographs of nude men embracing, where Leo takes my hand and strokes the inside of my wrist. Outside the gallery, a café is playing music loudly. As a new song comes on, Leo stops.

"I love this song," he says. "You know it?"

I listen, then laugh.

"ABBA. 'Super Trouper.' It's super old."

"But it was in that movie," Leo says, starting to dance a little, right there on the street.

"True," I say. "That movie is kind of old, too, though."

"It's a good song! They play it at the gay club a lot." He's dancing bigger now, enough so a few people are looking at him.

"You go to a gay club?"

"If the bouncer knows me that night," he says, putting his hands around my waist, making me move in time with him. "Here, dance with me, one-two, one-two."

I laugh, following him forward and backward to the beat. I put my arms around his neck. "I think every gay man knows this song, actually," I say. "One of the old gay ones."

"Probably," Leo says. We're really dancing now. He moves with much more confidence than I do. His hands slide down to the small of my back and I take a deep breath. People are staring, amused, at the two boys dancing on the street. But I don't care. We've managed to get in sync. He gives me a little spin, and a few people applaud. Then he pulls me close, and I want to kiss him. I want to kiss him so badly. It rises up inside me like the feeling of finding an old tomb, the sudden overwhelming urge to explore, to run, to feel that thrill again, knowing how my body will pulse, how out of breath I'll be.

The song ends, and without saying anything, I take him by the hand, pulling him down the first alley I see. Then I grab him and put my mouth to his.

It's different than kissing David, or even Gabe. It's like it's not even me kissing him. I'm some stranger in Athens, and so is he, and he tastes like cinnamon more than I thought he would. His arms wrap around my lower back, and he leans against the wall, drawing me closer. His hands creep down, grabbing my ass and pulling me fully into him. I kiss him for a moment more, then pull away.

"Maybe we can go back to your hotel?" he asks. I grin. I'm not a virgin. But . . .

1. Bring him back to my hotel and have sex. Sex with someone who isn't David for the first time. Oh god. What if I'm bad at it? What if only David liked weird stuff, or he cheated on me because I'm bad at sex, or—

2. There is no option two! Not anymore!

"It's not that I don't want to," I say quickly. Because I do. I want to embrace that me-that-isn't-me, that stranger in Athens, take him back to my hotel room and sneak him out in the morning so my parents don't see. But I'm also, suddenly, terrified. I've leapt over literal pits of flaming bones, but this is what's scary? This is ridiculous.

"But?" Leo asks, and I realize I've been quiet for a while.

"I . . . I just got out of a relationship. Back home, and I'm just afraid that . . ." I'm looking at our feet. His sneakers are kind of beat up. He runs his hands down my arms until I look at him.

"He was your first?" Leo asks.

I nod.

"You're afraid?"

I nod again.

He kisses me again, his whole body pushing against mine, and then releases and I miss it. I miss being wanted and wanting, and I realize now that David hadn't wanted me in months. That he'd always wanted to break up with me. Cheating was just the coward's way to do that. What he and I had was never wanting, not like this is. Not like this other me wants Leo right now.

"Don't be afraid," he says.

"Okay," I say.

❧ SIX ❧

The alarm on my phone goes off at seven in the morning and I roll over. Leo is next to me in the hotel bed, somehow sleeping through it, adorable. The sheets only half cover him and I enjoy looking at him in the light, the curves of his body, the diamond of dark hair on his chest. I suddenly want to take a picture, and then remember Gabe asking me to send him photos of hot men. Sadly, Leo really needs to go before my parents see him, so I shake his shoulders until he blinks groggily awake.

For a moment, he looks around the room, confused, almost panicked, but then he sees me and smiles and leans up to kiss me.

"I need to get ready to leave," I whisper. I don't know why I whisper. Dad's room is across the hall, but I don't think he'd be able to hear us.

"Are you sure you need to do that now?" he asks, kissing me again, more deeply.

"I mean . . . I wish I didn't, but I have a schedule to keep."

"All right," he says, frowning a little. "Okay." He stretches.

"Can I take a picture of you?" I ask.

He wiggles his eyebrows. "Which side?"

I laugh. "Just from the waist up. A friend asked me to get photos of hot Greek guys."

"Ohhhh, I see. Showing off." He leans back on the pillows, grinning at me, posing. "Take the photo, then."

I laugh and take a shot with my phone.

"Good?" he asks. I nod and he crawls across the bed at me, kissing me again. I thread my fingers through his hair.

"I need to get ready," I say. "And pack." I kiss him again.

"Can I shower here first?" he murmurs between kisses. I nod and he gets up, walking naked to the bathroom. The shower goes on and I follow him in, watching him in the mirror as I brush my teeth. I hope this wasn't a bad idea. I was so worried about David and being bad in bed last night I didn't even get to the part where I should have worried about sleeping with a guy I just met. We used protection of course, but was it too fast?

Even if it was too fast, it was worth it. Last night was . . . is there a word for something that's both a relief and a joy? I understand why people have rebounds now. I feel like I'm someone else again, a new head sprouting where the old one used to be. Not the stranger in Athens, but not David's boyfriend, either. I'm someone new, someone I like. I've been through so many someones in just the past handful of days, each of them running through my fingers like sand, but now there's this stone left in my palm—me.

I finish brushing my teeth and hop in the shower with Leo. He grins and kisses me again, his hands pulling me into him, but I shake my head, reaching for the shampoo instead. We wash, stealing kisses and gropes, but hurriedly. When we've dried off, he throws on his clothes and kisses me again as I open the door to the hallway. He pauses, kissing me again, which is when I hear Dad chuckling.

I freeze and look up. Dad is standing across the hall in the door to his hotel room, wearing one of the hotel robes, holding the newspaper that's been left outside his door.

"Good morning," he says, clearly trying hard not to laugh. I feel myself blush. I guess it could be worse, right? Dad at least looks kind of proud. I feel like Mom would be embarrassed.

"Uh, hi, Dad," I say.

Options:

1. Push Leo back into my room, slam the door, tell Dad he didn't see anything, he's imagining it.

2. Jump back into my room with Leo, slam the door, live there forever.

3. Maybe Leo has an idea?!

4. Pretend he's a bellhop! Bringing me breakfast! With his mouth . . .

5. Just man up and accept this is awkward and awful and it'll be over soon.

Leo doesn't say anything, he looks just as in-the-headlights as I feel, so I guess option three is out.

"Who's your friend?" Dad asks.

Number five it is. This is going to be the worst. "This is, uh, Leo," I say. "We met yesterday, and . . ."

Dad holds out his hand to shake. Leo looks nervously at me, and I motion for him to take it. They shake.

"Nice to meet you," Leo says.

"You too," Dad says. I can see Leo trying to pull his hand back, but Dad won't let go. "Where'd you meet?"

"A museum," I say, my throat dry.

"And Mom just let you go galivanting off together?"

"Um . . . yes?" I say.

Dad laughs. "And you speak English, Leo? Or was this a situation where you didn't need words?"

"Dad," I say. I'm still blushing. That can't be healthy.

"I speak English," Leo says. "I, um, learned from TV."

Dad drops Leo's hand finally, putting his hand on his waist instead and tilting his head.

"So you can translate?" he asks Leo.

"Translate what?" Leo says.

"Greek. To English. My translator bailed yesterday. I like having a translator to help with road signs, talk to the locals, stuff like that. Maybe a little light camera work."

"Oh, well, I do speak Greek, of course," Leo says, looking back at me. I shrug.

"And English. I think I speak it well. I'm not sure how much I'd need to know as a translator, and I'm still in school, so . . ."

"Ah. I see," Dad says.

"Dad, let him go." I can hear myself pleading.

"But you're how old?"

"Seventeen."

"So that's legal adult here, right? You can take some time off, sign your own disclosure forms."

"I could," Leo says, looking confused.

"It pays five hundred US dollars a day," Dad says. "You sure you can't take off school early? You must have a break soon, right?"

Leo's eyes nearly bug out at the number. But then he shakes his head. "I don't know," he says. "I've seen your show. It's very dangerous."

"Six hundred," Dad says.

"Dad, come on, that's not right, he and I—"

"I'm not doing this because of whatever you two did, Tenny," Dad says. "I'm doing it because we need a translator and if he speaks English well enough to seduce an American—"

"Ew, Dad, don't say seduce."

"What do you say, Leo?" Dad asks. Leo looks nervous. I remember what he said about being scared of our show when he was young.

"Leo, you don't have to," I say.

"Seven fifty," Dad says. "Final offer."

"I could use the money," Leo says, turning to me. "Plus we could spend more time together. That's not bad, right?"

"Well, yeah, but I'd kind of be your boss, so . . ."

Dad laughs. "I'd be his boss. And if you tell me to fire him because you have a fight or something, I will ignore you. This has nothing to do with that. Well, except that you literally brought him to my door, Tenny. Thanks for that. We need a translator, we're out of time, he's perfect. So, Leo, what do you say? You in? Money, adventure?"

Leo swallows. "Okay, I'm in."

I stand there, not sure what to say. But part of me is happy—thrilled, even. I wanted him to say yes. I wanted to show him how much fun this can be. I wanted to share it with someone, the way Dad shares it with me, I guess.

Dad turns to Leo. "Go home, pack some clothes—you want stuff to block the sun and keep warm. And good boots. And get a waterproof case for your phone, just in case. Here, I'll give you money for one."

He goes back into his room for a moment, closing the door behind him.

Leo turns back to me, smiling. "This is okay with you, right?"

"Yeah," I say, though I'm not really sure. "If it's okay with you. You can skip school?"

"Just a few days. It'll be fine. We had finals already, so we are just on the coast until the end of the year?"

"What?" I ask, then laugh. "Coasting. Not on the coast. Unless your school is seaside."

He tilts his head, considering. "Coasting," he says, finally.

Dad's door opens again and he hands Leo some bills. "Good boots. That's important. Meet us in the lobby at nine, okay?"

"Yes," Leo says, taking the money. "Thank you, sir."

"Just call me Henry. Now get moving, we have a tight schedule."

Dad closes the door to his room again and Leo turns to me. "See you soon?" he says.

"I . . ." I'm so confused, but then he leans forward and kisses me. "Okay," I say. Sure, this could be a disaster, but . . . it could be fun, too. Dad always brought women on his adventures before the show, like Mom, so it must be fine. Wait. Am I like my dad?

Leo smiles and takes off down the hall. I stare after him, enjoying the view. Once he's gone and I've taken a minute to process my weird new reality, I get dressed and text him a checklist of things he should pack, if he can. While I'm on my phone, I check my email. I have one from Anika:

It's sweet you want to bring the rings to my little exhibit, but I doubt the Greek government or whatever museum it gives the rings to—if you find them—is going to lend them to a tiny museum in America for a queer show. They're going to keep those things under lock and key. But I hope you find them. Keep me updated!

I frown. I know our museum is small, but the show is important. I worked on it. If I find the rings, you'd think they'd let me borrow them, right?

Then I send a text to Gabe along with the photo of Leo.

TEN

This what you wanted?

I start packing but he texts me back almost immediately.

GABE

Yes

God yes

What's his name?

I grin.

TEN

Leo

GABE

Mmm, I hope he's a lion in bed

I laugh. Why didn't I ever talk this way to David or our friends?

TEN

A gentleman doesn't tell

GABE

What time is it there?

TEN

Early
Breakfast, then headed to the dig site

GABE

I've been watching your show
Never seen it before, sorry

TEN

That's okay

GABE

Well, it's pretty cool

But be careful, okay

I like that we're friends now

I smile at that. It's true. Just a little making out and now he's probably my closest friend at school. A new friend for a new me.

TEN

Me too

GABE

So be careful

I don't want to have to go to your funeral

and be like, we were just starting to be

friends after he made out with me to make

his ex jealous

TEN

And cause you're cute

GABE

As cute as Leo?

TEN

I don't play favorites

GABE

> Well, maybe you can bring him back as a souvenir and we can all play . . . whatever

I throw back my head and cackle. I don't know what Gabe and I are exactly, or what exactly Leo and I are, but I like them both, and I think they'd like each other, too. It's not like how it was with David, with his very nice dates, and his very nice bringing me flowers, and his very nice kisses. "I want to show them we're just like them" is what he said when he asked me to the winter formal last year. It was . . . boring.

Who wants to be "just like them" when we can be better, right?

TEN

> I'll see if he's interested
> I need to go, though
> Talk later

GABE

> We'd better
> Be careful

I put down the phone and start packing. Dressing for adventure isn't easy. On a dig site, the main worry is sun protection, so you need a hat, long pants, a collared shirt, all lightweight enough they won't get uncomfortable. I have a waterproof parka, the kind skiers use, in case we end up underground, or somewhere wet. Bright green, so I'm easier to spot in the dark, too. Under that I wear a long-sleeved collared shirt unbuttoned over a tank top, and khakis.

My bag is light: sleeping bag, flashlight, satellite phone, trowel, and several of the tiny water- and shockproof video cameras I use to film everything, along with extra batteries and memory cards, all in waterproof cases. I have my phone, which I put in an intense thick clear case, and a few changes of underwear. Once I have everything ready, I take the rest of my stuff to Mom's room.

"You have fun yesterday?" Mom says, opening the door. She's getting ready for another day of sightseeing: wrap dress, earrings, makeup.

"Yeah, thanks for letting me go," I say. I'd texted her when I'd gotten back to the hotel but hadn't mentioned Leo coming along.

"You deserved to have a nice time, and I know at your age having your mom hover around isn't going to let that happen. Leo seemed nice, too."

"He is," I say. "And, um . . . Dad hired him. As our translator."

"Oh." Mom turns to me, narrowing her eyes. "That was nice of him. He can take off from school?"

"I guess so," I say, staring at her earrings to cover my lie. "He's meeting us in the lobby at nine."

"And how did Dad meet Leo?"

"Accidentally?" I offer, praying silently that she isn't about to give me another sex talk. I've gotten one a year from her since my bar mitzvah, and they're usually forty-five minutes long and involve explanations of ancient sexual rites.

Mom glances at her watch. "Well, bring in the stuff you're leaving here, then. Let's go get a good breakfast in you before you go."

I sigh with relief and drop off my stuff in her room.

Downstairs in the hotel restaurant, we order eggs and drink orange juice as I look out the window of the restaurant, waiting for Dad to show up.

"You'll be careful, right?" Mom asks.

"Yeah," I say.

"I know it's hard, with your father, but when I watch the show I'm always happy you don't just leap headlong into danger."

"I don't need to," I say.

"Fair enough," Mom says, sipping her drink. It's a mimosa.

"You're okay with this?" I ask.

"Of course," she says, in the same voice she always used years ago, which suddenly sounds different to me now.

"Really?" I say.

"I told you I was."

"You don't sound it."

Mom smiles and bites into a piece of toast, then dabs the crumbs away with her napkin. "I don't love it. It's dangerous. You're my son. I don't like my son in danger. That's . . . obvious, I hope." She takes another sip of her mimosa.

"But I was your age. And I was wild. Snuck out of the house, drove drunk—things you should never ever do. And when I had you, I thought the best way to make sure you never did them was to make it clear that you should tell me, and we would work out the safest way to let you do what you want, be who you are."

"But you didn't want me to go at first," I say, remembering when Dad asked me to go with him when I was thirteen. They had the only knock-down screaming fight I can remember.

"And you snuck out anyway," she says, pointing her fork at me. "You think you get that from your dad, but you get it from me." She cuts into her eggs and eats a piece. "And then I remembered what I told myself. So that's my deal. You go, I know you're going, and we make sure you stay as safe as you can. And, generally, I trust your father. He kept me safe on our adventure. He can keep you safe."

She glances out the window and smiles and I follow her gaze. Dad is walking up to the hotel, a backpack on over his leather jacket, fedora shading his eyes.

"He loves you. He's a good father at heart. Sometimes I just have to have faith."

She takes another long sip of her drink. I've never thought about how scared she is while I'm gone. I suddenly realize it's a lot.

"Come on, let's go see you off," she says, putting down her drink. She hasn't finished her eggs, but pays the bill and we go out into the lobby, where Dad is sitting on one of the green sofas in the middle of the room, staring at his phone.

"Hey, Dad," I say, walking over to him.

He looks up at me, smiling. He has the same look every time we're about to set out: a little wild, eyes too wide, grin too big, and also impatient somehow. Mom once called it his "junkie about to get another hit" look, but I like to think it's better than that, somehow. It's about the thrill of adventure.

"Hey, Tenny. Hi, Sarah. You have plans while we're out there?"

"Sightseeing, shopping, maybe some dancing," Mom says, spinning her hand in the air like she's not even sure. Then her hand drops and she stares hard at Dad. "You know the rules: if he gets hurt, you'd better be dead, otherwise I'm killing you."

"As always, your justice is fair," Dad says, with a slight bow.

I roll my eyes and then spot Leo coming in. He's changed and is wearing thicker boots and a black T-shirt with a white button-down open over it. He smiles and waves at me and I bring him over.

"Good to see you again, Leo," Dad says. "I'm glad you were able to get home and change and get back so quickly. Good thing you showered here, I guess." He raises his eyebrows at his joke, and I stare directly at the floor. I can feel Mom's eyes on me, wondering if she can take me aside for a little while to explain condoms, PrEP, and ancient Sumerian blow job considerations.

"We should go, right?" I say.

"Yeah," Dad says, "as much fun as this awkwardness is, we'd better head out. I have an address and a jeep, but not much else to go on, so I'm counting on Leo to read road signs for me."

"That I can definitely do," Leo says. His voice cracks a little. He's as embarrassed as I am.

"Bye, Sarah," Dad says to Mom, kissing her on the cheek. "I'll bring him back safe and sound."

"You'd better," Mom says. She turns from him to me and hugs me tight. "I love you," she says softly. "Be careful."

"I love you, too, Mom," I say, hugging her back. There's always a chance that this will be the last time I see her. That I'll die. And so we promised those would be the last words we said before I left. I'm not embarrassed that Leo can see it. Maybe I should be, I don't know.

And then Dad walks out of the lobby, Leo and I following him. I glance back at Mom once, and she's just standing, watching us. She gives me a wave goodbye.

Outside, Dad takes us around the corner to where he's parked a rental jeep. Leo sits in front with him, to better read road signs, and I sit in the back and take out one of the video cameras and train it on Dad as he pulls out onto the street. Here we go.

❧ SEVEN ❧

I take a deep breath. I'm really doing this. I'm going on an adventure with Dad again even knowing everything he's done. Emotions well up in me like vomit. I'm angry, thinking about the last time I did this, what Dad did, our fight, how he left me alone. But I'm happy, too, because before that, I loved our adventures, and I've missed them so much. I can practically smell the old stone of the ruins I'm sure is waiting for us. And then I feel guilty for feeling happy because I should be angry, but I'm too excited, and it's just a wave of too many things that I feel like I'm drowning and I don't know how to feel about that, either.

Leo turns around and smiles at me, and I feel better. He's the new thing, the different thing, the line between old adventures with Dad and this one. He'll remind me to hold Dad accountable, make sure he does this right. He gives me permission to be excited, just by being excited himself.

I look down at the camera. It's been a while since I handled one—more complicated than a phone, and I take a few minutes to remember the buttons that film and stop and zoom and reduce glare. It's not the same camera from when I used to do this, but it's similar enough it all comes back to me. And then it's time to start. Same, but different. Same, but better, if I do it right.

"So, Dad," I say, focusing the camera on him. "Where are we going today?"

He turns back briefly to smile. "We are headed to a dig site in the mountains to the east of Thiva, which in ancient times was known as Thebes. We are looking for the Sacred Band of Thebes, which is a little name you and I have given to a set of rings we're going to be hunting for." He pauses. "But you know what, Tennessee? I feel like this is your adventure. Your treasure to find. I think you should tell the folks at home about them."

"Yeah?" I say. Normally we open with Dad driving us to the dig and talking about what we're looking for. The producers edit it over some footage I shoot of the environment, of us arriving. But him telling me to do it feels like a trick.

"Yeah," Dad says. "I'm driving, but you're in the driver's seat. Tell us about the bands."

Me on camera, doing the lead-in?

1. Absolutely, this is my history, my story, and maybe Dad is just giving it to me to try to get me back into his good graces, but I can say yes and still remember he's not a good person.

2. Reject him out of spite. Watch him explain the rings on TV.

It has to be option one, so I grin and turn the camera on myself and talk about the Sacred Band of Thebes and the references to their rings in a few old fragments of writing. I talk about how they were founded by Epaminondas and Pelopidas, two ancient Theban warriors who had once disguised themselves as women to take back Thebes from invading Spartans. How they had taken their city back and decided to use an idea from Plato, to create an army of lovers, one united by Eros—passion—that would be unstoppable. And for decades, they were, until they fell battling Alexander the Great.

"That's why Dad says I'm in the driver's seat," I say to the camera without looking at it. "Because I think these bands, if they're real, if we can find them, they're part of my history as a queer man. I know not all of you will love that. I saw the comments online after I came out, and you can change the channel, I don't care. But queer people are part of history. People keep trying to erase that, but if we find these rings—well, no one can erase the rings. No one is going to erase what we find."

I try to imitate Dad's smile into the camera, but I falter. Is that true? Will finding the rings mean no one can erase their queerness? I think about David for a moment, and the Good Upstanding Queers. What would they think of seeing themselves as an army? They were so intent on seeing themselves as one thing—pillars of society—that they shunned other queer people who were different. Maybe I don't just want to show this history to the world because it's mine. Maybe I want them to see it, too.

"I'm proud of you," Dad says, shaking my thoughts from my head and making me blush. I quickly turn the camera back on him. "And I want to find those rings for you."

I roll my eyes, but grin. He wants to find them for the audience, for the museum, for the glory. But also, maybe for me. Maybe a little.

"Why don't you introduce our other passenger?" Dad says, nodding at Leo, who's kept quiet this whole drive.

"What?" I ask. We normally don't make the translators part of the show.

"This is Leo, our translator," Dad says when I don't start in. Shrugging, I turn the camera on Leo, who grins into it. Damn, he's hot.

"Tennessee here picked up Leo last night at a museum," Dad says, and I turn the camera on him, glaring.

"I didn't pick him up," I say. "I met him."

"That's what I meant," Dad says, all innocence. I'm not sure what he's doing, so I turn the camera back to Leo. Leo waves.

"Leo's my age," I say. "And he's helping us with some of the modern Greek. Dad and I know some Ancient Greek—well, kind of—but modern Greek is a whole other thing and it's what all the street signs are in."

"Right here?" Dad asks.

"No, left!" Leo says, almost grabbing for the wheel, not realizing it's a performance.

Dad laughs, turning suddenly left as we head out of Athens.

I roll down the windows and film the scenery as we go by. This part has always been easy. I'm not some great cinematographer or anything, but I don't need to be. I just film what I see. The landscape, Dad talking, ruins we're looking at. I film it all. I leave the camera on and strung around my neck, recording everything, most of the time. Dad will go through it later, cut some stuff, send a rough edit to the producers. That's when he gets rid of the supernatural stuff that's too unbelievable, and when he cuts out the boring stuff, too, like us star-ing at an engraving for three hours or reading books. So yeah, we look way quicker on the show than we really are because hours of us actu-ally figuring stuff out is not exciting TV. Aside from that, and not showing the supernatural stuff when it happens, it's pretty honest. It's documentary TV, not like *Real Housewives*, after all. Though people do tune in 'cause Dad is charismatic. I know that, and so does he, the way he looks at the camera all the time.

We drive for almost an hour, me filming the landscape or Dad or Leo, and sometimes me or Dad talking about the bands a little more.

"You didn't tell them the most exciting thing about the bands," Dad says as we get to the foothills, which are dense with forest.

"What?" I ask.

"That they might have been the reason the army was so unstoppable."

"They were unstoppable because of love," I say, flinching at how sincere I sound.

"Sure, and the rings were a symbol of that. And supposedly they let those who wore them move as one, think as one mind. I don't know what that means, it could just be a metaphor, but . . . could be some-thing more. Something magic," Dad says, smiling that smile he does for the camera. That "we're gonna get it" smile.

"That was in two fragments," I say. "And it's unclear if it meant the rings or being part of the army. And it was probably a metaphor. They're not magic."

"No?" Leo asks. "Why not?"

"Because . . ." I pause, aware of the camera and Leo watching. Stay illusive, that's what Dad always says. "Magic is metaphors. Or mechanics. Or weird herbs or an animal . . ."

"I've seen your show," Leo says. "Sometimes those things look like magic."

"Those are unusual, though. We're historians. That's what we focus on. Lost history. Lost *queer* history this time."

Leo turns around, smiling at me. I train the camera on him. "We, us queer people, we can be unusual, too. And we can definitely be magical."

He wiggles his eyebrows. He means last night.

"Okay, so maybe there's something special about them," I say after too long a pause. "But we have to find them to find out."

"Well, let's see what we can find here," Dad says. We're driving uphill pretty steeply now. "The Temple of Iolaus, who was one of Heracles's lovers, was where the men of the Sacred Band took their vows, so we should be able to find something there, if not the rings themselves. And I think . . ." He pulls sharply off the road onto a narrow dirt pass between the trees. "This is it."

The trees part and Dad stops the car. I lean forward to look out the front window. It's definitely the dig site. The trees are gone, and the dirt's been turned over. And sticking out of the side of the mountain, still mostly buried, is the front of a temple, recently uncovered. I know from Mom that archaeology digs usually consider it a success if they find some walls and a coin or two. They look for context, for history that they can piece together from broken bits—the formation of the walls means this was a bedroom, or this spot here signifies a kitchen—and through that, they learn about life in the past. That's real archaeology. What Dad does is sort of like that, but on steroids. He maps things out, documents everything (or, more likely, I do, with the camera), which is good, but he's never interested in the day-to-day life of people in the past. He wants stories. Legends. Treasures.

But even he's impressed by this: what looks to be a nearly entirely intact temple. That's practically unheard of. It's going to be the talk of archaeology for the next decade, probably. And it's beautiful, too. Columns like the one at the Temple of Zeus at the Acropolis thrusting out of the soil, three on each side, framing a door in the wall behind them. The columns are topped with a triangular roof, which has a carved frieze facing us. But we're too far to see it from here.

"Wow," Leo says, and I nod in agreement.

"Let's get a closer look," Dad says, opening the door.

We all get out. The air smells different than in Athens. Like green leaves and jasmine. The actual dig site isn't too big, but a large chain-link fence has been put up around it, and as we approach the swinging gate, two men step forward. Under their coats, I spot guns. That is definitely not normal. Dig security isn't uncommon, but usually it's just hired locals. These guys look like ex-military.

"Tell them we're here to see Jean," Dad says to Leo.

"We speak English," one of the guards says in a British accent before Leo can translate. Definitely not locals, then. The two guards exchange a look and one of them walks a few steps away, taking out a walkie-talkie and mumbling something into it. The other guard stays, watching us, his hand resting on his gun. A minute later a woman comes running up to the fence, arms wide.

"Henry!" she calls out. "You're here!" She has an accent, Scottish, I think. She pulls the gate open from inside and says something to the guards in Greek. They go back to their posts as she runs up and hugs Dad.

"It's been too long, but look at you," she says. "Still handsome. I always thought that was video editing."

"All me," Dad says, turning his charisma up to a ten. They hug, and I make sure to film it all. The woman—Jean, I assume—is decked out for a dig, white pants and a white button-down open over a purple tank top, and a white safari hat complete with mosquito veil, which doesn't stop her from kissing Dad on the cheek. She's a little flushed despite the sun protection, or maybe her cheeks are pink because of Dad. She looks around Dad's age, fifties, with a pointed face, big eyes, and brown hair in a low bun. She also very obviously has the hots for Dad. This isn't unusual, but it's always embarrassing. When they break the hug, she keeps her arms on him, holding him at the elbows, grinning widely.

"Oh, it's been too long," she repeats. "I'm so glad to see you."

"This is amazing," Dad says, turning to the temple. "When you told me, I thought . . . well, not this."

"Can you believe it? It was just supposed to be a quick rescue—they were going to put a solar farm here—but we got out the lidar and it showed something big enough I said we'd better dig fast, and . . . look."

"Hope they had a backup location for the solar farm," Dad laughs.

"We're still looking for a tomb. Some sources say this is where Iolaus was buried, but . . ." She looks out over the temple and shakes her head, her eyes wide with disbelief, even though she was the one who discovered it. "I just hope they can find the funding to keep it open," she says. "Once we finish, of course. We're going to shut down for the holidays next week, and resume in the New Year. Strange schedule, I know, but . . . it can't be helped."

"Well, I'm glad we got here before you started laying down the geotextile. What's with the guns, though?" He nods at the guards.

"Ah, well, once it became clear it was going to be a big dig, I needed a bit more funding." She pauses, looks at her feet. "So I paired up with Bulwark, and they . . . want to keep their investment safe."

"Bulwark?" Dad frowns. "Really, Jean?"

"Not my call," Jean says, frowning and shaking her head. "Henry, trust me, I'm just as upset as you are. But the university couldn't fund this one, so they found a partner and when I protested made it very clear if I don't give Bulwark everything they want, my academic career is over."

"Jean . . ." Dad looks sad for a moment. He takes her hand and squeezes it.

"What's Bulwark?" I ask, keeping the camera on them.

Dad turns as if he'd forgotten I was there. "Tenny, put down the camera, say hi to my old friend Jean." He turns quickly to Jean and says in a low voice, "Don't worry, I won't let them use that."

But Jean is already looking at me, her worried expression vanishing into a sudden smile as our eyes meet. "Oh my goodness, hi. I know this will sound ridiculous, but I'm such a fan of yours. Much bigger than I am of your dad."

"Hey," Dad says.

"It's true. As a bisexual woman, Tennessee, your coming-out—it really touched me. You inspired a lot of queer archaeologists."

"What?" Laughter bubbles nervously from my throat. "That can't be true."

"It is," she insists, coming over to me and giving me a hug. "Like a lot of academic professions, there's some homophobia. You're like a breath of fresh air. And you're on TV, so everyone sees you. Or you were. But I'm so glad you're back now! And at my dig, no less! I'm honored, seriously." She keeps her hands on my arms like she did with Dad, but it's not flirty with me; it's more like that feeling I get walking through the Village. She looks straight into my eyes, and I look into hers, and we see each other. Even without the rainbow pins or whatever. There we are.

"Oh, well, thanks," I say. "I don't know what to say. I just . . . like history."

"Well, I hope you'll love this," she says, gesturing at the temple. "Come on, let's get you in. Oh, and who's this?" she asks, spotting Leo. "Boyfriend?"

Leo laughs. "Translator," he says, extending his hand.

"So young!" Jean laughs, shaking his hand. "Or maybe I'm just old."

"You look the same as you did in grad school," Dad says.

"Liar," Jean says, smiling. "Well, come on in, everyone. I can't wait to show you this. It's even more impressive inside."

"Inside?" Dad asks as we follow her through the fence.

"Oh yes," Jean says. She looks very excited, like she can't wait to tell a secret. We follow her across the dig. Other archaeologists are around, many of them on top of the temple where it's still covered by the hill, carving the dirt away with trowels. Some are taking photos and video, too. I try to film everything.

As we approach, I stare at the carved frieze at the top of the temple. It shows what looks like a dragon, but with many heads. It's too high up to really make out the details, but below it the temple entrance is wide open and beyond—

"It's all intact," Jean says, leading us in. And she's right. Somehow, miraculously, the temple is untouched, like a time capsule. There are columns inside, carved walls, and two statues of men, still painted, which you never see because the paint has chipped off over the centuries. They stand at the end of the temple, facing the door. On the left is Heracles. I recognize him easily because of the lion's pelt he wears like a cape—though I've never seen it so bright sunflower yellow. On the right, I think, is Iolaus—it's his temple, after all. Iolaus isn't nearly as famous as Heracles, so I'm not sure about his symbols, but he looks younger, blond, with a wreath in his hair and holding a curved sword and a torch.

"Iolaus," Dad says, as if reading my mind. "He helped Heracles fight the Hydra. After Heracles sliced off each head, Iolaus was the one who went around using his wide-bladed sword and torch to brand their neck stumps, so the heads couldn't regrow." I film as he points and talks. "This is truly astounding, Jean. I was amazed when you sent me pictures, but this is just wow. You're going to win awards for this."

"I hope so," Jean says.

"You had pictures?" I ask. "You didn't show me those."

"I wanted to see your face when you first saw this place. Surprise!" Dad grins for the camera, or for me. I don't know which.

We walk quietly around the temple, our footsteps echoing on the stone floor. I film everything. Jean has brought in floodlights, their wires running back outside, so the place is well lit, even without windows. It's not huge for a temple, but it's tall—the statues are twice the size of Dad—and there are carved friezes along the walls like stained-glass windows in a church: one of Heracles and Iolaus fighting the Hydra, Iolaus searing its neck stumps. One of Iolaus running a chariot race, and opposite the door, behind the statues, one of Heracles and Iolaus standing facing each other, hands entwined. Behind them, a winged male figure is in the air, standing perfectly in the center of the image, his wings sloping down.

"Is that Eros?" I ask.

"That'd be my best guess," Jean says.

Dad comes closer to inspect the frieze and nods. "It must be. This is Heracles and Iolaus blessed by Eros, god of love."

I zoom in on their hands with the camera. Rings are carved onto each hand.

"Look," I whisper to Dad, though it echoes, "rings."

Dad nods, smiling. "They must be real."

"So this whole temple was devoted not just to Iolaus," I say, "but to his relationship to Heracles?"

Dad and Jean nod and I feel a thrill run through me, like the stones are vibrating. A temple devoted to gay love. I turn to look at Leo, who's already staring at me, smiling.

"I'm going to write such a paper on this," Jean says. "Maybe a book."

I practically jump at that. "That would be so special," I tell her, raising the camera up to her again. "A book out in the world about this temple devoted to an ancient queer relationship. You have to."

"Oh . . ." She smiles at me and walks closer. "Obviously this frieze is proof of their romantic relationship, yes. It's Eros behind them . . . people might argue that, but I feel like the archaeological community will come around. It'll be important, historically speaking. But . . . it'll be a textbook, Tennessee. And even then, people will say I'm misinterpreting it, that there were no queer people in the past—all the usual arguments until we're forgotten again. I don't see it ending homophobia, if that's what you mean. I'm sorry."

"Well, no," I say, but I feel kind of sad. "I don't think it'll do that. But it could show the world we have a history, no matter how much they try to eliminate it."

"Well, maybe for people who want to look for it," Jean says, nodding. She puts her hand on my shoulder. "I just don't want to disappoint you when I'm not a bestseller."

I shake my head. "You wouldn't. I just . . . want people to know. That we've always been here."

"Me too," she says.

"They'd better not cover it back up," Dad says.

"Cover it back up?" Leo asks. "Why would they do that?"

I swallow. I hadn't even thought of it. My stomach curls at the idea, sinking into the lowest part of my abdomen.

"Sometimes," Jean explains, "with a major discovery like this, if it can't be turned into a heritage site or museum because of a lack of finances, the best thing to do is just bury it again and mark where it is so it can be dug up again later when it can be properly preserved. They did it with the Rose Theatre in London for a decade, and Hattusa is still mostly buried. It also prevents looting." She shoots Dad a look. "What are you here for anyway? What's the big treasure this season that you think this place might help you find?"

Dad glances at me, as if asking permission. I shrug.

"The Sacred Band exchanged rings when they took their vows here, supposedly," Dad says. "We'd like to find those."

"The warrior bands?" Jean raises an eyebrow. "With the magic powers? You believe in those?"

"We believe they're worth trying to find," Dad says.

Jean nods. "Mmmm. Well . . . this is all we've found, as you can see. So you can inspect the carvings and statues—carefully, of course—but I don't think there's much evidence the rings existed, aside from that frieze and those few snippets, which can be interpreted so many ways. And the frieze is just Heracles and Iolaus. So there's no proof every couple in the Sacred Band of Thebes wore rings."

"Well, we're going to see what we can figure out."

Jean nods. Her walkie-talkie suddenly squeaks and a voice comes through in Greek. She sighs. "I'd better get back to this. But come tell me if you figure anything out. You know I'd love to go on another adventure with you, Henry."

"We will," Dad says, and winks at her, because he's terrible. I make sure to film it.

Jean leaves us alone in the temple, barking into her walkie-talkie as she exits the room. Suddenly, we're all alone in the temple, and I can feel the history vibrating me down to my bones. Something is close. We just need to find it.

❧ EIGHT ❧

"They'd really just cover it all up again?" Leo asks, staring up at the friezes, the statues, his eyes horrified. "Hide it away?"

"If they can't afford to keep it open," Dad says. "Then . . . yeah."

"In school, there's a teacher, he calls me a *poustis* sometimes," Leo says. "It's like *faggot*. I want to keep this place open just so he has to have field trips here."

"A teacher calls you that?" I ask, going over to him and putting my hand on his lower back. Dad turns away, studying the walls.

Leo shrugs. "Some teachers are better. But some not so much. Part of the reason I work at the museum is because I wanted to meet other people like me. If this place exists, and they don't keep it open . . ." He sighs. "I don't know if it will be a top priority for the government. Even if they do have the money."

I shake my head. I feel angry. This is what always happens, I think. It's what Anika has taught me. Queer history is erased, or at least the queer parts of it are.

I think of how I came out again, how Dad handled it. How he told me my history. And for a moment, I'm so, so grateful to him, I just want to hug him. Even with everything he's done wrong, that one moment of doing it right is something I can never thank him for enough.

And I want to do for every queer person what he did for me. That's why I want this, I realize. For David, for everyone, to show us we've been here forever, that we can be whoever we want. That's what the Good Upstanding Queers were so afraid of, I think—that if they weren't good and upstanding, then they'd be forgotten, brushed off as stereotypes, ignored. Because our history always is.

But not today. I have to save this temple, this history. I have to make sure I find those rings and that their queerness is celebrated. But now, this temple . . . it could just vanish again. Like all the rest of my history.

"Maybe the people funding Jean can help," I say, sounding a little desperate. I feel a little desperate.

"Nope," Dad says. "Not Bulwark. And let's try not to talk about them here. Or about anything in front of them. It's not like Jean to be partnering with them. She hated—" He shakes his head and then turns back to the frieze of Iolaus in the chariot.

"What is Bulwark?" I ask. Surely they can't be so bad it's worth giving up this history.

"Private military, essentially," Dad says. "Security force, they call themselves, but they go into a lot of ruins and clear them out, looking for . . . whatever."

"Like you?" I say, arching an eyebrow.

Dad turns and glares at me. "No. They blow stuff up to get at what they want. They've killed people who've tried to preserve sites. I know you don't think highly of my methods, Tenny, but trust me when

I say these guys are way worse. And dangerous." His voice is low and serious. It's a tone he hardly ever uses, and never on camera.

"Okay," I say, "sorry."

"Just be careful," Dad says. "With Jean, too. Just in case."

"Okay," I say again, narrowing my eyes. Dad turns back to the wall. He seems scared, which I don't see from him too often. So not Bulwark. They can't save this. But maybe the show can. If it's a big success, if we find the rings, then they'll have to keep it open, right?

"Well, we know this temple is here," I say to Leo, stroking his arm. "No matter what. They can bury it back up, but it'll still be here, even if no one comes here on class trips."

"I thought you wanted to uncover all of it," Leo says. It's like he can tell I'm saying it to reassure myself, too.

"I do. We will. And it's all on tape now. I don't know what's going to happen, but that's a lot."

"Yeah," Leo says.

I take my hand off his arm and go back to filming everything, making sure I capture every angle and every bit of carving, both close up and far away. Even if it's only on the show, this temple will be preserved. Shown to the world.

"Dad?" I ask, looking at the frieze with Eros between the lovers again. "Where would the light come from in here? Just oil lamps?"

"Probably," he says. "Most of these temples were dark inside, just lit by lamps. Why?"

"There's something about the way the statues frame the frieze behind them, when you stand at the entry," I say. Dad walks over and joins me at the door. From here we can look down the temple. The frieze is centered at the far end, and the statues are on either side, almost like they're holding it.

"Huh," Dad says. "So what are you thinking?"

"I don't know yet," I say.

"Well, I think there's writing in the stands around the chariot race," he says, leading me back to the frieze end points. "I saw it in the photos Jean sent me, but they're still too busy cataloging to start interpreting everything."

I look at the frieze: Iolaus is racing in a coliseum of some sort, and behind him at the distance are seats, filled with small, careful carvings of people watching. Some of their arms are up in strange positions. Maybe cheering, but—

"That does look like a sigma," I say, looking at a tiny man, his arms and the belt around his toga creating the suggestion of the letter.

Dad nods. "I'm going to see if it means anything," he says, taking out a notebook and writing things down.

"Why didn't you show me the photos?" I ask. "Really. You could have come here without me. You knew about it how long ago?"

"A week," Dad says, staring at his book. "So we're already behind. I need to work on this. I brought you because I couldn't do this one without you, Tenny." He looks up and smiles. "It's ours. But only if we're quick. So go see if there are letters in the other frieze, too."

"Okay," I say. He's right. It's weird he waited a week, took the time to get me involved, and then let Mom and me have a day to ourselves. Maybe he's actually trying to make things right. But now we have to catch up.

I go over to the other mural, of Heracles and Iolaus fighting the Hydra, looking for more letters. And after a minute, I see them: in the Hydra's scales, one for each long neck. "Here, too," I tell Dad.

"Write them down."

Leo comes over and the two of us start searching for the letters, making sure we're not missing any. Once we have them, we start translating, which takes a while. I put the camera on a ledge, standing up to move it when I want to stretch my legs. Dad knows some Ancient Greek, and Leo knows the modern tongue, which is sort of helpful, and I man the books—computer, really, which has access to hundreds of libraries and private collections filled with not just e-books but scanned images of ancient texts—looking up definitions, previous uses of words, just to try to figure out the meaning from context. This is the part Dad will cut down to mere seconds for the TV show, but I film it all anyway.

After a few hours, we have the words: On the Hydra mural it says WITH ONLY THE LIGHT OF DAWN and on the chariot mural it reads LOVE FLIES TO THE BINDINGS.

"What does that mean?" Leo asks. He's been watching us work, sometimes taking the camera from me to film us.

"Well, 'only the light of dawn' means no other light. Torches out," I say. "The door faces east, so the light would be coming directly in through the door."

Leo glances at the door. It's after noon now, so the light coming in through the door is dim.

"Let's move one of these floodlights to the door, and shut the others," Dad says.

With a little effort we move the light and shut out all the others. The light in the doorway shines brightly down the center of the temple, but all I can see that's changed is that the Eros frieze at the far end is well lit, and the shadows of the two statues are cast next to it.

"Well?" Dad asks. I shake my head. Leo shrugs. Dad comes back to stand with us and stares at the statues. "All right, the bindings, let's assume, are the rings, right?"

"I hope," I say, excited. "And 'love' must mean Eros. I don't see Aphrodite around here."

"Eros was usually used to represent love between men, anyway," Dad says. "And he's got wings, right there. Why isn't he flying to the bindings?"

We stare at the temple for a while longer. I make sure to film it all. Something bothers me about the statues, I'm not sure what. It's like they're twisted slightly. Heracles is a little hunched, and Iolaus is leaning backward for no reason.

I walk down to the statues and stare up at them. They're twice the size of Dad, carved from stone; they must weigh tons. They stand on carved stands as high as my knees. There's no way they can be moved by me. Still . . . I reach out and try turning Iolaus.

"Careful, what are you doing?" Dad calls down the temple.

I lean into the stand, pushing, and to my surprise, Iolaus starts to turn, some mechanism under his feet clanking as I do. The statue was made to turn. I can feel the old stone mechanisms falling into place as I push. I look up and see Leo filming me, and I smile.

"Wait," Dad calls. "Okay, yes, keep going . . ."

I keep turning.

"Stop." I stop when Dad calls out. Iolaus is facing Heracles now, not the door like he was before. "Come see," Dad calls. I jog back to the end of the temple and look at the statues again. Iolaus's shadow now looks exactly like Eros's wing. The same shape, just dark, cast on the edge of the frieze.

"Wings," Leo says.

"So if we turn Heracles . . . ," I say.

"Yeah," Dad says, "but wait." He glances out the door of the temple. "Let's turn him back for now. Turn all the lights back on, too." He waves at Leo and me while he goes to the statue and starts turning it back.

"Why?" I ask. "We almost have it."

"Lights," Dad says. "Tenny, now."

I shake my head but help Leo turn all the lights back on. Just as we finish, Jean walks in. I glance at Dad, curious. He said we had to be careful around her—but does that mean hiding everything from her, too? Or is this just some excuse to steal the rings out from under her? I've never seen him rob a friend before, but he's robbed everyone else. Well, maybe I can give them back to her, then. Or make sure she's involved with where they go. If they're here.

"Hello, boys," she says. "Figure anything out?"

I look at Dad and he says no with his eyes before looking back at her.

"Just studying the stonework," he says, patting Iolaus's knee. "There's a lot to admire before we get to the actual investigation part, and we want to make sure we document everything so the editors can show it off in the show. Actually, Tenny, we should get a shot of Jean in the center of the temple. It's her discovery. Jean, you mind?"

"Oh, well, all right," Jean says, joining my father between the statues.

He's flattering her, we all know it. I feel bad about this. After all, it's her discovery.

1. I could tell her what we found, show her our shared history.
2. Or I could do what Dad asks.

I'm about to open my mouth to tell her, when a guard walks in. He crosses his arms, staring at Dad. There's a pistol in a holster on his belt. I shut my mouth. I don't know what Bulwark is, but I know I shouldn't say anything until I know more.

So I film the two of them. Dad guides Jean through some background shots: the two of them talking, pointing, stuff they can use in the background with voice-over. When they're done, Jean shakes her head, amused. "I know you're just buttering me up to sign that release form," she says. "Where is it?"

Dad grins and takes out his phone and hits a few buttons. "In your inbox. Virtual signatures these days."

"I'll sign it, don't you worry. But I wanted to invite you all to lunch. It's nearly two now. You must be hungry."

Dad nods. "Where's the dig house, anyway?"

"Nice family about a mile up the road has a big farm. They're putting us up in their barn, which we've strung some cloths around and put cots up in. They cook for us, too. Not sure they understood what they were getting into, with all of us, but they seem to like the company. And the money. The food is good. Come on, I'll show you the way."

We follow Jean back out into the dig, where it's less crowded than it was before, though the guards are still there. Jean hops into a car and drives out of the gate to where our jeep is parked. We move to get in and follow her, but she stops and rolls down her window.

"Leo, why don't you ride with me?" she asks. "I want to talk to you about some translation issues I've been having talking to my contact at the Archaeological Society. I could have more work for you when these boys go back to America."

Leo looks at me and I nod, not that he needs my permission. He gets in the car with Jean, and I sit in the rental jeep with Dad, following her as she drives up the road.

"Why don't you want Jean to know what we found?" I ask him.

"I'm just being cautious," Dad says. "It's Bulwark. They make me nervous. I had a run-in with them two years back—the first season you left me?"

I blink at that phrase, "the first season you left me." I didn't leave him. He left me. And for a moment, I want to scream or hit him. I feel my hands clenching into fists of their own accord, ready to fight. But I don't let them. The rings are more important. I swallow the anger back down.

"I watched it. I don't remember Bulwark."

"I cut it out. Didn't want legal troubles. They shot at me a few times, and they might have sued or tried to twist the narrative, claim I'd attacked them first, just to save their reputation. I decided it was better to just leave them out entirely. But they're hunting for artifacts, same as us. I think they're after the rings."

"You think Jean knows?"

Dad shakes his head. "I don't know. I don't think so . . . That's not the Jean I know. She's a lover, not a fighter."

"Dad, gross."

"I just mean she's not like that. But I haven't seen her in years. We email, but people change, y'know?"

I think about David and nod. "Can't be too careful," I say. "I get it."

"Good. Try to make sure Leo does, too."

Jean pulls off the road and drives through a large field to a farmhouse where she parks. There are a bunch of cars here and Dad leaves our rental with them.

Jean grins at us as we close the jeep doors. Leo looks up at me and smiles, but then looks away.

"I like him," Jean says. "He sorted my issue with the Archaeological Society, easy. Something about my accent. Let's go eat."

Dad and Jean head toward the farmhouse but I hang back with Leo.

"Dad says we shouldn't tell Jean anything yet," I say in a low voice, "because of Bulwark."

"Okay," he says. "I thought she didn't like them, though."

"She doesn't," I say, "but Dad wants to be careful. Just in case, I guess."

"She seems cool."

"You didn't tell her anything about what we found, right?"

"No, no." He shakes his head. "She wanted to know if you were actually looking for the rings. I said you were. Then she asked me about a conversation she had with someone from the Archaeological Society and asked for my number so she could hire me again."

"Okay," I say. "Good. I mean, she does seem cool, but Bulwark is scary. I'm sure she's okay, but just in case—Dad says Bulwark shot at him."

"Then we should definitely avoid them," Leo says, his eyes widening.

"Yeah," I say, nodding. I take his hand and he squeezes mine back. His palms are a little damp, though, and I let go before we head into the farmhouse. "I'm sure it'll be fine. We'll just stay out of their way."

Over lunch, Dad regales Jean and the other archaeologists with stories of his adventures, and a few anecdotes about Jean that make it clear they've definitely been lovers in the past, which . . . ew, but it's not the first time I've met one of Dad's old flings. After lunch, we leave the rental at the farmhouse and hitch a ride back to the dig site with Jean. I'm ready to go inside and turn the statues and see what happens, but Dad wants to film the site, rather than going back in the temple. Once we're on-site, we wander away from Jean, who's overseeing the excavation at the top and sides of the temple, and get long shots of everything.

It's winter, so the sun sets pretty early, and it's nearly sunset when Dad finally ushers us back into the temple. He peeks outside, then turns out all the lights except the one by the door again.

"We have to be quick," he says. "We don't want anyone knowing we're doing this."

"Dad, we have to do this properly."

"Properly isn't going to happen with Bulwark around. We tell Jean we found something, then they're going to go in there first. Do you really want to risk some private security company finding the bands before you do?"

"Well then, they'd have to give them to the Greek government, at least," I say.

Dad laughs. "They'll do whatever they want with them, Tenny. Trust me. We have to figure this out on our own. We'll do it right, film everything, take notes and photos, and make sure Jean gets everything she needs for her textbook. But I'm not letting Bulwark figure anything out before we do, all right?"

I take a breath. I don't want Bulwark getting anything before we do, either, but I thought we were going to do this right this time. Archaeologically right. And that means not breaking anything, documenting, telling Jean.

But I guess we'll be filming everything. I look at Leo, who nods at me.

"We should be the ones to find the rings, right?" he says.

I nod. "Okay," I say.

Dad peeks outside again. It's dark. The archaeologists are probably going back to the dig house. Leo goes to the statues and starts turning them as Dad keeps a lookout and I watch the shadows turn into wings.

I keep thinking the grinding stone sound of turning statues is so loud someone will come in to see what's happening, but no one does. Iolaus is turned back into place, facing Heracles, and Heracles, without much effort, turns to face Iolaus. I study their faces as Leo turns them and I see their expressions more clearly now. Before, I thought they were just staring ahead, vacant, regal maybe, like lots of statues. But facing each other, it's two men in love. Heracles clicks into place, his shadow extending as another wing, and suddenly there's a loud echo, the sound of stone on stone as something below us clicks, making the floor shiver. We did it. We did something. I look around the room for a sign of what, though. Will the rings just emerge on a pillar? The frieze at the back of the temple slowly sinks into the floor, revealing a dark stone staircase behind it, spiraling down into the ground. So that must be where they are. Maybe there are traps or puzzles down there, but they must be down there. The rings. We've found them. We're so close I can feel them in my hand, warming from my body heat after being lost for so long.

"Get out your flashlights," Dad says, and with that, we head into the hidden part of the temple.

❧ NINE ❧

Flashlights don't make much of a dent in real darkness. On a starry night or in a city, they can make things clearer, but in true underground darkness, even the strongest flashlight just sort of carves out a small piece of brightness.

Dad and I have learned to see the world in those small pieces. I shine my light there, and see stairs. I keep the light on them as I walk down. When they stop, I walk forward a few steps, then swing the light around, taking in the space in chunks: a low ceiling, so we've come far down.

The floor is smooth stone, not dirt, so this area was important. The walls are smooth, too. There's a statue by the side of one wall. Below it is a raised platform of some kind. I put the night vision filter on the camera, but it doesn't help much in this level of darkness. Just makes the cuts through the dark greenish.

"How do you see anything like this?" Leo asks.

"You can go back up," I tell him. "If you want. This is the dangerous part."

"No," he says. "This is thrilling. I just . . . wish I could see it." He sounds so excited. Maybe more excited than I am—this is his first hidden temple, after all. I reach out in the dark and find his fingers, squeezing them for a moment. He squeezes back, our joy at being close to the rings, to our history, flashing back and forth between us like lightning.

"Can you smell oil?" Dad asks.

I inhale, then nod as it hits me—olive oil, sort of musty. Then I remember he can't see me. "Yeah, I smell it."

Dad shines his flashlight around, taking in more little details—carvings in the floor in the distance, I think; vases along the walls.

"Amphoras," Dad says, approaching the vases. He shines his light directly on their sides, which are between the wall and what looks like a valley carved into the floor. "Ah." His flashlight stops on what I think is a tap, like in a keg, but facing up. "Make sure you get this, Tenny," he says, and I switch the camera back to regular mode, shining my flashlight on the tap as Dad reaches out and carefully turns it. It rotates smoothly and is suddenly pouring ancient oil onto the floor.

"What does that do?" Leo asks.

"Get the other side," Dad says, and I look at the opposite end of the room and quickly find amphoras there, too. There's a tap in one and I turn it, the ceramic feeling too delicate under my hands, until oil spills over my hands. It pours into the carved riverbed on this side, too, flowing from where we stand, by the stairs, at a slight slope down into the rest of the room.

"There's our lighting," Dad says. "Let me get my lighter."

"Won't the amphora explode?" I say, thinking of the accidental explosion he caused in France. Luckily, the only things that were damaged were an unremarkable door, a camera, and one of Dad's eyebrows, but I'd like to avoid it happening again.

"Then it would be a pretty weird design," Dad says as he roots around in his backpack.

"Sure, but we don't want to blow everything up, so—"

"Got it," Dad says, and a light flickers in the dark over his flashlight beam.

"Dad, you promised—"

But he's already set the flame into the river of oil on his side. I duck behind the stairs, pulling Leo with me, and crouch, bracing for an explosion.

But no explosion happens. For a moment, there's nothing, then the oil on Dad's side of the room lights up with a *whoosh* and a flash—but nothing else. One side of the room is lit now, though, by a low crackling fire that runs down in the carved oil river, down to the wider room at the end of the hall. There, the river—now totally on fire—pulls away from the wall and wraps itself in a strange design before meeting up with the river I'd started and coming back on the other side of the room. The fire has been carried by the oil outline and lights up the entire room. It's huge, but the focus of the room is the flames on the floor at the other end, where the floor widens slightly.

I record everything as we walk down to the wider part of the room. It's hot, too. The flames reach higher than my knees. I don't know how the amphoras haven't exploded, but maybe some device in the taps is keeping the fire from getting inside the actual containers.

"Look," Dad says.

"This is wild," Leo says, and I film his wide eyes, staring at the firelit chamber.

"It is pretty cool," I confess. I'm annoyed Dad didn't pause; he could have destroyed the amphora, or worse, us, but it seems to be fine now so . . . here we are.

I turn the camera up, at the slightly domed ceiling. It's all just plain stone, but it has the same feel as the temple above. Someplace quiet. Holy.

"Recognize it?" Dad asks, pointing at the pattern the river of flames has made in the floor at the far end of the room, where we stand now. I look at the way the flames curve and create a sort of shadow puppet, but in reverse. A line drawing in fire.

"It's the Hydra," I say after a moment of studying. A dragon with nine long necks and heads, all made of flame, is in front of us. And we can't make our way around it without lighting on fire, probably. "But I don't see rings."

"Me neither," Dad says. "But this has to mean something."

"Look," Leo says, pointing at something on the ground and moving toward it.

"Careful," I say, filming him.

Leo laughs. "I know fire burns, Tennessee."

"Sorry," I laugh.

"You two are cute," Dad says, but I don't turn to look at him.

Leo gets close to the flames and I'm about to pull him back when he picks up what looks like a miniature sword. It's bronze, not very fancy, with a slight curve and a broad blade. But it's only a half foot long. It had just been laying on the tiles, and I'd been so focused on the walls before I hadn't noticed.

"Like the sword Iolaus used to brand the Hydra's neck, after Heracles chopped off their heads," I say, remembering it from upstairs. "But what do we do with it?"

Leo shrugs, bringing it over to me. I hand him the camera and take the sword to study it. It's plain and blunt, not a real sword at all, with a notch in the blade. Not an accidental one, though, I realize, looking closely at it. It's intentional.

"I think it must move something," I say, "or open something? Like a key or lever?"

We look around the room some more, careful of the flames. Everything glows from their light now; the stone walls and floor are polished and gleam like bronze, reflecting the fire, making it seem bigger. And it's hot. I shrug off my jacket and wipe the sweat from the back of my neck.

Then I study the way the rivers of fire curve and think of Iolaus and Heracles, two men in love, fighting off a monster that only grew as they fought it. Like homophobia, I realize with a smirk. Silence one homophobic asshole or politician, win one victory, like marriage, and within a year it's something new, like banning books and making it illegal for trans kids to transition. *Hydra* even sounds like *homophobia*, a little. But Heracles and Iolaus won their battle. They have a temple. That makes me feel strong.

"There are notches," Dad says, pointing at the flames rising from the floor. "In the actual . . . streams of fire, I guess. In the necks." I carefully approach the Hydra and look at the necks. There are in fact thin slits, not actually across the river of flame, but in the border of stone around them. Carefully, I push the sword into one of them, one of the middle necks. It fits, and when I try angling the sword, I can feel something vibrate through it, and hear a low click. Suddenly, across the neck I just put the sword into, a wall rises, cutting off the flames from the head. Then the head itself flips around, into the ground, a flameless head appearing in its place. From around it, steam rises with a fizz, as if the flames on the other side have been doused. I can see now, without the flames, that there's an actual carved dragon face at the bottom of the river where the oil poured out. Or at least there is on this side.

"I think you just cut off and branded one of its heads, Tenny," Dad says.

I grin and turn around to look at him, and he's giving me a thumbs-up. Then I glance over at Leo, who's been filming everything.

"Okay, so I just have to cut off all the heads," I say. "Easy."

But then, suddenly, two other heads, nearby, flip over and go out.

I look back at Dad, confused. "I didn't cut those off, though."

"That's not how it goes in the myth, either," Dad says, also looking confused.

Three heads extinguished, six to go. But clearly, we're not understanding how it works yet.

I move to two necks over, past the other one that went out. "I'm just going to see what happens," I say. Dad nods.

I find the slot for the sword and repeat the process. The wall rises up, the head turns around, and the head goes out. But then I hear something else click and look back at the head between this one and the first one I put out. The wall that had been put out falls back down with a thud, and the flaming oil rolls back into the head, setting it on fire again. At the same time, another head, above the one I just cut off, flips over and goes out.

"Okay . . . ," I say, even more confused.

"Cut one off, two grow in its place," Dad says. "That's the myth. This is more . . . ambiguous."

I step back and look over the Hydra, Dad behind me, as we consider what to do next. Leo turns the camera on both of us and laughs.

"What?" I ask.

"You have the same expression," he says. "You both are doing the same thing with your hands, too." I look down at my crossed arms, my right thumb rubbing my left elbow, then look behind at Dad, who is in the same pose. I sigh and drop my arms.

"Don't stop," Leo says. "It's cute."

I shake my head. But it's true, Dad and I are most alike at moments like these. Puzzles, ruins—it's when I feel closest to him, too. I didn't even yell at him about lighting the oil on fire, even though I thought it was dangerous, because, well, it's fun. I'm having fun. And I like knowing that we're in this together, trying to figure it out.

I look at the carving of the Hydras. Their necks all weave and curve around the floor but they end up looking a little like a grid of three-by-three. I chopped off the one in the lower right first and took the lower middle and right middle with it. Then I chopped off the lower left, which took out the middle left, but grew back the lower middle.

"I want to try something," I say and walk to the head in the center. I plunge the sword in, and it goes out; so do the ones above and below it. But the ones to the left and right, which had been out, light on fire again.

"Smart," Dad says. "So knocking off a head flips all the ones next to it."

"Looks that way," I say.

"Is the fire getting brighter?" Leo asks.

I look around the room, and the flames lining the walls, which were once knee-high, are now nearly to my waist.

"Yeah . . . ," I say, and run back up to the vases the oil is pouring out of. The amphoras next to the ones we opened are open now, too, adding more oil and more heat. "I think every time we get it wrong, it's going to get hotter in here," I call to them, running back.

"So we solve it or get cooked alive," Dad says.

"We could leave," Leo says, his voice very high. "Or get help."

"No." Dad's voice is firm. "No Bulwark."

"And we if leave, we wouldn't find the rings," I say. "We can solve it."

"What if it's on a timer?" Leo asks.

"Then we'd better solve it fast," Dad says. We stare at the burning Hydra in front of us. I take off my outer shirt. I'm sweating hard now, I can feel it pooling down my lower back. The room is like an oven, growing hotter and hotter.

I wipe my forehead with the back of my hand and study the grid of heads. I tune out everything else—Dad behind me, staring at the grid; Leo beside me, looking anxiously at the growing flames. I focus only on the puzzle in front of me.

"I have to undo what I did first," I say.

"Will that make the fire get hotter or cool it down?" Leo asks.

"I don't know." I shake my head and carefully step around the flames to the middle head again. I plunge the sword in. The heads flip back, but the fire on the sides of the room raise a fraction of an inch. Every move I make brings us closer to a very hot death. I can't afford to undo all my other moves and just restart.

I swallow, my mouth dry, and look at the grid again. It's as it was after I chopped off the second head: the center left and right and the lower left and right are dark. I could take out the top center, and everything would be extinguished except the center middle. But I couldn't slice off that one without lighting up three others.

"What if you took out the top center?" Dad asks. "Then only the bottom—"

"No," I interrupt.

I focus again, considering my options. There are so many, they flicker in front of me. I can feel myself getting dizzy as I think.

1. Right middle, then top middle, then . . . no.
2. Right upper, then center, then . . . no.
3. Undo the lower left, then upper left, then center, then . . . almost. No.

Finally, I see it. Without saying anything more, I go to the upper left and plunge the sword in.

"Tenny, what are you doing, you just lit one again!" Dad says as the center left head relights.

"I know," I say, moving to the upper right head. I plunge the sword in and look at the heads and smile. Only the four corners are out now. A fiery cross is in the center.

"We can't be in here any longer," Leo says. "It's too hot."

He's right. I can feel myself roasting. My skin is already hot, and I have to stand back from the flames or risk a blister or worse. But I'm almost done. I go to the center of the grid and plunge my sword down again into the neck of the Hydra.

"There," I say. I know I'm not actually slaying a beast or anything, but it feels like a triumph anyway. There's a hiss, and the sudden *thwunk* of a breeze blowing through the room, but I can't tell from where. The entire Hydra goes dark, and the flames lining the walls go back down. Very suddenly, the room is colder, and darker. But that's it. Was that right? Or have we made a mistake? Goose bumps break out over my skin. I check my elbow. I'm burnt, and it stings, but it feels good, too.

"Nice job, Tenny," Dad says. "You okay there?"

"Just a burn."

"Hold on, I got some cream," Dad says, going into his bag and taking out a bandage and some burn cream. He walks over to me and applies it, the cream so cool it stings. I'm still wet with sweat and now that it's cold, I'm starting to shiver.

"So . . . now what?" Leo asks.

I turn to Dad, wanting to ask the same thing. But he's staring at the ceiling. I follow his gaze. So does Leo, pointing the camera.

Above us, the ceiling's dome is suddenly no longer just worn stone. Behind it is fire, and it's shining through carefully carved holes, like stars in the night sky.

"Wow," Leo says, and I nod. It's strangely breathtaking, this beautiful dome of fire and stone. I walk up to Dad to stand next to him and he puts his hand on my shoulder, squeezing me.

"Good work," he says. "Real good work."

I grin in the dim light and feel warm again. Not flames-about-to-bake-us-hot, but warm, cozy, standing next to Dad, with his hand on my shoulder, proud of me. I'm proud of him, too. I'm proud of us. I missed this. This feeling in my body like I just fought an army and won, Dad and I back-to-back, taking on the ancient world. The traps, the skeletons. Together, we can triumph over anything. I'd forgotten that. Forgotten how good it feels.

"Make sure you get all of it," Dad says to Leo. Leo pans the camera over everything. "Look." I point to the very center of the dome, where a faint symbol is glowing—two rings, interlocked. "What does that mean?"

"I think it's a map," Dad says. "That's where the bands are."

I feel a little disappointment because he's right. That means the bands aren't here. But we're closer. We know where they are now, or at least the next step. That's something. More than something. I think of the stones of the Acropolis, the ones walked on by people thousands of years ago. I'm doing it again now, but I know these people were queer. I'm walking in their footsteps.

I take out my phone and snap photos of the ceiling to consult later. "So, it's a star map," I say. "We'll need to find charts of what the sky looked like thousands of years ago."

"I have a friend, an astronomer, who should be able to help us out," Dad says. "And good thinking not just assuming the sky is the same."

"So, is that it?" Leo asks. "A star map, and then the rings?"

"We'll see when we get there," I say.

"Hellllloooo!" comes Jean's voice, echoing from the temple above.

"Shit," Dad says. "Tenny, put out the oil on that side."

Dad and I run up the side of the room and quickly turn off the taps from the amphoras. I know we're hiding what we've found from Jean, but the way he says it just makes me run and obey. I don't like it, but then I remember what he said about Bulwark.

"Off?" Dad whispers. The flames flicker out in answer. We're in the dark again.

"What's going on?" Leo asks, turning his flashlight on and coming back to us, by the stairs.

"Just don't say anything about what we just found," Dad whispers.

I can feel Leo staring at me in the dark, but I don't say anything as I quickly put my shirt and jacket back on.

"Did you boys find a secret door?" Jean asks, coming down the stairs. "Oh, it's dark."

Dad shines his flashlight on her. "We were just coming back to tell you," he says. "We wanted to see if it led anywhere."

"I can't believe you found this!" Jean says, nearly breathless. "Now it's going to have to be a book."

I hate not saying anything. This is her discovery. She deserves to know.

"You should—" I start.

"Jean?" A deep voice comes from up the stairs. British accent.

"Aye, Luke, I'm down here. Henry found some kind of chamber. Come see!"

There's the sound of heavy boots coming down the stone stairs. Jean has her flashlight on and is shining it around the room, exploring like we did at first. I open my mouth to speak again, to correct Dad, tell her everything, but then Luke appears and immediately shines his flashlight in my face.

"Why the hell didn't you come find us the moment you opened that door?"

"Hey, get that out of my son's face," Dad says.

"Calm down, Luke, they were just seeing if the space was intact," Jean says, shining her light at him, so we can see him for the first time: tall, broad, in a blue Bulwark uniform complete with beret. A gun in a holster at his hip. He's got reddish hair and a five-o'clock shadow and nasty green eyes that are now focused on Dad.

"They shouldn't have been doing anything without supervision," Luke says. "We've dealt with him before. He's a liar and a thief."

"I'm an archaeologist," Dad says, smirking.

"Let's go back upstairs," Jean says, ignoring them. "We're going to need to bring some real lights down here to explore this place."

Luke steps to the side, waiting for us to go up first. Jean starts and we all follow her back up to the temple. Outside, it's pitch-black.

"When I realized you weren't at the dig house but that you also hadn't said goodbye, I figured you were still here," Jean says. "So I came back. Good thing. You'd have to walk a few miles to get back to your car from there." She crosses her arms. "Unless you were trying to hide from me."

Dad leans against the wall, smiling at her. "We were just really involved in figuring this puzzle out," he says. "There are Greek letters in the friezes, see, and they spelled out—"

"I don't care how you did it," Luke interrupts, coming up from the stairs. "You should have notified someone immediately. This dig is controlled by Bulwark, and anything found here is ours. Including those rings I know you're looking for."

I look at Jean, who shrugs, apologetic.

"Those are just a myth," Dad says, rolling his eyes.

"Like all those other artifacts you've beaten us to?" Luke asks, walking closer to Dad. "Which you just throw up in museums so people write articles about you and keep you on TV? We could find much better uses for them."

"Uses?" Dad asks, his face passive. "For antiquities?" I know he's thinking about the scepter we found, the one that can control fire. What would an institution like Bulwark do with it if they knew? What would they do with the rings?

"Certain antiquities, yes. And the rings are one of them."

"But shouldn't they be somewhere queer people can appreciate them?" I ask, looking at Jean. She looks nervously at Luke.

"Oh, please," Luke says to me, rolling his eyes. "The gay thing? The love that those old texts write about is obviously the love soldiers have for each other during war. Brothers-in-arms. Why does your type always need to sexualize everything? No way a group of gay men were the most fearsome warriors in the world."

"Why not?" I ask, raising my chin.

Luke scoffs. "I don't have a problem with gays," he says. "But be serious."

"You think the rings are real," I say. "Those are just a legend. And what were they for if the army wasn't made of lovers?"

"To make them better warriors. To give them powers—" He stops, suddenly. "This is all classified. Stop filming," he says to Leo, who immediately lowers the camera. "Any of that ends up on the show, I sue. I didn't sign a release."

"Okay, okay," Dad says. "We didn't show Bulwark last time, either."

"Yeah," Luke says. "I was there, you know. Missed you by this much." He holds up his hand, his thumb and forefinger an inch apart. "Begged the higher-ups to let me have another shot at you." I swallow, thinking of the bullet coming that close to Dad.

"I thought we were finally rid of you with the ratings falling," Luke says. "People lose interest without the family angle, huh? And then no network to finance your little escapades. I thought you'd be out of our hair. But I guess you don't mind bringing your kid back if it means you get another season. Viewers love him."

I take a breath, not sure if I heard that right. "What?" I feel the boulder again, rolling, but this time it's just in my stomach.

He brought me back for another season? I don't want to believe that, but it makes so much more sense than anything else. I can feel my brain fighting, not wanting to believe, having to believe. He said he wanted to do this with me.

"That's a lie, Tenny, ratings were just fine." Does he sound desperate or is that just in my head?

Luke grins at that, flashing sharp white teeth. He's all predator now, going in for the kill. And I can't tell if the kill is me or Dad. "You were going to be canceled. Everyone knew it. No show, no financing. Viewership has plummeted since your kid left. The father-son thing was what sold it." Luke turns on me, grinning. "He didn't tell you? What, after two years he wants you back and you don't ask why?"

I look down. I hadn't asked why. I'd been so focused on the rings, but of course that's why Dad asked me to come back. He had photos. He took a week off to come get me. He could have done this one all by himself. Not because he missed me, or wanted to spend time with me, or even because he wanted me to help find the rings. But because he needed me. As a prop. As a good story for the viewers: father and son, reunited, exploring the son's history. He's a good dad. We have great adventures.

"I . . ." I look at Leo, who takes a step toward me. I look at Dad, who's shaking his head, and then at Luke, who's rolling his eyes, and then finally at Jean, who won't meet my gaze. That's how I know it's true.

❧ TEN ❧

I try to look at my options, try to see them now that I know I'm just a prop to Dad, brought along for ratings, but my eyes are starting to blur. I don't know what to do. I feel like they're all staring at me, but it must have only been a second since Luke said what he said. The truth.

"I'm going outside," I say finally. I swallow, my throat suddenly hard and dry, and walk as calmly as I can out into the night.

The dig site is empty aside from a few Bulwark guards at the gate. I look for the darkest shadow I can find, between the columns in front of the temple, and go sit between them and let myself cry. Not because Dad didn't want me here—well, maybe partially because of that—but because I'm stupid enough not to have realized it. He just waltzed back into my life, dangling the thing I wanted most in front of me, and I fell for it. Just like when he promised that family he'd retrieve the sword, or when he conned his way into the treasure cave. He never lies, not really. He just never tells the whole story. *Yes, I plan to sell your family heirloom to a museum. Yes, I'm going to loot the place. Yes, I'm just using you to keep my lifestyle the way I want it, but I don't give a damn about you, Tenny. If I did, I would have at least called at some point over the past two years.*

"You all right?" I glance up to find Leo standing next to me. I wipe my face, which is a mix of sweat, dirt, and tears. I must look disgusting.

Leo sits down next to me anyway. "I think that man was lying."

"He wasn't." My voice sounds so soft.

"Then so what?" Leo asks. "This isn't about your dad, right? It's about those bands, about our history."

"Yeah, I guess." That's why I came back, after all. The rings. But it was Dad, too. It was doing all this again, adventuring, exploring, solving puzzles, the things he and I had always done together. Just did together again. Dad finally came back. And I liked that. I liked us reasoning the puzzle through while the flames burned hotter and hotter. It was exciting, dangerous. But I felt safe the whole time because he was there, looking out for me, the way a dad does.

Except he was just looking for his meal ticket. Or worse, his ticket to keep doing what we both love to do. He just needed me this time. But he didn't *want* me.

I swallow and smear all the grime off my face. I'm done crying. I lean on Leo's shoulder and he puts his arm around my waist. This is someone who wants me here for me. Not because his producers told him to bring me. I accidentally got him a job, sure, but if he was doing his job, he'd be with Dad. Instead, he's out here, not saying anything, just holding me. That's what it is to want someone, to care about someone. And I don't mean romantically, but maybe with Leo it is, I don't know, but . . . he cares about me. Maybe it's just a queer thing. Queers caring for queers. That's not always how it works, but it should be. You can't trust straight people after all—not even your parents.

"Thanks," I say to Leo. He looks like a statue in the dim light, his skin glowing where the light hits it, the rest of him dark in shadow. I lean up and kiss him and he kisses me back. He tastes like dirt, and I realize his face must be dirty, too, he must be almost as filthy as me, but I didn't even see it, and maybe that's how he sees me.

I wrap my arms tight around him for a moment before breaking the kiss and just holding him. I realize I can always leave. Call Mom, walk away.

1. Walk away, which would be what Dad deserves.

2. Go with Dad to find the rings, act like nothing is wrong, like I'm not just a pawn to him.

3. Or maybe something better than that . . .

"We'll get the rings," I tell Leo. "And then, I'm going to get my own show. I'll be eighteen soon. I'll negotiate the contract. Make sure Dad can't do anything with the artifacts. He'll become my assistant. The cameraman. Just my co-star. I'll never treat him like a father again."

"Ten . . ." Leo whispers.

I pull back from the hug, waiting for him to tell me I'm wrong. But he doesn't say anything.

Then Dad comes out of the temple, looking around, his face worried, before he spots me and breaks into a smile. That same charming smile. I recognize it now. He uses it on Mom. Used it on Jean. And he uses it on me. I thought I was special somehow. But he uses me the same as everyone else.

"You okay, Tenny?" he asks.

"Sure," I say, keeping my voice even as I stand up.

"Luke was lying about all that," he says. "It was nothing to do with ratings. I wanted to see you again."

"Can we go?" I ask.

It's quiet for a moment. Dad staring at me, me staring at Dad.

"Sure," he says after a minute, his voice quiet. "Jean said one of the Bulwark guys would give us a lift back to our car. Just don't say anything about what we found around those guys, okay?" He dips his voice down to a whisper. "Say nothing. We'll talk when we're back in our car."

I nod. And I do what he asks. I don't say a single thing as we get into one of the big Bulwark Humvees and the guard drives us back to the dig house. We ride in silence, the guard barely looking at us. When he lets us out, he immediately turns right around and drives away. Dad gets into our rental jeep, and I follow, sitting in the back with Leo.

"Okay," Dad says. "Let me make a few calls. I bet I can find out where that map was pointing and get us there. Sound good, Tenny?"

"Sure," I say.

"Is he mad at me?" Dad asks Leo.

Leo's eyes go wide, and he stares at me.

"Dad, leave him alone. It's fine. Leo, give me the camera so I can change out the memory card."

Dad takes out his phone and calls someone while I go about the business of changing out the memory card, sealing away the old one so it's safe.

"Hey, Isabelle," Dad says into his phone. I roll my eyes. Of course it's a woman. "It's not late in Paris, is it? Oh, well, I'm sorry, but I have a favor to ask, for the show, a pretty big one, but it's exciting. I'll be sure to mention you. Here, Tenny, get this on tape." I sigh and hold up the camera with its fresh memory card, filming Dad like I always do. "I'm on the phone with Isabelle Montague. She's an astronomer based in Paris with a focus on historical astronomy. Because like you said, Tenny, the stars have moved in the past thousands of years, right. Probably not too much, but enough that this map could be off. So, Isabelle, if I send you this map, you think you can figure out where it was pointing in around 380 BCE? I know, I know, it's a huge world, but it'll be somewhere around Greece, I'm almost sure of it." He turns to look into the camera. "They needed to be able to retrieve the rings pretty quickly when new guys joined up, right? So it can't have been too far. Yeah, Isabelle, just talking into the camera. So let me send you the photos I got with my phone, and you can tell me what you find? Fast as you can, please, we're not the only ones on this treasure hunt. Yeah? Thanks so much. You are an amazing woman, and I am going to take you out for a night on the town when this is done. I'll fly into Paris and take you dancing. Yeah. Okay, okay, I'll let you get to work."

He hangs up and grins into the camera like he's just done the actual stellar cartography himself. "It'll probably be ready by the morning. Let's drive into Thiva proper and get cleaned up, okay? I don't want to hang around the dig house. We need to get as big a lead as possible, now that we know for sure Bulwark wants the rings, too."

I frown. I'd been so caught up in my feelings about Dad I hadn't really lingered on that part: Bulwark, a paramilitary group, wants the rings.

"Why would they want them?" I ask.

"Money?" Dad shrugs, pulling the jeep away from the dig house.

"Except it sounded like he believed in the powers of the bands," Leo says. "You don't just sell that."

"Well, they are a military. Maybe they want to put the rings on their soldiers, give them powers like the original Sacred Band had."

"Are they all queer?" I ask.

"Bulwark?" Dad snorts. "I'd be surprised."

"Then they won't work," I say.

"You sure about that?" Dad asks.

I take a deep breath. I'm not. And Luke seemed to think the rings could have power, or at least was hunting them down to make sure. So Dad is probably right. Bulwark wants them to make themselves a better army. A straight one, it sounds like. And the thought of those rings, that magic, if it's real, helping out a man like Luke who doesn't even believe the Sacred Band was queer, doesn't seem to like queer people . . . My mouth tastes like metal suddenly. I can't let them have the bands. They're worse than Dad, way worse. And I'm so angry at Jean, too, for helping them.

I sigh and stare out the window. Thiva is coming up on us quickly, small warm lights in the blue night. No matter how mad I am at Dad now, I know we need to get the rings. I can't find the rings without him, and if he finds them, I can't trust him to do the right thing. But if we don't get them at all, then Bulwark will, and the rings, their queerness, will be erased. They'll become weapons of war. Which I guess they always were, but the Sacred Band protected Thebes. They protected themselves. They were for queer people. Bulwark just wants them to make super soldiers. And I don't think they can. Even if the rings are magic, I don't think they'd work for straight people.

They can't, right?

Dad pulls into a garage under a hotel and we head up to the reception desk.

"You two okay sharing a room?" he asks.

I nod, trying not to smile. He books two rooms and Leo and I head up to ours.

"I'll wake you when Isabelle calls me back. And I have a guy in Athens who can fly us wherever, if it's nearby, on a moment's notice. So be prepared to go at the drop of a hat. This is a race now."

"I get it," I say, covering a yawn.

"Wash up, sleep," Dad says. "We'll be heading out soon."

Alone in our hotel room (two beds, I didn't have the nerve to tell Dad we could use a king), Leo kisses me, then immediately gets in the shower. I'm so tired it's hard to stand, so we don't fool around, just wash up, stealing kisses sometimes, before falling into one of the beds naked together. I lie on his chest, his hair tickling my face, but in a nice way.

"You feel better?" he asks. The light is out.

"Yes, I think so," I say. "I'm angry, though. At my dad, at Bulwark, at Jean for working with Bulwark . . ."

"She was just doing what she had to do," he says.

"I know, but it doesn't make it right."

I sigh and his hand strokes my back, running down my spine and making me shiver.

"How about you?" I ask. "Your first adventure. Almost baked to death. Was it fun? You want out?"

"No," he says, and I can feel him smile in the dark. "It was exciting."

"Yeah?"

"Mmmm," he says, already falling asleep. I let him drift off but take out my phone. I think of Luke again, the look in his eyes, and google Bulwark: Private Military Contractor operating out of London. Hires out to governments and private citizens alike. The web page is clean and corporate, all white and pale blue. Founded in 2002, controlled by an anonymous board. They mostly seem to do bodyguard work, but searching the Internet reveals a few "incidents" of friendly fire in the Middle East that were reported on briefly, and with no real lasting consequences.

Back on the corporate page, I see if I can find Luke, and I do: Luke Welles, Director of Research and Retrieval. "Heading up a small, specialized unit, Luke Welles searches for new forms of outfitting our soldiers with state-of-the-art technology created from historic war philosophies." Uh-huh. Fancy talk for he looks for old artifacts, same as my dad.

Dad says that from what he knows, only like three people before him had found artifacts with any weird properties, and even he's not sure they're all real or do what they're rumored to. The first artifact was discovered sometime in the twenties, but it vanished right after it was found: a mirror that aged people who looked into it.

Then, in 1936, another find: a teapot that made perfect tea. All you had to do was add water. The teapot heated up the water and turned it into tea somehow. People think it's a layer of ancient tea on the inside of the pot itself that flavors the water, though some scientists say it's not. No one uses it anymore. It's under glass at the Natural History Museum in London—though it should be in China, I think.

In 1945, in Canada, an explorer found an oil lamp that, when it was lit and you looked into it, made time disappear—people just stared into it until it went out, not realizing they'd been in a trance the whole time. That's when the UN first got involved. Dad thinks it's one of the reasons they were created. They studied the lamp for years, eventually cutting the wick so it could never be lit again, and even then, they provided guards to watch over it in Gatineau. And what it could do was never made public. No one person could have it, it would be too dangerous, which is what they've done with every artifact since, or at least that's how they explained it to Dad before they told him a guard would be watching over the first magical artifact he found.

The UN likes that he doesn't tell the world about the magic. They think it'll be chaos if everyone knew. Instead, it's an "Oh, maybe it's just science we don't understand" or "It's fake special effects" or the other stuff people say online. Dad has only found four magical artifacts: Two were from before I joined up. The first was more of a location, a temple in Central America where sound just doesn't exist. Then, during his second season, his first on the network, he found a flute in Romania that played by itself. Not mechanics, not a music box, just a beautifully carved flute that kept on playing. People think it's something about the carving creating pressure when a breeze passes through it, but I've seen it—it's just magic. That was a great season because in the ruins of the sunken fort that Dad was exploring, you could always hear the flute playing faintly in the background.

The UN sent guards to both of those, too, but then on my first season, we found the scepter. It controlled flames. It couldn't produce flames, or make them bigger, but it could shuffle them out of the way so we could pass through, and it could take already roaring fires and make them lash out, like a whip or sword. That's when Dad decided some stuff was too unbelievable to show entirely. He showed the scepter controlling fire in the castle where he found it, and even said on camera it was probably due to "particles" the scepter was spraying, an "ancient chemical formula," but the footage of him lighting a match and making the fire from that dance into words and patterns he didn't even leak online.

That's when the UN showed up, worried. If the scepter were controlled or replicated, it could save lives—or destroy them. So they tagged the scepter and assigned guards to it, like they always did, but they also appointed an international group of scientists to study it under careful watch from their officers and historical preservationists— no access otherwise. It was too dangerous, they said.

People objected, of course, especially the French aristocrat who bought it, but the UN said it was radioactive, made from a meteorite probably, and it was for everyone's safety. They didn't want the truth getting out, either. But all their scientists couldn't find anything, so they eventually released it to the public. Most of the time it lives on display in the Louvre, under careful watch by UN soldiers. The plaque underneath doesn't mention that it can control fire, and mostly you can just find out about that on the Internet, right next to the post about aliens building the pyramids.

The Misumune katana was the same. Geotagged, UN scientists, then a museum with the UN watching over it. People were way more curious about the skeletons that season, so no one asked what the katana could do—and freezing water isn't as dangerous as controlling fire. The island we found it on is totally locked off now and under constant guard. Most people think the skeletons were robots, like Dad said on the show, just with skeletons on the outside.

But if Luke finds the rings, if they really are magic, then Bulwark isn't going to want to put them in a museum. They're going to have their own scientists look them over, probably with no care for destroying them. They're going to keep them as weapons. They're going to make sure they never come to light, that my history never comes to light, so that they can keep them as a secret tool in their battles. Probably charge extra. "The Sacred Band Package."

I shut off my phone and lie down next to Leo, who is snoring. I close my eyes and it takes a while, but eventually my mind rests. The sleep that comes for me is a blackout sleep, where you fall like a weight into the ocean, and not a single dream stirs in your wake.

❧ ELEVEN ❧

We don't hear from Dad's friend that night, and we get some real sleep. The next day, Leo and I go out to a café across the street for breakfast, where he makes me try *tropita* and some of that dark Greek coffee, which is like a hit in the face to my weak Frappuccino taste buds.

"Thank you," I tell him, feeling the caffeine singing in my veins. I glance out the window of the café. I wonder if Bulwark is watching us, has someone following us.

"It's good, right?" he asks, taking another bite of the delicious cheese pastry.

"Yes," I laugh, "but I mean for yesterday. It was a lot. And you didn't freak out or walk away, and I barely know you."

"True." He smiles, sipping his coffee. "But it wasn't so bad, really. And even if we weren't, um, sharing a bed, I still would have done it. You're my friend. Even if we have only known each other a few days. I know you enough to know that."

I smile, then take a sip of the coffee and flinch. He laughs, which makes me laugh.

"Still," I say. "Me crying because my dad doesn't love me—that's intense for a second date."

"I don't think your father doesn't love you."

"He didn't visit me for two years, and when he finally showed up, it was only because the producers made him," I say, shaking my head. "I feel calmer about it today, I guess? But I'm sad. He didn't want me with him. And I was an idiot to think he did."

"I think . . . you should tell him all that. You should talk to him. You can't know what another person is thinking, what his reasons were for staying away or coming back."

"Two years." I draw the words out.

"I don't mean forgive. I mean . . . understand before you decide. My mother and I didn't have the best relationship. I was never out to her. But if she were here . . . I'd be grateful."

"Right." I close my eyes. "I'm sorry, me whining to you about my dad must seem so callous."

"Callous?" he asks. "Like in your fingers?" He stretches out his hand and looks down at it. I take his hand, linking my fingers through his.

"No, it means cold."

"Oh, no then, I don't think you're callous. Just angry your father didn't tell you the truth. But you should tell him that."

My phone pings and I take it out.

GABE

You still alive?

I laugh.

"What?" Leo asks.

"A friend back home," I say.

"Oh?" he says. "What do they say?"

"He just wants to know if I'm still alive."

"This isn't your ex, though?"

"No." I scowl. "I blocked him."

"What happened with him anyway? If you want to tell me?"

"He cheated on me."

"Ah," Leo says.

"And so then I made out with a random guy in front of him—Gabe, the one who texted. And now we're friends."

Leo laughs. "Is he the one you sent the photo of me to?"

I feel my cheeks warm. "Yes."

"Video chat him," Leo says.

"What?"

"I want to meet him. If he's seen a photo of me, it's only fair."

I laugh. "Okay," I say, hitting the video chat button. It rings a few times before Gabe picks up. He's close to the camera but then backs away and I can see he's in what I guess is his bedroom. Black sheets on the bed behind him, gray walls, and a bunch of posters of punk bands I've only half heard of. There's also a zebra stuffed animal on one of the pillows, which is adorable.

"You're videoing me?" Gabe asks. He's in a loose neon pink tank top that matches his hair where the dye hasn't grown out. "To what do I owe the honor?"

"Leo wanted to meet you," I say, turning the camera so he can see Leo.

"Oh, hello," Gabe says, fussing with his hair. "So you've been spending some time together, huh?"

"He's our translator," I say.

"Nice," Gabe says. "Well, hi, Leo."

"Hi," Leo says. "I thought it only fair since apparently you've seen my photo, that I see you."

Gabe laughs. "Yeah, yeah, but I didn't choose to send it to me."

"You asked," I say.

"I'm very impressed you delivered," Gabe says. "I didn't think you'd have time to find a guy. Where'd you two meet, anyway?"

"Queer museum," I say.

"There's a queer museum?" Gabe asks. "That's awesome."

"Athens Museum of Queer History and Culture," Leo says. "It's very small. Tennessee was hoping for something else, I think."

"Looks like he got something better, though," Gabe says. "Is there a lot of queer culture there?"

Leo shakes his head. "Athens is probably the most queer place, but it's not like America."

"Well, it's not like New York, you mean," Gabe says. "Plenty of places in America you still can't really be queer. That's cool, though. I'm glad you found someone queer to hang out with, Ten. I can't imagine being around just straight people for that long."

"It's been like three days," I say.

"Yeah." Gabe makes his eyes serious and shakes his head sadly. "Way too long." Leo and I both laugh.

"Well, I'm glad, too. If only so it's not just me and my dad." Gabe nods. I realize he doesn't know the whole story.

"It's complicated," I say.

"You'll tell me about it when you're home," he says. "But I'm fading, guys. So unless you're going to do something to keep me awake . . ."

"You were just texting me," I say.

"I like texting you before bed," Gabe says. "Though now I'm going to text Leo, too."

"Sounds fun," Leo says, smiling. "We can have group text."

Gabe cackles.

"*A* group text," I correct.

"I know what I said," Leo says, the corner of his mouth raising like a devil's horn.

"And with that thought, I'm shutting out the lights. Night, you two. Stay safe."

"Sweet dreams," Leo says as Gabe ends the video.

"You flirting with my friend?" I ask him.

"I like flirting. Besides, you made out with him," he says.

"Should we—" I pause. "Do we need to talk about—"

"Tennessee, you're on a trip. You won't be here long. We're friends. That we've also had sex is just . . . an extension of that friendship. I have no expectations, but I hope when you go home, you'll still text and email me."

I grin, a small relief rolling down my spine, my shoulders a little lighter. "Good," I say. "That's exactly what I felt, too. And I'm definitely going to call you. After last night, that thing with my dad, how you were there for me . . . you mean a lot to me."

Leo takes my hand and leans forward to kiss me lightly on the forehead. I feel his hands weave with mine, and for a moment, I feel like I'm woven with all the queer people in the world. That's what's important about him—not just as a person but having another queer person here with me. Not being alone.

Then suddenly, there's a banging on the window we're sitting next to. Dad is there, filming us. Seeing him breaks the moment. I'm not part of some great queer tapestry anymore, I'm the kid whose dad didn't want him again.

Dad says something, but we can't hear it through the glass, so he waves us to come out. I pay for breakfast and we head outside, where Dad is grinning from ear to ear.

"We have a location, and we have a plane."

"Really?" I ask. "Already?"

"Computer program made the chart easy to read and my friend with the plane is dying for some work. Go grab your stuff while I check us out and we can drive to the airport now."

"Okay," I say, heading back toward the hotel. Leo follows but crashes into me when I suddenly stop.

"What?" he asks.

I turn around and take his wrist. "You don't have to come. I just wanted to make sure you knew that. Because it could be danger-ous again."

"You might need a translator."

"I just wanted to give you the opportunity," I say. "I care about you, and I don't want you to get hurt tagging along just because—"

"Because I like you?" Leo grins. "Don't worry. I'm not risking my life for you, Ten. I'm doing it for money and fun, and maybe a little for you. But it's third on the list."

"Okay," I say. "That makes me feel better."

We head back to our hotel room and pack everything up before meeting Dad in the lobby where he's checked us out. Then we pile into the car and drive to the airport. I sit in the back seat again, filming Dad. I'm still angry at him, very angry, but a new lead, heading to maybe find the rings, takes over everything else. Excitement is my only emotion.

"So," I ask Dad, filming from the back seat, "where are we headed?"

"Well, Isabelle used a computer program and her own genius to calculate where the rings are based on the star map we found below the temple. It's a private island off the coast, acquired by a hotelier about a decade ago with plans to build a resort there. They started building, but then the hotelier had some financial troubles, so building was halted indefinitely. The island hasn't been inhabited since then. Historically, there's nothing interesting about it, unless it had a different name once upon a time. Now they just call it Psephos."

"That means, like, small stone," Leo says. "Smooth, like the kind people use to vote."

"The hard part is going to be the landing," Dad says, ignoring Leo. "I'm not sure if there'll be enough clear land to work as a runway. Luckily, my favorite pilot, Sonny, is in town. If anyone can get us down safely, it's him."

"Sonny?" I ask, scowling over the camera. "You're using Sonny again?"

"What's wrong with Sonny?" Dad asks.

"He's a drunk," I say.

"Oh, he's not that bad. He's just a little wild."

"He literally keeps an open bottle of gin next to his seat on the plane."

"That's just for the nerves," Dad says, smiling.

"Seriously," I say, turning to Leo, "get out now."

"I'm having too much fun," Leo says. Dad laughs and claps him on the back. I sigh.

"So, what do you think we'll find there?" I ask. "If we survive the flight."

"I don't know," Dad says. "I'm hoping some sort of warehouse filled with rings, but considering the little test we had back at the temple, I'm expecting something more complicated. I brought rations, just in case."

"Oh." I take a deep breath. I hate the sponsorship moments, but know my part. "What kind?"

"The kind from our sponsors at QuickFix Foods," Dad says, turning briefly to wink.

"I feel like being cheesy and obvious about the advertising doesn't make it better," I say.

"The producers want it."

I sigh. "Will we really need the rations?"

"I don't know, Tenny. It could be a warehouse, like I said, it could be an underground temple filled with puzzles that'll take us a week to unravel if they don't kill us first. You uploaded everything we filmed so far?"

"It's in the cloud," I say, nodding. I'd done it this morning after I'd emailed Mom to let her know we were still alive. The cloud is encrypted. Not to be sent to the producers until Dad has combed through and edited the footage, or if we don't check in after two months—that's the time limit he set to determine if we're dead.

"I'm just worried about Bulwark. I'm glad you got all that. Not for the show, but just in case."

We go quiet at that. Throwing ourselves into certain danger is one thing, being chased by it is another.

"Hopefully it'll take them a while to figure out what the puzzle meant," Leo says.

"Hopefully," I echo.

We make it to the airport and pull through to the private terminal. It's just small hangars here, rented by the day, to people like Sonny, freelance pilots who work as carriers of packages; or to rich people who aren't rich enough for a private jet; or to crazy people like us who want to land somewhere there's no landing strip. Sonny's in the third hangar, waiting for us. His plane is an old Cessna he's painted bright yellow, with a child's rendition of a sun in black on the side. He calls it Luna, though, to go with his name—Sun and Moon. He's the sort of guy who finds that hilarious. He's refueling it when we pull in, but he looks up, grins, and waves. Of course, he's in a Hawaiian shirt—every pilot Dad uses wears Hawaiian shirts for some reason, maybe it's a uniform. What's left of his blond hair is combed over his scalp, which is sunburned.

"Hey, Henry," he says when we exit the jeep. He draws out his words too long, but I've never been sure if that's just the way he speaks or because of alcohol or pot or what. "Oh man, and you got the little man back with you . . . and some other little man," he says, spotting me and Leo.

"I'm seventeen," I tell him. "And five eleven."

"Yeah, but you're little in terms of age. But look at you . . . wow, man. Why are you back? Didn't you and your dad have some big blowout because—"

"You have the plane ready?" Dad asks. "We're kind of racing to this one."

"Yeah, yeah," Sonny says, putting down the fuel and closing the tank up. "We can go whenever."

"Shouldn't you like . . . check it before we just take off?" I ask.

"Check what?" Sonny asks. He stares at me a moment before hopping up into the plane. I sigh and grab my backpack and jump in behind him. Leo and Dad follow. It's a small plane, can only seat four besides the pilot and copilot (Dad says he can copilot because of all the times he's seen other people fly). Leo and I strap ourselves in behind them as Sonny starts talking over his radio, asking for permission to take off and arguing about why he should get to go to the front of the line.

"I don't see any open gin," Leo whispers to me.

"I don't know if that's better or worse," I whisper back.

"You didn't talk to your dad," he says, after a moment.

"I . . . will," I say. "When the time is right." And I guess I will. I'd like to see him sputter to explain: *No, I stayed away for two years because you wanted me to, and I came back because I needed you again. You're just a tool to me, Tenny.*

Maybe I won't steal the show from him. Maybe I'll just start my own YouTube channel, talking about the adventures from my perspective, bashing him, explaining everything he did wrong. I'm not sure what the contract I signed allows. I'll have to go over that with Mom.

"Are you okay?" Leo asks. "You look so angry."

"Just thinking," I say.

He puts his hand on my knee and squeezes.

"All right, you guys ready for takeoff?" Sonny asks, turning around. He spots Leo's hand on my leg and suddenly blushes. "Oh man, sorry, little man, didn't mean to interrupt whatever. Um, just buckle up, okay?"

"You didn't—" I stop, sighing. Who cares?

A moment later we're pulling down the runway and then blasting down it as we launch into the air. I've been in these little prop planes before but looking over at Leo, it's clearly new to him. They rattle—a *lot*. Always feel like they're going to fall apart midair, even when they're not being flown by Sonny.

"Hey," I say, taking his hand. "You okay?"

"This is noisy," he says, but I can tell he means more than that. It's scary.

"Hey, you almost just got baked alive in an ancient underground temple, right? This is just a shaking plane. You can do it."

"I've actually never been on any kind of plane," he says.

"Oh," I say.

I should have thought of that. I squeeze his hand tightly. "Okay, so what helps me is I like to imagine a Frisbee being thrown. It catches the wind, right, like we are, and then it glides back down to earth. That's all we're doing. Catching the wind and gliding back down."

"Frisbees don't always do that. Especially not when they're thrown by drunk people," he says, his face melting into anxiety.

"I was just kidding about that." I shake my head.

"No you weren't," Leo says, laughing nervously.

"Okay, I wasn't—but I'm here, okay. And we're in the air, right? So let's just hold hands and hope we glide gently to the ground?"

"Because that's all we can do?" he asks.

"You wanna jump?" I ask. "There are parachutes. We can bail now."

"No." He shakes his head quickly and clutches my hand.

"Well then, I'm not sure what other options we have. Plus, hey, if you've never flown—look out the window." I nod at the window behind him. "It's cool, too. Not just scary."

He turns and looks out the window, and his hand loosens its grip a little.

"It looks like we're moving so smoothly," he says.

"We are," I tell him. "As smoothly as we can anyway."

We sit like that, Leo holding my hand and gazing out the window, for about an hour more. I film out the windows and Dad and Sonny talking up front, the noise of the plane impossible to hear them over.

The island isn't too far off the coast. I wonder if, as a private island, the Greek laws surrounding antiquities still apply. It's still technically Greece, so they must, I think. But it does mean it'll be even easier to get the rings out of the country. Just have Sonny fly us from the island to Turkey or Egypt, hop on a bigger plane out of there. No one is on the island to even know we're going to be there, much less what we'd take out. But I don't know if that's the right thing to do. I wish I could give them specifically to the queer museum in Athens, but there's no way they'd have the security or insurance to be able to hold on to them.

And that's if we find anything. The rings could all be gone. We could be on a wild goose chase.

"All right, all right, get ready back there," Sonny says. "I see a dirt road down there I'm going to try for, but it's going to be rough."

Leo turns to me, his eyes filled with panic. "What does *rough* mean?" he asks. I hold his hand tighter.

I've only experienced one other "rough" landing with Sonny, in Guatemala. We'd crashed through the upper canopy of the jungle to land close to these ancient ruins that an earthquake had recently revealed. It was hard, that landing. Sonny had to repair the plane while we explored the ruins, but it wasn't so hard he couldn't do it alone.

This one looks easier. After all, it's just an overgrown dirt road on a rocky island. The wheels come down hard enough we bounce up in the air, my teeth knocking together like I've been punched in the jaw, and I lose my grip on the camera. But there are no branches, no broken windows. Except then comes the braking.

"Keep holding," Sonny screams. "It's a short road."

Leo's hand is still firmly around mine, cutting off circulation, as we feel the pressure of the plane stopping sharply and suddenly, trying to slow down before we crash into a large boulder at the end of the road. I hold my breath as the rock gets closer and closer. We're not slowing down. I feel like a crash test dummy. I push myself farther and farther into the chair. Maybe this is finally it. Maybe this is how I die: not drowned in a flooded temple or impaled on a spear under a trapdoor, but in a plane crash, nose first into a mountain on an island in the middle of nowhere. That would be funny, I think, swallowing as the rock gets closer. Dying just feet from the first treasure we uncovered that was for me. The velocity pulls my head back and I bite down a scream.

Maybe not really so funny.

❧ TWELVE ❧

Suddenly, we stop. The tip of the plane is less than a foot from the stone. I take a big gulp of air and then reach into my backpack for a bottle of water. My hands are shaking enough it's hard to grab, but then I drink and pass it to Leo, whose hands are also shaking.

"Not bad, right?" Sonny asks, turning around. "You get it all on camera?"

"I lost my grip," I say, my voice steadier than it should be.

"Well, shit," Sonny says, turning back around. "Some of my best work."

"You guys okay?" Dad asks.

"Just a little shaky," I say.

"Well, let's get out of here. That'll help. And we have an entire island to explore."

"Right," I say, standing. I grab the camera and check it's okay as Dad opens the plane door. We hop out onto the barren road. Maybe it was cleared by the people building the hotel? I'm not sure. At the far end of the road, toward the coast, I can see the metal skeleton of a tower peeking out of the woods. It reminds me of my date with Leo, the towers over Athens. It's just a frame, once the beginning of the hotel, I guess, but now it's ruins—didn't even have a chance to finish building before it became archaeology.

"We can assume they dug around there, to pour the foundation," Dad says, following my gaze. "If they'd found anything they would have destroyed it or reported it, so we should start on the other side." He turns around and I follow. The boulder we almost crashed into is just the first of many, growing larger in size, leading up to a mountain. Dad pulls up a map on his phone. "There's not much geographical information online," he says. But it's pretty much just this mountain and the beach where they built the hotel. I think we need to start with the mountain.

"We're climbing it?" Leo asks nervously.

"We'll look around the base first," Dad says.

"It's probably not that steep all away around," I tell Leo, taking his hand again. "Besides, we didn't bring equipment for full scaling."

"Yes we did," Dad says.

"Oh," I say, shrugging.

"Bought it last night," Dad says. "Just in case."

I nod. I forget how single-minded he can be about expeditions. How prepared for anything. He's good at it. Until he isn't. I sigh, feeling proud of him and then in the same moment remembering I'm only here because his producers forced him to bring me back. Why couldn't he just want me here? Enjoying myself feels dirty now, like I'm falling for a trick. Again.

I pull on Leo's hand. "Let's start looking around."

"You good to stay here?" Dad asks Sonny.

"Sure," Sonny says. "How long?"

"I don't know," Dad says. "But there might be some folks on our tail. If you see anyone else land, hide. They're dangerous."

"Roger that," Sonny says, hopping back into the plane. "I gotta find a better place to park her anyway."

I pull Leo away, walking toward the mountain. Once we're off the road, we're quickly surrounded by trees, which twist around us. The bushes grow up past our knees in places. Tall and leafy enough to hide under.

"Olive," Leo says, pointing the camera at the unripe berries on the branches. "Maybe this was a grove once. Maybe when whatever was built here was built."

I grin. He's thinking like an archaeologist. "Maybe," I say. "If there was, then we should follow the olive trees."

I look around. There are a bunch of trees, but the olives stand out because of their dark bark and curved trunks. There are several of them, mixed in with other trees. We try following them through the woods, the dirt crunching under our shoes.

"Tenny?" I hear Dad call. "Where'd you two get to?"

I sigh. I don't want to answer.

"Here," Leo calls.

I keep following the olive trees, pulling Leo along, getting farther from Dad. The trees lead to the remnants of a low wall, barely to my knees.

"A fence?" Leo says.

"I don't know," I say.

"Hey," Dad says, coming up behind us. "There you are. Trying to get away from me?"

I don't turn around. "Leo said the olive trees could be from an ancient grove, so we were following to see if it led to anything. We found this." I point at the wall.

Dad bends down to look at the wall. "Could be ancient. Definitely not modern building."

"So it could lead to the temple?" Leo asks.

"It might," Dad says.

"So how about we follow it this way?" I say, pointing toward the mountain. "And you go that way, and if either of us finds anything we can come back to get the other."

"Oh," Dad says, looking me over. His brow scrunches a little like it does when he's working out a puzzle. "Sure, Tenny."

I turn around and walk away from him, Leo following a step behind. I barely look to see if I'm following the old wall, I just want to get away from Dad. My anger is swelling up in me now. It does that when he smiles, when he's around too long, like some sort of allergic reaction. Hives of rage. He should have said something by now, apologized for not telling me why he brought me back, at least, instead of just denying it and moving on. Just like he did with the two years he was gone. Just like he's done with everything my whole life. Acts like everything is better and hopes I'll play along.

Well, I won't this time. Not yet at least.

I stomp forward, dirt and fallen leaves crackling underfoot.

"Ten," Leo says, a few feet behind me. "You're going too fast." I stop and wait for him to catch up. "We need to follow the wall, right? And I'm trying to film everything."

"Right, sorry," I say. "Just wanted to get away from him."

"I know," Leo says. "I think he knows, too."

"Good," I say.

He doesn't say anything more and a chilly breeze wafts over me. It smells like fish and olives.

"The wall turns there," Leo says. "Let's follow."

I let Leo lead, filming, as we follow the wall. It's turned at a right angle and continues south, taking us farther from the mountain.

"I think this is the edge of the grove," I say. Leo turns the camera on me. "So if this is the end of the grove, we should look for something else—evidence of an old road or maybe a home, though that's unlikely."

"But wouldn't a road be overgrown by now?" Leo asks.

"Roads last," I say. "Not paved or anything, but people tend to walk the path of least resistance, trample the same dirt. That can last way beyond buildings. Although this island seems so abandoned . . ." I look up at the mountain. It's dark gray, overgrown with trees like hanging moss. It looks like a headstone. How long has this island been dead, though? Did the surveyors who were going to build the hotel inspect this side?

"Let's follow it a little longer," I say, walking along the old wall again. It vanishes in places, crumbled to nothing. But we can spot it if we look carefully. We follow it a half mile or so before I notice something odd in the wall—a post. Before, it had been just rocks piled up, or falling down in most cases, but this is a stone column, thin and broken, but definitely carved. I kneel down to check and study it.

"What is it?" Leo asks.

I turn toward him and the camera. "So this is different. This is a carved stone post, which probably means there was a gate or entry here. If this was an olive grove—and it was definitely something—then maybe this was the way people went in and out." I stand and study the ground, walking away from the grove. "And that means if there was a road, it would be here."

I stare at the trees in front of us, looking at their heights, the grass and stones between them. There's definitely a pattern of younger trees weaving ahead like a river.

"There was a road here," I say, pointing. "See how the trees are younger? That's because the dirt has been cleared more recently than the older trees around them."

"So we follow the younger trees?"

"Yes," I say. I feel electric. Something is here.

"Should we go get your dad?"

I sigh. "I guess." The electricity leaves me.

We turn around and head back, following the wall, but meet Dad coming toward us after ten minutes.

"It vanished on my side. You?"

"I think we found something," I say.

I lead him back to the post and point out the young trees.

"Nice work, Tenny," he says, slapping me on the back, and I smile. And then I frown at my smile. I hate how easily he charms me again. Makes me feel wanted.

I start forward, following the young trees.

"If this was a grove," Dad says into Leo's camera as we walk, "it means maybe there was a small village here. Possibly they were in charge of safekeeping whatever it was having to do with the sacred bands that we're going to find. A village of guardians, maybe."

"I wonder if they were all queer, too," Leo says.

"Maybe," Dad says.

The young trees end with the forest as the island suddenly slopes down to a rocky beach. It's all gray and beige stone in front of us, but the mountain rises up close on our right.

"So if the road ends here, there were no people?" Leo asks.

"Could have been a small harbor," I say.

"Yeah," Dad says, looking up at the mountain. "A dead end. Or . . ."

I follow his gaze. The mountain's incline is gentler here, and right by us, it almost looks like there's a valley in the gray stone.

"Think that was steps?" I ask.

"Yeah," Dad says.

We walk up to the valley, which is almost like a natural slide in the stone. It's unusual, but if it were carved stone once, worn down now, it would make sense. I start walking up it. It's a gentle incline, but only goes up and forward a little before ending in another sheer face of stone. I walk up as far as I can, then turn to the left, and smile. A small path curves around the mountain, heading up, invisible from the shore.

"Up here," I say. Dad and Leo follow me, and Dad smiles at the path.

"Yes," he says. "Something was definitely here."

I feel it again, that electric energy of discovery.

"Looks narrow," Leo says. "Is it safe?"

"No," Dad says, grinning widely.

"You can stay if you want," I tell Leo. "There's no shame in that." Leo stares at the path.

"It's not so narrow," he says.

I smile at him and start walking up. It's not just a thin path, but steeper, too, and if there were steps here, they're even further gone than the ones below. I can feel pebbles punching up into the soles of my shoes, a few of them tumbling loose under my feet. I step carefully, leaning into the mountain, especially as what little jutting stone there was on my left fades away into a sheer cliff face. We move quickly, spiraling the mountain, and soon we're twenty feet up, then thirty. The path is just a grassy cliff face now, narrow enough for my two feet pressed close together and not much else. Every time my backpack hits the mountain and rebounds, it almost takes me over the edge, so I shrug it off, carrying it ahead of me in my hand.

"I have spikes," Dad says. "Climbing claws back with the plane, too."

"There's no time to go all the way back," I say. "It's fine. We've seen worse." I take a deep breath and keep walking, flattening myself against the wall of the mountain and walking sideways when it gets too thin.

Once, the rock crumbles under me and I nearly fall, but Leo, just behind me, catches my shoulder, which gives me enough time to move my foot to a more stable part of the ledge. I smile at him, but we don't say anything. Both our faces are covered in sweat.

I don't know how long we walk for. It feels like it could be hours. The sun moves lower and lower on the horizon by the time the path stops. It spreads out like a puddle, an outcropping with high rocks at the edge that hide us from anyone below, and a few bushes growing in the thin dirt. For the first time in a while, the ground feels steady under my feet, and I take a deep breath and sit in the dirt. Leo crumples down next to me, panting, and then comes Dad, who leaps onto the plateau and grins.

"I should have gone first," he says. "I think the camera Leo is wearing just has footage of you, Tenny."

"It's a better view, you should thank him," I say, lying down so I can stare up at the sky. Clouds have come in thick, and I worry it might rain soon.

"Uh-huh," Dad says, rolling his eyes. "Get some shots of the way we came," he says to me, and I take the camera from Leo and film the side of the mountain, our little path. We're high up. Much higher up than I realized, at least a hundred feet in the air. "So is this it?" Dad asks. "What's here?"

I turn the camera around, naturally focusing on him as he studies the walls of the mountain, the ground beneath us. It doesn't take long before he finds a tunnel carved into the rock that was hidden behind the bushes. He turns to the camera and wiggles his eyebrows as he pushes the bush out of the way, and we follow him in. The cave starts small but gets taller as we walk into it. I film every inch, the way it goes from a natural-looking cave opening to carved hallway with worn friezes in the walls. They look like the symbol we saw in the temple. The interlocking rings. Just that image over and over again, at about eye level along the walls. Dad and Leo shine their flashlights on it as we walk farther from the light.

"This has to be it," Dad says.

At the end of the tunnel is a large set of stone double doors, the interlocking ring symbol over the front of them, much larger now, big enough to spread your hand out in one of the rings. I feel excitement rising in me. This is it. We're so close to the rings and we found them before Bulwark, before anyone else. Soon, I'll be holding them in my hand. I can feel it.

Dad goes to push the doors open, but they don't budge. There are no handles, but he tries latching his fingers into the space between them and pulling anyway. Nothing. I hand the camera to Leo and push with Dad, but it's not even like we're pushing against doors. It's just a stone wall. There's no give at all. Dad gets out a pickax and tries to use it like a crowbar to pry them open, but all it does is scratch the stone. The three of us try shoving with our shoulders in unison. Never once does it even shake.

"Is this . . ." I sigh, sitting on the floor. Dad has set his flashlight up as a lantern, so it's a dim little corner. "Is this wrong somehow? A distraction? Not even where the rings are?" I feel my heart sinking with every word.

"Where else could it be?" Dad asks, pounding the wall with his fist. "Everything led us to this island, and there's nowhere else the rings could be stored."

"Maybe something inside is broken, and it's locked," I say, trying to stare the stone open.

"We could get some dynamite, blow it open," Dad says.

"Dad, you promised, no destruction. We could pry it open, carefully. Maybe Jean knows some way to—"

"No. No Jean. Jean brings Bulwark."

"But if we blow it up, we might ruin whatever is inside. What if the rings are just beyond these doors?" I ask, folding my arms.

"I . . . don't know," Dad says.

Outside I hear the first heavy pellets of rain dropping; then all at once, a thousand more like a landslide. I stand and go back to the entrance of the tunnel. It's pouring rain, so thick I can't see past the edge of the small cliff. I sigh and turn back, walking toward Dad and Leo. The temperature has dropped with the rain. I rub my shoulders as goose bumps break out.

"Raining?" Dad asks.

I nod. "Heavy. We're stuck here for a while."

"Well," he says, "then let's keep thinking. We have nothing else to do. Let's imagine this is still the right place."

Leo stares at the doors-that-probably-aren't-even-doors and films them, corner to corner. I take his hand. I feel like I've let him down somehow. Like all this was for nothing. Dad must feel he's let himself down, as he leans against the wall and then slides down it.

"So that's it," he says. "Nothing. Are we done with the adventure, then? Because you won't let me risk some dynamite just to open a—"

"Dad, stop." I sigh and put my hand against the doors, in the center of the ring on the left. Leo squeezes my other hand and then lays his free hand in the center of the other ring.

And suddenly, the doors move.

Just a little. Just a tremor under my hand.

"Do that again," I say to Leo.

"What?" Leo says.

"Did you feel something?" Dad asks.

"Give the camera to Dad," I say to Leo, "and put your hand in the center of that ring again." Leo does as he's told and Dad films us. I feel it again when he pushes into the ring. A slight tremor. But the doors don't open.

"I saw dust fall," Dad says. "You moved it."

I feel the stone in the center of the rings. It's smoother there, worn down. Leo and I both try pushing in the center of the rings, and while we feel more movement, the doors still don't open. Dad tries, first with me, then with Leo, then by himself, pushing with both hands in the centers of the circles. But still nothing more than a little shake.

I give the camera to Dad again when he's done and then I take Leo's hand and hold it right over the ring on his side. I hold my hand over the ring on the left side.

"If the rings really were magic," I say, "and they made two minds one . . ."

Leo nods, understanding. "On the count of three?"

I nod. "One . . . two . . . three!"

We surge forward in unison, pushing into the doors. And then we fall forward as the doors swing open, collapsing onto a worn stone floor. I look up. All I can see is darkness, but the doors are open. We're going to find the bands.

✯ THIRTEEN ✯

With our flashlights on, we can't see much more of the space. It's too large. Our footsteps echo and then fade like it's an auditorium. Bigger. We're about halfway up the mountain, but from here, it feels like the entire mountain has been hollowed out, a giant room extending above and below us.

"Hello?" I shout, and my voice echoes back in the darkness. We follow the floor about ten feet forward. It's tiled with stone, very plain, but then, suddenly, the floor ends. There's a tile, then a border, and beyond that, just darkness falling down. We look for steps leading up, but nothing. The room just ends in a cliff.

"Are we supposed to jump?" Leo asks.

"Let's leave that as a last resort," Dad says, walking along the cliff's edge until we hit a wall. There, we find a large lever sticking out of the ground. It's not stone like back at the temple, but a big iron lever, almost up to my neck, and it's at an angle, waiting to be pulled. It sticks out of a beautifully done curve of stone that's been carved like it just flows out of the tile.

Dad goes to pull it while I film. It doesn't budge. He pulls again harder, and then again, bracing himself on the wall that the lever stands next to. Still it won't move.

"It must be locked somehow," he says.

"We can try the other side," I say, pointing to the far end of the room opposite us, past the door. "We haven't looked there yet."

"Sure, good idea. You check it out," Dad says.

I hand the camera to Leo, who stays filming Dad, and then walk back through the darkness, along the cliff's edge, until I find the other wall. There, sticking out of the floor, is an identical lever.

"Found a lever!" I shout, my voice echoing. "Pulling . . ."

I give it a tug. It doesn't move. I pull harder, but it doesn't even give. "This one is locked, too," I call.

"Did we miss something?" Dad calls back. I can't see him, and his voice seems to come from everywhere. There's only a little spot of light in the distance, which I know is his flashlight. "A lock in the wall or something?"

"Maybe," I yell back. And then a thought occurs. "Or maybe not. Think of the door. Leo and I had to push at exactly the same time."

"So you think these are the same?" Dad asks.

"Let's try," I shout back.

"One," Dad says.

"Two," I respond.

"Three," we say in unison as I yank down the lever. It moves smoothly this time and clicks into place, level with the floor. I hear Dad whoop from the other side of the hall, so it must have worked for him, too.

And then, I hear a clattering. And the ground seems to shake. I look around for what could be causing it, but it's so dark I can't see anything. I check the cliff's edge, to see if platforms have magically appeared or anything, but nothing. Except light.

Beams of light are shining down into the darkness, and I look up to see where they're coming from: panels high up against the wall are lifting and behind them are windows. Small windows, most of them are circular, but some are oval, or rectangular, and some are weirder shapes. They're all shining the gray, rainy light of outside into the hall.

"Looks like quartz windows," Dad says. He and Leo are walking toward me, their flashlights out. We don't need them anymore. The hall, though huge, is lit dimly enough to see now. "Covered by rock, so from a distance the mountain might look a little frosted, but . . ."

"This is amazing," I say, staring at the hall. Now that there's light, I can see more beyond the cliff. Another cliff ahead of us by about forty feet, and maybe ten feet higher. It's hard to see what's on it, but I can see along the slanted ceiling of the hall now, and there's a system of pulleys, suspended from which is a kind of gondola, like a ski lift. It's already moving slowly toward our cliff. We must be meant to ride it up.

"It's astounding work, no doubt about it," Dad says. "Good work on the simultaneous pull thing," he adds, patting me on the shoulder. I pull away. I'm excited about everything but I haven't forgotten who he is. He doesn't seem to notice. He just points at the gondola and starts walking toward where it will land. Following his finger, though, I see something else—in the walls between the two cliffs, along the same angle as the gondola's path, is a series of carved Hydra heads. Small holes for mouths.

"Did you see the Hydras?" I ask. The gondola pulls to a stop in front of us, perfectly lining up with the cliff's edge. It's wooden, about the size of a door, so we'll all fit on it, but tightly. There's a shoulder-high wooden fence around it, too, with gates that swing open on the front and back. And inside, on either side, are wooden cranks with copper handles.

"Yeah, I see them," Dad says. "And since it looks like we'll be cranking ourselves across, what do you think—they shoot spears?"

"Fire," I say. "If the temple was anything to go by."

"Mmmm," Dad says, stepping onto the gondola. "Well, maybe that part is broken. Nothing happening yet."

Leo and I get onto the gondola, too. It swings back and forth under us but holds firm.

"So, think one of these takes us forward and one back?" Dad says, putting his hand on the crank nearest him and giving it a shove. It moves, but the gondola doesn't.

The Hydras do, though. They pull out slightly from the wall and begin shooting fire from their mouths. The flames reach so far they meet the fire coming from the Hydra opposite, creating a burning barrier. Nine heads on each side. Nine beams of fire we have to pass through without burning alive or burning the gondola to ash and falling to our deaths. Leo shrieks. Thankfully, none of the beams face us directly, though there's one a foot or two ahead. I can feel the heat coming off it.

Dad takes his hand off the crank. The fire stops.

"Okay," he says. "So this crank turns on the fire."

"Why would they have that?" Leo asks, his voice very high. "Why would anyone *want* to turn on the death fire?"

"I bet it's not just that one," I say, giving the crank on my side a little tug. Again, we don't move, but the Hydras spit fire until I let go of the handle. "Yep. I think it's like the door, and the levers—we have to turn the cranks in tandem, or else we get the fire."

"A theme, huh?" Dad says.

"It makes sense, right? If this is where the rings were stored for new members of the Sacred Band, maybe they had to show they worked as one. Maybe that's how the rumors of their magic powers started."

"Or maybe they sent people already wearing the rings to retrieve more," Dad says. "Make sure no one but members of the Sacred Band could pick new members."

I shrug. "Either way, we should try winding in unison."

"Sure," Dad says, putting his hand on his crank. I put my hand on mine. "One."

"Two."

"Three," we say together, and start winding. The gondola moves, starting up toward the next cliff. Then it stalls and the Hydras spit fire again. We're even closer to the first fire now. I'm worried that the gondola might catch fire.

"What did we do?" Dad asks. "Do we need to wind in time, too? Like, match our exact timing?"

"Probably," I say, staring at the fire and swallowing. "We'll have to move very carefully."

"Otherwise we stall," Dad says.

"In front of the fire?" Leo asks.

"I think the stalling causes the fire," I say. "So we have to turn in time and stop when we're clear of the fire."

"Why do we have to stop?" Dad asks. "We'll just keep in time winding the whole way."

"How?" I ask. "We couldn't get two turns of the crank before we weren't in time."

"I didn't know we had to be in time," Dad says, waving me off.

"Sure," I say, my voice cold. Like the two of us have ever been in sync. But he never seems to realize that. "Fine. So let's try to do it in time this time. I think it'll be eight seconds per turn? That sound right?"

"Okay," Dad says. "I'll count."

I take a deep breath and we start turning again as Dad counts.

"One, two, three, four, five, six, seven, eight." He goes a little faster than I would, but I keep time with him, watching the Hydra faces as we creak by them, the gondola swinging slightly over the bottomless pit. The gondola moves way too slowly, and I swear the Hydras are staring at me. For a moment I think they might breathe fire again anyway and I lose count but keep moving at the same rhythm, picking up again with Dad's count. After we pass the first face, I let out a sigh of relief.

"Stop," I say, then wait a beat and let go. The gondola breaks suddenly, swinging back and forth as fire erupts around us. "I said stop, Dad."

"I thought we said we'd keep going," he says.

"Well, I lost the beat."

"We were moving fine," Dad says, sounding a little annoyed. "Keep up so I don't leave you behind."

Those words hit me like ice. "Like you did in Japan?" I ask. Beside me, Leo stiffens.

"What?" Dad turns on me, confused. "What are you talking about? Can we get back to this? I don't like swinging over nothing. I want to get through this so we're back on solid ground."

"Me too," Leo adds, his voice a whisper.

"Fine," I say, because he's right.

"One—" Dad starts again. We wind the cranks in time past the second Hydra, then the third and fourth. After that we stall when he starts going too fast again. The fire is so close I could reach out and burn my hand off.

"Careful," Dad says when the fire stops. "Again."

We wind past the fifth Hydra, then the sixth. My arm is starting to hurt. We pass the seventh and eighth and finally the ninth. The gondola stops at the edge of another stone-tiled cliff, swaying slightly, and smelling singed.

Dad takes a deep breath as he steps off the gondola and sits down on the stone. "Much better."

It does feel good to be back on solid ground. The crystal windows are closer to us now. I can see raindrops on them, hear their pattering. Moss creeps around the edges of some of the crystal windows, as though it's grown in from outside. And one of the windows is totally gone, worn away or shattered, letting in a cold wind.

I take a deep breath and study the room we're in now. It's just a huge square, practically empty, but at the far end is a large door, covered in stone panels, each carved with a unique design. Over the door, carved into the wall, is some lettering in Ancient Greek.

"All right, so . . . another test," Dad says. "Guesses?"

"It's pictures," Leo says. "Maybe we pick the right one?"

"Or the right order," I say, walking toward the wall. "Or we have to hit the ones that match at the same time."

"Tenny, look." Dad points at the walls on either side of us. By the door, there are a bunch of small, dark holes in them. I step back.

"More fire?" I sigh.

"Spears, I'd guess," Dad says. "Classic."

"There'd better be rings in there. And maybe they are magic. Otherwise these guys had way too much time on their hands."

Leo laughs, filming me, and Dad walks up beside me.

"Okay," Dad says, "so the writing over it probably tells us what to do. Let's hit the books."

He pulls down his backpack and takes out his laptop and charts for us to consult.

Thankfully, it's short, so it doesn't take us too long to translate it: "From One to the Other."

"So I'm guessing matching," I say. "By meaning."

"Well, let's look at what we have and try it—just be ready to jump. We should be clear of the spears if we can leap back here," Dad says, drawing a line in the dust with his foot. "You get that, Leo?"

Leo dutifully films it as I roll my eyes. Then I turn to the actual images in front of us. The tallest I can just barely reach, but they form a grid of four by four—sixteen images, eight pairs. If it is pairs we're trying to figure out.

"Make sure you get a shot of each one," Dad tells Leo.

This is a puzzle that feels custom-fit to my brain, as I start putting two symbols together and eliminating others, like options on a list. Some of the pairs are obvious—there's a left wing and a right wing, like the ones on Eros back at the temple. Grapes and the wine goblet probably go together, too. There's a helmet and spear that are probably a pair, but also a curved sword—but I think that goes with the Hydra symbol. Unless the fire symbol does. There's the symbol of the rings we've seen all over, a symbol like an oval with two curves taken out of either side, which I know is the ancient symbol of Thebes; an image of two men holding hands, a bow and arrow, a shield with arrows flying into it, and then finally, a skull and the upside-down V I know is the symbol of Sparta, Thebes's enemy. I hope those last two are a pair. But we should start with the easy one, just to test if we're even right about this.

"So you want to start with the wings?" Dad asks, as if reading my mind. It's amazing how when it comes to puzzles, we're always on the same page. But when it comes to everything else, it's the opposite. "Press them at the same time, then jump back real fast in case we're wrong?"

I nod, standing in front of one of the wing panels. "How much force you think they need?"

"They're stone. A good shove?" Dad says. "Use it to launch yourself back. Careful."

"Yeah, don't want to get hurt and worry the producers," I say in a low voice.

"What?"

"Can we do this?" I ask. It comes out in a nasty voice. Oh well.

"Um, sure," Dad says. "One, two . . . three."

We push down on the wing panels and leap backward at the same time, jumping out of the range of any spears or fire that might come flying out of the walls. But nothing happens. We wait in silence for a good ten seconds.

"Okay, well, we thought we'd get that one right," Dad says. "And that means it is about pairs. So we just need to figure the rest out."

"Skull and Sparta," I say, pointing. "Death to their enemies, right?"

"Yeah," Dad says. He brings one hand to his chin, that gesture he does—we do—when thinking. I hate that we both do it. "Could be the helmet for Sparta, too, though . . . Let's do grapes and the wine goblet first. Do the easy ones."

"Sure," I say.

"You okay, Tenny?" Dad asks.

"Sure," I repeat. "I'll take grapes, you wine?"

"Yeah, okay," Dad says, and we get in front of our buttons. "One, two . . . three."

We repeat what we did last time, pressing the panels and leaping back in unison. And again, nothing happens.

"Okay," Dad says. "Two down . . . six to go."

"I still think skull and Sparta. The helmet could go with the spear, for Ares, but the skull wouldn't make sense with anything else."

Dad nods. "All right, let's try it. But get ready to jump again."

"All right."

We position ourselves, Dad in front of the skull, me by the symbol of Sparta.

"One, two . . . three."

We press and leap backward. Again, nothing happens.

I grin. "Told ya."

"Good work," Dad says. "Now, I've been staring at the fire. That's got to be a hearth, right? It's not a bonfire."

I hadn't thought of that. "Yeah. Then the curved sword goes with the Hydra for sure, not the helmet, so the helmet and spear go together, for Ares, like I said."

"Right," Dad says. "So hearth means home. And that means family, right, so I think the two men."

I laugh. "Family and home?"

"What?" Dad looks at me confused.

"It's just funny, coming from you," I say.

He takes a deep breath. "Is there something you want to say, Tenny?"

"Ten . . . ," Leo says. "Don't be mean. Just . . . talk."

1. Don't be mean.

2. Be honest.

"Fine," I say, crossing my arms and turning on my dad. "I don't believe you that the show isn't failing. You only asked me back because the producers made you."

Dad clenches his jaw. "That's not true. You can't believe what someone from Bulwark of all places says."

"I don't care who said it. It makes perfect sense. You left me alone in Japan. I didn't hear from you for TWO YEARS. Not even a phone call on my birthday."

"Tenny, I—"

"And then all of a sudden you reappear, acting like nothing's wrong, pretending like you never did anything bad and offering me a chance to go after the thing you know I want." I laugh, suddenly realizing. "You don't care about the rings at all, do you? You only went after them to convince me to come along. For ratings. So you wouldn't be canceled. Get more articles about what a great dad you are, like after I came out. That's all you care about. The show."

"Tenny," Dad says, his voice firmer now. "Stop. I came back because I love you."

"Is that all?" I ask. "I can ask the producers, you know. When we're out of here. I can look up ratings, viewership. In fact, Leo, can you bring the camera up, I'll just ask them on this."

Leo shakes his head a little and I turn back to Dad.

Dad sighs. "Look, the producers suggested I bring you back, yes, but—"

I roll my eyes. "Uh-huh." I can feel my jaw clenching.

"Let me finish," Dad says, his voice loud. "Look. Yes. They suggested it. But it was what I needed, okay? I needed someone to make me go to you, because I missed you! I wanted you back. You're so good at this, Tennessee. You're better than me. I love having you along to see how good you are at it."

I feel a little wobbly now. Rage had been holding me up like steel, but now it's turned to jelly. I can feel myself looking for a way to forgive him, and I try to stop. Do I want to stop? Should I stop? Is this real or just more of his charm?

"Then why didn't you come back in Japan?" I ask.

"Because you called me a thief!" Dad practically snarls. No charm now.

"You are one," I hiss back.

"You know what?" Dad says, his voice rising. "Maybe this was a mistake. Maybe I was right that if you can't respect what I do, I should have just left you out of my life completely. Yeah. That's why I didn't call. Because what would you want to say to me—a thief, right? You're so much better than me, Tenny, with your high moral ground. Never mind the money from the show since you were thirteen. Or that I do most of the prep work while your mom takes good care of you. Must be nice. Just come onto my show, get famous, and then start judging. Instead of thanking me, like you should have. No, you just come for the thrill, then go back to your cozy life while I do work for the next season."

"Oh, please, you're doing fine. You have a penthouse in LA. You've never had me over, but I know about it. You don't sell the artifacts to the highest bidder to put food on the table. You do it to get rich. And I help you get richer."

"I don't sell to the highest bidder," Dad says, rolling his eyes. "I've explained this. I sell to the person who will give the artifact the most attention, make sure it's appreciated. But I guess you'd just give it to nice old ladies whose great-great-great-great-grandfather maybe owned it. She could keep it in her closet, and you could feel smug."

"I would make sure it at least went to the country it was found in," I say. "I would make sure it went to the culture it belonged to."

"Oh really?" Dad asks, crossing his arms. "So who are you giving the rings to? They're probably just past this wall. What are you going to do with them, Tenny? Give them to Greece? I'm sure they'll be nice in one of the museums, maybe get their own case, their own plaque." He holds up a hand like he's describing a show marquee. "Rings worn by the Sacred Band of Thebes. Maybe they'll say 'to demonstrate membership.' That sound right? That have all the queer history you wanted to show the world?"

I take a long breath. Then I sit down. He's right. I have no idea what to do with the rings.

"So this was all a test?" I ask. I don't sound as angry. I still am, but I'm more tired now.

"No," Dad says, walking over to me. His voice is lower, too. "I wanted you to figure out what to do with the rings because they're your history. Because if we find them, this is your story, the story of finding them. That's their history, too. And it should be told. I know . . . sometimes the stuff we find ends up places maybe it doesn't belong. But I can't fix the world, Tenny. The places with money can tell the stories. That's what I care about. Tell the stories, get enough promotion for the show, another season, another treasure. That's how I keep getting to do this, the thing I love. And that I thought you loved." He pauses. "Honestly, part of me doesn't even care where it ends up. I just want to find it, I just want to do the show. Solve puzzles, like this. With you."

He kneels in front of me.

"You left me for two years," I say. I can feel the tears starting. "You left me alone in Japan."

"Yeah," he says. "But I knew you'd be fine."

"I don't want to be fine. I want you to be my dad. And I want you to do the right thing."

"I . . . don't know how to do that, Tenny. All I know how to do is find treasure. And that's all I want to do. I thought you wanted to do it, too."

That's all he wants to do. He doesn't know how to do anything else—not even be a dad. He's a thief. That's all, and that's not going to change. He's not even going to apologize. He's a glory-seeker, an adventure addict, and a grudge holder. And no one has ever really shown him how to be different. And he's never tried.

"Come on," Dad says, standing and reaching down his hands. I give mine to him, and he pulls me up and hugs me. "I'll tell the producers you won't be back after this season, okay? This clearly isn't working, but you're right. I shouldn't have cut you out like that. I promise I'll still be around, okay? I'll call on your birthday."

"Sure," I say. He doesn't want to change. For a moment, I thought maybe I could show him how to still be the adventurer he wants to be and do it right, but he doesn't want that. He just wants the thrills. And those will be easier with me gone. Mom always said Dad was like an addict, always looking for treasure. That's what's most important to him. Not me.

Dad lets go, and I stand alone for a moment, the breeze from outside smelling like rain, the trap-filled mountain we're in smelling like mold and stone. It's chilly. I hug myself. Dad is already studying the panels again, not looking at me.

"You all right?" Leo asks softly, coming up behind me.

"He can't be something he's not," I say in a whisper. "He can't be someone who thinks of me before he thinks of the next temple, the next puzzle. He can't be someone who thinks of where the stuff we find should go. He needs these adventures more than anything else. And he needs the show to pay for them, which means he needs to give the stuff he finds to someone who will promote it, promote the show. It's a cycle. One I'm not actually part of, except that I make him look better."

"Ten," Leo says, and hugs me from behind. "I think he loves you. In his way."

"Maybe," I sigh. "But not like he loves . . ." I gesture around me. "This."

"You love it, too," he says. "Maybe it's not about rankings. Maybe it's just about being together."

"That's sweet, but too simple," I say. "He'd rather get rid of me than try to do better for me. That's what he just said."

"You ready, Tenny?" Dad calls, still staring at the panels. "I'm thinking sword and Hydra, spear and helmet, two men and hearth. The bow, I think, is a symbol of Eros. So that and the rings, maybe? But then what is the coin going to be?"

"Coin?" I ask, walking up to him. I look behind me. Leo is filming again. He smiles at me.

"This is a coin," Dad says, pointing at the symbol of Thebes.

"It's the symbol of Thebes," I say. "It was on coins. I guess it could be a coin."

"So maybe it goes with the rings. Sacred Band of Thebes?"

"Maybe," I say. "Or it could be the men. And then what's the shield with arrows going into it? Protection?"

"Hmm," Dad says. "Well, let's try the Hydra and sword first. We're agreed on that one, right?"

"Yeah." I nod.

He looks me in the eye and smiles. "I am glad you're here, Tenny. You know that, right?"

"Sure," I sigh. "Me too." I make myself smile at him. "You take the Hydra?"

"You got it," Dad says, taking his place in front of the symbols. "One, two . . . three."

We push the symbols and fall back. Again, nothing happens.

"Great," Dad says, clapping. "How about the two men and the hearth next? I know we're less sure, but—"

"Yeah, okay," I say. I just want to finish and get the rings. I stand in front of the panel with the two men on it, hand ready, as Dad gets in front of the hearth.

"One, two . . . three," he says. We push and I can immediately tell it's wrong. The panel doesn't give, and there's a creaking noise as I leap back, running away the moment I land. I look at Dad just in time to see him leap, too, but not far enough. Arrows come flying out of the holes in the walls, whistling as they fill the space in front of the panels, Dad still in their path.

❧ FOURTEEN ❧

I run forward. Everything seems to go in slow motion. All the anger and disappointment vanish out a trapdoor and leave only cold fear behind. He's my dad, and now he's caught between a hundred flying arrows. He lands on his back, just out of range of the arrows, which keep flying. I kneel next to him. His head is fine. His torso's fine.

His leg, though, has an arrow sticking out of it. His calf. He groans in pain.

"Okay, you're alive, that's good," I say.

"Arrows," he says. "Should have guessed arrows."

"Leo, come over here!" I yell, looking at the arrow stuck in his leg. It's old, beautifully designed—hawk feathers, I think, but I can't linger there. The arrowhead is only halfway in him, shallow enough to pull out.

"It's halfway in," I tell Dad. "Pull it out or snap it off?"

"Snap the ends off," Dad says. "Bind it up best you can over that."

I laugh, even as I feel like crying and my heart is going to burst out of me. I reach into his backpack and quickly find what I need—a knife, peroxide, bandages, antibacterial cream.

"What do I do?" Leo asks.

"Hold his leg," I say. "I need to cut as much off as I can."

"Make sure you record it, though," Dad says. "I'll look heroic."

"You'll look like a man hit with an arrow," I say, tearing his pant leg up and past the arrow. "Because he thought that two men meant home."

"Well, it did for them," Dad says as Leo braces him. "It will for you one day. Hell, it does for me . . ." His eyes go a little fuzzy. He must be in a lot of pain.

I swallow, pushing that thought aside for a moment. "Get ready, this will hurt." I grab the shaft of the arrow and the knife. The shaft is thin enough I think I can do it in one quick cut, but it'll probably hurt him. "One . . . two . . ." I cut before I say three. I've seen doctors do that on TV. Dad screams as the shaft splinters off. Blood flies everywhere, hitting my face, which I was not expecting. For a moment, I'm not sure what to do. Then I look at the wound on his leg, now looking like a cork in a broken bottle, and remember. I grab the peroxide and just pour it over the wound. He screams again. I ignore him and grab the bandages and cream. I smear the cream over the wound.

"Keep holding him," I say to Leo, who is struggling against Dad as he squirms from the pain. I take the bandages and wrap them around his leg several times before taping them down, right.

"Good?" I ask.

"Yeah," Dad groans weakly.

"That was . . . a lot," Leo says. "You have blood on your face."

"Yeah," I say. "Now let's move you away from the arrows, and keep your leg above your head."

Dad snorts as we help him up, but winces as he takes a few steps, clear of the arrows' range. Though they've stopped flying. I don't know when.

We lie Dad down and use his backpack to prop up his leg.

"But now what do we do?" Leo asks. "Go for help?"

"What?" Dad asks. "Absolutely not. You finish the puzzle. You bring back the rings. Then we carefully help me out of here. And then maybe go for help, because I don't think I can get down the path we came up."

"You want us to finish the puzzle?" Leo asks, looking at me concerned.

"We're almost there," I say, forcing a smile. Dad is fine, and he wants us to go on, and I can feel the rings. They're close.

Leo shakes his head in disbelief. "You're so alike."

I shrug. Maybe. Maybe I should forgive Dad for putting these adventures first, even at my expense, the expense of the people he steals from. Maybe, if I didn't have him to take me with him, I'd do what he did. I hope not, but who knows?

I stand up and get some water out of my bag to rinse the blood off my hands and face.

"Give the camera to Dad," I say.

Leo hands Dad the camera and stares at me, nervous.

"Look, if you just want to go, we can go," I say. "I need you to get the rings, but I'm not going to force you—clearly it's dangerous." I point at Dad, still lying on the ground, the camera to one side as he fishes out a bottle of aspirin from his backpack.

"No, no," Leo says. "You're right. We're close."

"And Bulwark is probably right behind us," I say. "So let's see if getting one wrong has reset the panels?" I nod at the wall and Leo and I walk over to it. The pressed panels have all popped back out again. "Okay, well, at least we know some of them already. You want to practice the leap back, though?"

"Yes," Leo says quickly.

"Okay, put your hand over that wing panel, then. Get ready to push yourself off it and jump backward as far as you can, and again. Don't worry about the ledge, it's twenty feet back, no one can jump that far."

"Okay," Leo says. I look at him. He's nervous. "Ready."

"It'll be fine. We know this one works. Just practice," I say.

He nods. "I know."

"One, two . . . three."

We hit the wing panels and I turn to watch Leo jump. He gets pretty far back, and quickly, too.

"You'll be fine if you keep doing that," I say.

"You didn't jump!" Leo says.

"We knew this one was fine," I say. "Only you have to practice."

Leo laughs. "Okay, well . . . I'm going to practice again."

"Sounds good," I say, grinning. We repeat the process with the wine and grapes, then the skull and Sparta symbol, and then the Hydra and sword.

"Okay," Leo says, shaking his legs and arms out like a track runner in front of the starting line. "Okay, I'm ready for the next one."

"If we get it right, we don't even need to worry," I say. "Now, I think the hearth should be with Thebes. Home is Thebes, right? If it's not a coin, I mean."

"Ohhhh," Dad says, filming from the ground. "That's good, Tenny. You should have said that before."

I smile weakly at him. He's right. I should have. I was so wrapped up in being angry at him I didn't speak up when I should have. It's my fault Dad got hurt. Well, partially. "Sorry," I say.

"So try it," he says.

I look at Leo, and we hover our hands over the symbols.

"One, two . . . three." We press the symbols and leap back, landing almost parallel and at the same time. But no arrows. We got that one right. I smile at Leo. His brow is sweaty, despite how chilly it is in here. I kind of want to kiss him, but Dad is watching, and filming, so I'll save it. He grins at me. I think he wants to kiss me, too. And he knows I want to kiss him, and that I know he wants to kiss me. I see all that in one look.

I wish Dad and I understood each other the way Leo and I do—not with kissing, obviously—but just in a way that connected. Sometimes we do, I guess. In Japan, with the sword, we sort of did. When he threw it and jumped. He trusted me. And that's more than a lot of people can do.

"Okay, so now I'm sure it's helmet and spear for Ares," I say. "Those next?"

"You're the archaeologist," Leo says.

"I'm a high schooler," I say. "Honestly, you're taking your life in your hands here."

Leo laughs. "I know," he says, and stands in front of the spear panel. I want to kiss him again. Instead, I turn to the panel.

"One, two . . . three." We press the panels and leap back, but again, no arrows fly.

Leo laughs. "Another down. So, what's next?"

"I don't know," I say. I'm stroking my chin, doing that thing Dad and I do. I stare up at the wall. We have four left to press, two pairs: the bow, which I think Dad was right about, a symbol of Eros, then the rings, the two men, and the shield taking arrows. I know we could just try anything and if we get it wrong we could redo it and get it right, but I'd rather not risk the arrows again, even if Leo's jumping is good.

"Okay, so first off, what does the shield mean?" I say. "It has arrows flying off it. That symbolize any gods or anything, Dad?"

"None I know of. Athena had the shield, of course, but the arrows don't make sense with her. And I don't know what else would match her. The spear and helmet are gone."

"Doesn't it mean protection?" Leo asks.

"Yeah," I say. "On the battlefield, anyway. To them, it would have meant protecting your husband, lover, making sure . . ." I pause, look at all the panels again. "I think the rings go with the two men, showing unity, pairing, and then the shield goes with the bow, because the bow represents Eros, love, and the shield is protecting someone you love. An act of love."

"Plus, the bow could be shooting the arrows at the shield," Leo says, pointing between the two symbols.

"That . . . also makes sense," I say. "Maybe I overthought it."

Leo laughs. "No. I like your explanation better."

"Okay, so let's try arrows and shield first?"

Leo nods and stands in front of the shield panel, his body tense, ready to jump. He knows this one is risky. I mimic him, getting ready, my whole body tense, and then count.

"One, two . . . three!"

We move in unison, reaching forward to press out panels and then leaping back. I check that he and I are both out of range before even looking up at the panels. But nothing happens. We chose the right symbols.

Leo lets out a whoop. "We did it!"

"We still have the last pair," I say, but I'm feeling it, too. The joy overcoming a test. Watching Leo experiencing this for the first time. "Let's be careful pressing these before we're sure we have it."

"Okay, okay," Leo says, shaking down again and taking his stance in front of the panel of the two men. I stand in front of the panel with the interlocking rings and stare at it for a moment. It's such a simple carving, a simple image. And the real bands, they could be just beyond us. I take a deep breath.

"One, two . . . three," I say, and reach forward to hit the bands, then leap back. No arrows this time, either. Instead, the wall itself seems to shake.

"That's good, right?" Leo asks.

With a loud groan, the wall separates, sliding open, leaving a cloud of dust in its wake, so thick I can't see through it and start coughing as it gets in my mouth and eyes. I turn away, blinking tears away, and when I look back, I'm hoping to see the rings.

"What is it?" Dad calls. "Is it the bands?"

"No," I say, my shoulders slumping. "Another puzzle."

Leo and I walk back to Dad and help him up so he can see. The new room is more like two rooms, or two hallways. In front of us is a narrow strip of stone tile, like the rest of the place. But five feet beyond that, a wall juts up in the middle of the room, about five feet tall, splitting the room into two five-by-five grids. The grids are made up of stone tiles, too, but they look different, each of them raising slightly like a mound, and larger than the tiles we've been on—they're at least three feet by three feet. Beyond the grids, the floor continues, ending in a small arched doorway. But I don't think we can just walk across.

"Another grid," I say. "At the temple, the Hydra was three by three, the match game was four by four, and now . . ."

"Five by five," Leo says.

"So what do we do?" Dad asks, starting to sit up.

"Keep your leg raised," I tell him. Then I look around the room for clues. I'm careful not to step on the grid, but from the side, I can see the half wall. On each side of it, a five-by-five grid is carved. There are carved dots in some of the squares on the grid. On one side, it's always an odd number of dots: 1, 3, 5, 7, 9, and on the other, even: 2, 4, 6, 8, 10. I tell Dad what I see.

"So, it's directions," he says. "Right? Across the tiles. Step one, then step two, et cetera, and you have to shout to each other where to go next. Left, right, forward. This should be a breeze. I could probably do it with you, if you want." He starts to get up.

"No," I say. "Leo and I will do it. And I think it'll be harder than that."

"Well, you should each take a camera, then," Dad says. "I can't film everything from here."

"Sure," I say, and fish a few more cameras out of my bag, check that they're working, and give one to Leo. "Now let's see what happens when I step on the wrong tile."

"Careful," Dad says.

I walk up to one of the grids and make sure I'm not stepping on tile one, then put some weight on a tile. It moves so quickly I almost fall backward. It's dropped slightly and swung away. Below it is nothing. I shine my flashlight, but it doesn't help. Just a deep, dark pit, like the cliff when we came in. A moment later, it swings back. But if I'd been on it, I'd be falling now.

"That's a drop," I say.

"So step on the right one," Dad says.

I look up at the map again and walk to the tile with one dot. It's right at the edge of the grid, so I know how to read the map. This time I get down on the ground and reach out and press it. Again, it drops and swings away almost immediately.

"Nope," I say. "We have to step on them in unison. And once we're on the tiles, we only have half the directions, so we need to shout out which way to walk."

"Oh . . ." Dad sighs. "That's a toughie."

"Let's double-check," Leo says, getting down on his stomach in front of the matching tile on the other side. "One, two . . . three."

We press down on the tiles at the same time. They stay firm.

"See?" I say, taking a breath. "So, it's going to be about stepping really carefully, like pushing the buttons."

Then the tile, still under my hand, swings open.

"That's not good," Leo says. "They just waited a few extra seconds."

"Did you keep the pressure on?" I ask. It should have worked.

"Yes," he says.

"Let's try it again. Count how long it stays. One, two . . . three."

We press down. I hold, counting. The tiles fall and open again. I swallow, but my throat is dry and dusty, so I cough.

"That's not very long," Leo says.

"Not at all," I say.

"How long?" Dad asks.

"Four seconds," I say. "We need to move from tile to tile in unison, shouting directions, at a steady pace of four seconds or less."

Dad whistles.

I stand and walk to the edge of the wall, looking past the tiles. There's a small arched doorway there. I can't see through it. But the rings have got to be in there, right? They're so close.

I turn to Leo. "You up for it?"

Leo looks nervous. "Maybe. I think—" His face goes blank for a moment and then he takes a step, then another, on a beat I can't hear. "Yes, it will work."

"What?" I say.

He walks up to me and holds me around the waist, and starts humming, making me move to the melody. I recognize it after a second: "Super Trouper." Like the night we danced in the street.

"Take a step," he says, singing the words to the melody. "On the beat, it should be short enough—bum bum, bum bum."

"You think we should cross them in time to 'Super Trouper'?" I ask.

He nods, still dancing and humming.

"Okay," I say. I keep dancing with him, and start singing along, making sure our bodies move together.

"What are you two doing?" Dad asks.

I glance over at him, and he's smiling, but clearly confused.

"Have you finally cracked, Tenny?"

"It's 'Super Trouper,'" I tell him. "ABBA. One of Leo's favorites. And the beat should keep us walking in time. And we can shout out directions to the melody."

"Okay, that's, um, smart. But why are you dancing together? You need to practice apart."

"Right," I say, and Leo and I take a step away from each other. I lose the beat for a second without his arms around me but catch it again.

"Don't keep dancing," Dad says. "You need to walk. And shout out left, right, or whatever."

I laugh and Leo and I change our dancing in place to more of a march. I try shouting out "left" on the beat, and then Leo calls "forward," still singing. Both times we lose the beat.

So we start singing from the beginning again, walking, calling, singing. All at once. It's hard. Like learning a dance while having to do it perfectly all at once. Dad and I have dealt with trapdoors and paths through trick tiles before, but we've never had to walk the same path in tandem without seeing each other.

Leo and I go through the song from start to finish enough times I think even he's growing sick of it before he stops. My feet keep tapping to the beat that now lives permanently in my brain.

"I think we can do it," he says.

I nod and look at the tiles. I can feel my heartbeat speed up. "All right, let's get in place, then."

We step up to the tiles, standing in front of the correct one—I double-check on my map. Then we start singing.

I sing the first line of the song, the beat playing in my head immediately. Step. I almost lose the beat, wondering if I'm about to fall, but it holds steady.

"Forward!" Leo sings from his side of the wall. I wait for the moment in the song and step again. And again it holds. Then I look up. I have to be reading the map, too, I remember. I look for dot three, figure out where it is in relation to us.

"Left," I sing and then step on the beat. That felt way too close. I'm shocked I'm not dead.

"Forward," Leo sings, and I step on the beat again, looking at the map.

"Right," I sing. We keep singing and marching as we call out directions. Right again, then forward, left, left, left, back, left, forward, forward, and then right one more time and forward—onto solid ground. I fall to my knees and stop singing. To my right, Leo has collapsed on the ground, too. My throat feels hoarse. I know it couldn't have been that long—we didn't even finish the song. But it felt long. My shirt is clinging to me from sweat.

"Tenny?" Dad calls. "You make it?"

"Yeah, Dad," I call back, getting up. I go over to Leo and help him up and hug him.

"ABBA saved our lives," he whispers into my ear, and I start laughing.

"Everything okay?" Dad asks. "What did you find?"

"We're just celebrating making it across," I say.

Dad goes silent, and I realize it sounds like I said we're making out or something.

"There's an arch," I call out, looking at the small doorway. "It's small."

I walk up to it. Inside is a smaller room, lit by one crystal skylight. Directly beneath are pillars, rows of them, each with a groove in the middle. In one pillar, the groove has a brass sphere in it. No rings. Maybe in the sphere? I call back to Dad everything we're seeing as I film it.

"Check the sphere!" Dad calls back. "They must be in there."

"One hundred and fifty," Leo says.

"What?" I ask.

"One hundred and fifty altars, one hundred and fifty of these orbs maybe . . . once."

I nod. Only one sphere left.

"Storage, I think," I say, looking around the rest of the room. No carvings, no explanations. Just pillars and one sphere left. If the rings are in this sphere, they're the last ones.

I go up to the sphere. It's about the size of a melon, and made of polished brass, somehow still gleaming after all these years, even with the coating of dust on it. I pull the sphere out of the altar. It's cool to the touch and heavier than I thought it would be. It's not hollow. It's bigger than a baseball; I can hold it in one hand, but just barely.

Around the circumference of it are what look like ivory wheels, with black markings on them, like belts. I don't have time to look closer, though, because the floor begins to shake.

"Tenny!" Dad calls. I take the sphere and Leo and I run back outside. The entire mountain feels like it's shaking. I look at the tiles—do we have to walk back across them the same as we got here? But they all suddenly pop a little higher out of the ground.

"What's happening?" I call to Dad as I tentatively put my foot out on the tiles. They don't fall.

"There's a bridge," Dad says. "Did you find the rings?"

I run over the tiles, and they don't fall. Leo follows. Dad is lying where we left him, now filming the way we came, which is changing. A heavy-looking wooden bridge is descending from the ceiling on chains. It falls into place at the edge of the cliff we came to by gondola. The other end falls by the entrance.

"An easy way out," Dad says. "Nice of them to do that. Let me see the orb?"

I hand him the orb, still staring at the new bridge in wonder. It's held by chains but doesn't sway at all. The gondola, right next to the bridge, starts making its way back to the entrance on its own.

"It looks like a puzzle-lock," Dad says, twirling the rings around the outside of the sphere.

"We should look at it outside," I say, holding out my hand to help him up. Leo gets on his other side. "I don't know how long the bridge will stay."

"Good idea," Dad says. He hands me the orb and I put it in my backpack and shrug it on.

Carefully, we gather our things and head for the bridge. It's more like a staircase, really, but also a bridge, of carefully placed wooden steps and tall banisters. When I step on it, it feels sturdy. The wood hasn't decayed.

We slowly make our way down, back to the entrance. I keep glancing at the Hydra heads, expecting them to spew fire, or looking up, waiting for the bridge to start raising before we're off it, but nothing happens. It's not another test. Just an easy way out, like Dad said.

We make it to the bottom of the stairs and go to open the door, but it's closed behind us, and won't budge when I push it.

"Maybe the same way we opened it?" Leo says. I nod, and we put our hands on the door and shove in unison. The doors open, and as they do, the room goes darker as the panels that covered the windows start to fall back to how they were when we entered. The levers on each side of the room start to click back. The bridge begins to raise. It's resetting itself.

I take a deep breath of the air coming from outside, and then help Dad limp out into the tunnel. It's still raining, but the sound is lighter now, like a drizzle. We walk down the stone hall and I breathe in the scents: the rain, the grass, the faint smell of herbs, and the sea. We're out. And we have the bands, I think. Or at least a locked case with the rings in it. I let that sink in finally. We have the bands! Sure, they're still one lock away, but we're closer than we've ever been.

Unless the orb is just another map. I hope it's not another map. I look over at Leo, who is helping Dad walk on the other side, and he looks over at me, grinning. He's a mess, and so am I probably, sweat sticking my hair down, clothes covered in dust and Dad's blood. But we did it. We made it out. I can't wait to sit down and look at the orb, try to unlock it.

At the end of the cave, I step outside into the rain—and the barrels of several guns pointed at me.

"About time," Luke says.

❧ FIFTEEN ❧

"I thought you'd be faster," Luke says. His arms are crossed and he's standing, smirking, behind his men. Behind him stands Jean, looking away from us, guilt etched in every line of her body. "You're supposed to be so good at this, after all. I was about to send men in, thinking you were dead." He notices Dad being held up by us and his smile grows wider. "Looks like you almost are."

He makes a few quick motions with his hands and soldiers come and grab Dad from us, holding him.

"Hey!" I shout. "You can't—"

I try to move after them, but another soldier shoves a gun in my face, pressing the cold barrel to my forehead. I wonder if I'm going to die right here. I wish I hadn't come. I wish I could say goodbye to Mom.

I try to think of what I can do. But around us, the soldiers have at least one gun on each of us.

1. Can I roll under this one and get away? No, they'd shoot Dad and Leo.
2. Maybe I can signal to them to roll at the same time—but the other men have guns, too.

3. Do we just give up, give them the rings? No, we can't.

4. We can lie. Say we don't have them.

"Stop it," Jean says, focusing my attention back on her. "You promised not to hurt anyone, and you definitely aren't holding a gun to a child's head, are you? I will tell people about this," she says to Luke.

Luke rolls his eyes and makes another motion. The gun pointed at me lowers and I feel the breath rush back into my body. At the other side of the cliff, the guards have laid Dad down and are looking at his wound. I make eye contact with him and I think I can read his expression. Choice four.

"He's got an injury," one of the soldiers says. "Hack job sewing it up. We'll need to pully him down the mountain."

Luke sighs. "Fine. Start getting that ready. You'd better have those rings on you, Henry."

"Couldn't," Dad groans. He's hamming up his pain for the guards. "Too injured halfway through. Arrow trap."

I swallow, feeling the weight of the sphere—and the rings—in my backpack. I hope this works.

"Right," Luke says with a sneer, then turns to his soldiers. "Search his stuff." They start going through Dad's bag and I try to stay calm, wondering if they'll go through mine next. Then I stare at the camera hanging from my neck. I quickly slip the memory card out and put it in my pocket. They can't have the footage from today.

Leo sees me and does the same, but Luke notices.

"Take their cameras," he says, and the soldiers grab mine, yanking it off so hard I can feel where the strap leaves a burn on my neck.

"There's nothing in his bags," one of the soldiers says, going through Dad's stuff. "Just medical stuff, food, water. No rings." I turn slightly, hoping no one notices that I have a bag, too.

Luke sighs. "Well, now we have to go in there," he says to Dad.

"Be careful," Dad says, smiling a little. He starts to cough. A lot. I try to go to him, but a soldier stops me again. Jean kneels down beside him, giving him some water.

"All right," she says, standing up. "You're here, I got you here. So now—"

"Well, no—*he* got us here," Luke says, jabbing his thumb at Leo.

My skin suddenly goes so cold I'm covered in goose bumps. I look at Leo, who looks away from me.

"What do they mean?" I ask Leo.

"It's my fault," Jean says quickly, glaring at Luke. "I gave him something. He didn't know what it was." She walks over to Leo and holds out her hand. He takes off his backpack and hands her what looks like a satellite phone.

"What?" I ask.

"I . . . didn't know," Leo says. "I thought it was just in case."

It suddenly feels like I'm not getting enough oxygen. I can feel my lungs filling up but it's like there's nothing in there. My head is fuzzy. I rock for a minute, and fall. I still can't get enough air. All that effort we just did. The dancing together. Being so in sync and the whole time . . . I look up at Leo. He still won't look at me. Dad is screaming something from where he's lying, but it's muffled by my own gasping for air. There's a ringing in my ears and I can't hear anyone, but then Jean is in front of me, helping me sit up, making me lean forward, telling me to breathe.

223

"Just in and out, Ten," she says. "Just in and out. I'm sorry. And I know Leo is, too. I took advantage of him. He was scared and I offered him a phone, just in case he got stranded without you."

"It's got a tracker," I say, staring up at Leo. "It's obviously got a tracker." And now he won't even look at me, because he knew, otherwise he would have told me. I told him not to trust Jean. I asked him what she'd wanted when they were alone in the car. And he had lied. Because he knew.

"I don't need any gay drama," Luke says. "Someone take them down the hill. Search their things." I'm dimly aware of the sphere still in my bag, but I almost don't care. I'm too focused on Leo, who still won't look at me.

"They're just kids," Jean says. "You think he's going to let them carry some ancient artifact?" She jabs a thumb at my dad.

"Why don't you take them down, then? Ask them what they saw in there."

"What if you need me for—" she starts.

"I have him," Luke says, sneering at Dad. "He can't go anywhere for a while. And he knows we have his kid. He'll cooperate."

"Bastard," Dad says, then breaks into another coughing fit.

"Fine," Jean says, her face cold. "I'll take them back to base camp."

"Jones," Luke says, pointing at a soldier, "go with them. I'm getting out of this piss." He motions to the soldiers with Dad, who lift him up and march into the cave. I stare after them for a moment, and then Jones steps between me and the cave entrance, holding his rifle with both hands.

"You ready to head back down?" Jean asks, frowning.

"I don't want to walk next to him," I say, staring at Leo, who still won't meet my eyes. I hate everyone here, I realize. Leo, for lying; Jean, for betraying; Luke, for being an asshole; and Dad, for not putting me first. I hate him the least, though. I almost laugh at that.

"Sorry, but I'll lead, then you, then Leo, and then Jones here," Jean says.

"Why are you even helping them?" I ask her. "Why give Leo a tracker and now let them hold my dad and me hostage? I thought you liked us."

Jean frowns. She looks genuinely sad. "I do. But I have a contract. They fund the dig, I help them find the rings. I just didn't think they were real . . ." She takes a deep breath. "Let's move." She starts down the cliff first. I don't want to move, but then Jones points his gun at me, so I follow.

The walk down is trickier. The light rain makes everything slippery, and I have to go slower, cling to the wall tighter. We walk in silence for a few minutes. I don't look behind me, but I can hear Leo breathing, can feel his body close to mine.

"I'm sorry," he whispers. "I didn't want to get stuck in the elevator."

I don't say anything back.

"I thought it was a safety. Just in case. I'd seen the trouble you got into on the show. She said to me, 'What if they leave you alone? What if they die and you just wait for them?' I was scared, I—"

"I told you what Dad said," I say, turning back to look at him. "You could have warned us. We could have gotten you your own satellite phone. Instead you took something from someone we told you not to trust. You didn't trust us. You didn't trust me."

I'm on a narrow strip of ground and slip, almost plummeting to my death. But Leo catches me. Pushes me back against the cliff side.

"You wanted me to trust you?" Leo asks. "Trust your dad? You don't even trust him, Ten."

"I trust my dad," I say. "I just know I'm second place to him."

Jean lets out a noise like she wants to laugh. I turn to look at her.

I swallow and move away from Leo, walking carefully down again. "You want to say something?" I ask her. "You were the one who said he only invited me back because his producers made him. He hadn't spoken to me in two years before that, did you know?"

"I didn't," Jean says, without looking back.

"So what don't I know at this point? Tell me what's so funny about me saying I'm second place to my dad?"

Jean shakes her head. We keep moving silently, carefully. Sometimes, Jones's gun clatters as he scrapes it against the rock. He keeps it pointed at us—but only raises it sometimes. I look back and see Leo staring at me. He looks scared. Sad. I feel bad. I shouldn't, it's his fault we're in this situation. But maybe I shouldn't be judging him so harshly. Maybe he really didn't know. Still, he should have told me. Then we could have figured it out. I asked what she wanted to talk to him about. And he didn't tell me, and now we're here. But maybe if we'd never met . . . everything would have been better for both of us.

In fact, everything would be better if I'd just never come. Leo wouldn't be here, Dad wouldn't be injured, I would be safe at home, working at the museum, crying over David, maybe making out with

Gabe. That would be so much easier. But I just had to see those rings. Needed to find them. Just like Dad. Maybe I have too much of him in me. Maybe he has regrets, too.

Probably, since he's on top of a mountain surrounded by men with guns to whom he's lied. I wonder how long it will take them to get through the traps and puzzles. How long before they realize they never searched my bag? And once they have that, and take the bands away, are they just going to leave us here, to find our own way back? They're not going to kill us, right?

I swallow, my foot slipping on a narrow part of the path again. Leo reaches out and grabs me, but I don't fall, and shake him off. No one says anything else the rest of the way down. The rain gets harder again as we reach the bottom, and the sun is setting, too. It's dark and we're all wet, even with our hoods up against the rain.

When we get to the ground again and are off the mountain, Jean takes a deep breath and bends over, her hands on her knees.

"That was frightening," she says, her accent heavier than normal.

"We'd better keep moving," Jones says, waving his gun at me. "We can dry off at HQ. They'll have a tent set up by now."

"Oh, I don't even remember which way it is," Jean says. "You lead."

Jones rolls his eyes. "I need to keep an eye on the prisoners."

"They're just kids, Jones," Jean says with a sigh. "We're on a tiny island. What are they going to do? Stop waving that thing around and lead the way."

Jones frowns but turns and starts marching back toward the olive grove, I assume leading the way. For a moment, I think about running. I look at Leo, and he's looking at me, and I know he's thinking the same thing. We could bolt. I still have my satellite phone. We could find someplace to hide and call Mom and she could send the police, maybe? Come by boat? I have no idea, but I'm sure she would know what to do. But then we'd be leaving Dad.

1. Run, alone, call Mom, hope the army comes in and Dad isn't dead. I guess hope Leo isn't dead, too.
2. Run with Leo. Same as above, but maybe Leo will rat me out again or has another tracker or something.
3. Stay with Bulwark, hope Jean makes sure we're not dead. Lose rings. Hope they don't kill Dad.

Three, I think. It's the only real choice I can make. I'm not sure I could even pull off one or two. I'm tired and wet and I don't know where to hide.

I start following Jones, walking past Jean, who's just getting up on her feet. She hangs back and I hear her grunt softly and turn. She's picked up a rock. A large rock, bigger than her head, and is quietly walking past me and Leo.

With one sharp movement she rams it into the back of Jones's head. He crumples.

"I can't believe I just did that," she says, dropping the rock next to him. She puts her hands to her face, her eyes widening in shock. "I hope I didn't kill him."

"What are you doing?" I cry.

"Your dad. He told me to protect you," she says.

I snort. Protect the rings, is what he meant. Protect his fame. But I don't say any of that.

"You have to believe I didn't want this, Ten," Jean continues. "I just wanted to unearth that temple, study it, write about it. But I needed the funding, and the university threatened my career. I knew it was a bad choice to stay, but I didn't think the rings were real and that temple means so much to me, Ten. I'd been looking for it for years."

She looks down at Jones, then kneels and puts her hand under his nose. "Okay, he's breathing, that's good." She carefully reaches out and takes his gun, holding it with her fingers like it's a snake that might bite her. "I don't like this, though. But . . . this is my fault. So I'm going to fix it. We need to tie him up, I think, right? And gag him maybe so he can't scream when he wakes up. Come on, help me, you two. And stop glaring at Leo, Ten. He thought he was being given a free escape beacon."

"I don't mind that," I say, kneeling and going through Jones's bag. I find some plastic ties and hand them to Jean. "I mind that he didn't tell me."

"God, why would they have these?" Jean asks, looking at the ties. Then she looks up at me. "What was there to tell?"

I look over at Leo, who's not speaking, standing apart. "I literally asked him what you talked about. What did you say, Leo?"

"I told the truth," Leo says. "I just didn't want you to think you couldn't protect me. That I didn't trust you to protect me."

"Except you *didn't* trust me," I say, watching as Jean fusses with the plastic ties and gets Jones's hands behind his back.

"I've seen the show, Ten," Leo says. "You barely make it out alive each time. You can't be angry at me for wanting a little extra safety."

He's right. I knew how scared he was, but once he agreed to come along, I ignored it. I was happy he was there. Finding the rings with me. Like Dad is with me.

But still.

"I can be mad when it means you lied," I say. I pull an undershirt out of Jones's bag and hand it to Jean. "Gag him with this."

"I'm going to gag all of you," she says, taking the shirt. "Stop squabbling. You've known each other less than a week and somehow you expect to have told each other everything?"

"Well . . ." I say. I think of home, the people on the street. The college kid who looked at me in front of his arguing straight friends and how I knew exactly what he was thinking. But Jean is right. It's unfair.

"I'm very sorry," Leo says.

I know he is. And I want to forgive him. He looks so sad, but still so cute in the rain. His hair is plastered to his face, like cracks in an old column. I open my mouth, maybe to forgive him, I'm not sure.

"We need to hide Jones and move," Jean says before I say anything, tying the undershirt around his mouth. "This can wait."

"Move where?" Leo asks.

Jean looks up and blinks. She doesn't know. She has no plan. Great.

"I have a satellite phone," I say. "If we have somewhere to hide, I can call my mom."

"I can call the Greek government," Jean says. "Explain the situation."

I think of the rings in my bag. "No," I say. I don't want to give them up yet.

Jean narrows her eyes. "Why not?"

"What makes you think they'll side with us?" I ask before Leo can give it all away. Again. "We're on some private island."

Jean shakes her head. "You have the rings." She looks up at the mountain we just came down from. "All right. We need to move, then. We can figure out who to call later. Where's the plane you came in on?"

"I don't know. Dad told the pilot to hide. We landed on the beach on the north side."

"I know, we saw the tracks. They set up camp there. Let's head for the old hotel site. No one was going that way, last I heard."

"Okay," I say. "Then what?"

"We'll figure it out," Jean says. "First let's get him out of sight." She nods down at Jones. I sigh and go to grab his legs, and Leo lifts his torso. Jean directs us to a cluster of bushes where we hide him, stripping him of his walkie-talkie and all his weapons before heading toward the old hotel. I look at the walkie-talkie, checking it for trackers, since that's apparently the game now, but it's basic, near as I can tell, and holding on to it will let us listen to them.

I wonder for a moment if the soldier might die there, but he's trained, I tell myself, strong. And once Luke notices he's gone, he'll look for him. He'll look for us, too. Thinking about that makes me swallow, and my throat feels sandpaper dry.

We walk silently toward the other side of the island. We're in the woods with the olive grove pretty quickly and it smells strong and herbal in the rain. We were here just a few hours ago, me and Leo, and he'd spotted the trees and come up with the idea of it being an old grove, and I'd been so proud of him. I'd been happy.

"I really am sorry," Leo says again, maybe remembering the same thing.

"What's the plan?" I ask Jean. "We still don't have a plan."

"Well, if you don't want to give up the rings, I think you should use them," she says. The rain is heavy and loud on the leaves and for a moment I don't think I heard her right.

"What?" I ask.

"They're supposed to make you into warriors, right? That's why Luke wants them. Bust them out. Put them on. Take back your dad. Find your pilot friend and his plane and get us out of here."

"That's just . . ." I sigh. This is her plan?

"Oh, don't give me that, Tennessee. You know better than most what they could be. I know the things you've found."

I narrow my eyes. "You do?"

"Your dad likes to brag. Did you try the rings on yet?"

"No," Leo says. "They're in a puzzle box. But are you saying that . . ." He lets the words hang there. The sound of rain is loud, and I nod at him. It's small, but his whole body shudders, trying to take it in. Then he nods back.

"Okay." Jean nods, talking to herself more than us. "We get to the old hotel, find someplace to hide while we figure out how to open the puzzle box, then we go from there, right? If the rings aren't magic . . . we have nothing. Except this gun, which I don't know how to use. The only option will be calling someone for help."

"I know," I say. That will save us, and hopefully save Dad, too, but it will mean giving up the rings. Greek authorities, the UN, anyone we could call will also take the rings with them. At least I'll get to see them before the Greek government takes them. Or maybe I can hide them. Probably not, they'll want to know what we're all doing here. But maybe it's for the best. I couldn't decide what to do with them if we found them anyway. Who they belonged to. Whose history they are. Mine, for sure, but the Greeks', too, and all the other queer people in the world. But there's no queer nation. We're scattered. No queer museums, except the one in Berlin, which definitely doesn't have a claim on something Greek, and the one in Athens, which couldn't possibly keep the rings safe.

I sigh and keep walking through the rain. We follow the olive trees back through the woods and then keep going past them. At the other end of the island, the ground dips a little into the old construction site. The ground has been blasted so it's flat. Steel beams rise up like half-built cages. There are several old bags of cement, probably bricks by now, and a few piles of beams. They didn't get very far in building this place, but there's a huge footprint of poured concrete that was probably going to be the base of the building. Beyond that, it's rocks and sand.

"There's nowhere to hide here," Leo says. "We should go back to the woods. At least they can't see us and pick us off like ants as easily there."

"There's got to be . . ." Jean says, looking around, then points. A small shipping crate is set up at the far side of the construction site, the kind that's been turned into an office with a window and door. "We'll wait there. It's quiet and should keep us out of sight."

As she finishes her sentence, the walkie-talkie on her belt squeaks. "Jones? Jean? You reach base camp yet?"

I look at Jean nervously, then at Leo. He looks as worried as I do. "Let's hurry," Jean says.

We all head down the hill toward the crate-office. The rain makes the ground loose and muddy and forces us to walk slowly, but the whole time I'm aware of how out in the open we are here. How the only thing blocking a direct gunshot at us are these thin metal beams rising up from the concrete. Barely any cover at all. And beyond that, we're leaving tracks in the mud.

The walkie-talkie crackles again, and then Luke's voice comes on. "Jones? Jean." There's a pause, and we clamor into the office, shutting the door behind us. It's pitch-black inside.

"Don't forget, kiddie, I have your dad."

I swallow, dig out my flashlight, and look around the office. There's a cheap desk, a file cabinet, a desk lamp, which Leo tries, but unsurprisingly doesn't work. Otherwise, it's empty. The whole place smells of dust. Jean sets down her flashlight like a lantern on the desk and checks all the windows are closed, not revealing the light to the outside.

I shrug my backpack off and take out the orb. I can't believe I'm actually doing this. This is the plan. Rely on some magic rings. I try to think of another plan, other choices, but aside from my mom, I don't know who to call. The satellite phone is in the bag, right next to where the orb was. I take that out, too.

"What are you doing?" asks Jean.

"I'm calling my mom," I tell her. "You figure out the orb."

"If she brings authorities—" Jean starts.

"I know."

I pick up the phone and turn it on, then dial Mom's cell. Jean takes the orb and starts looking at it. Leo walks over to her but watches me. I wait as the phone rings. And rings again. Voice mail.

"Hi, this is Sarah Russo. I can't get to my phone, so please text or leave a message and I'll get back to you as soon as I can. If this is a student who somehow got ahold of my personal line, I won't get back to you unless you email me, like the syllabus says to do."

Even before there's a beep, I can feel myself crying.

"Mom," I say into the phone. "Mom, we're in trouble. It's not Dad's fault. It's these men, this group. Bulwark. I guess they were after the rings, too, and they followed us to this island, Psephos. I'm okay, but they have Dad, and we're holed up away from them, but they have guns, and we have the rings, but if the Greek government comes in then they'll take the rings, and this will all have been for nothing, but if I don't give Bulwark the rings they might hurt Dad, but if I do give them the rings, they'll use them as weapons, somehow." I'm bawling now. My face was already wet from the rain, but tears are different, hotter. I glance up. Leo is still staring at me. Jean is twisting the rings set in the orb. I turn away.

"I don't know what to do," I whisper into the phone. "But I love you."

I hang up the phone and turn back around. Leo is behind me now. Closer. He hugs me, but I shake him off. He looks like that's enough to make him cry and I feel bad, but I'm just angry at everything. At Luke, at the situation. At the fact that I probably just said goodbye to Mom forever.

I hand him the phone. "You should call your sister," I say.

He nods and takes the phone, then walks to the other side of the office, where he dials and then starts murmuring in Greek. I wipe my face and go over to Jean.

"There's no code, no clue, no riddle," she says, turning the rings. "How am I supposed to know what pattern they should make without a guide?"

"Well, what can they make?" I ask.

"It's all dots or lines or circles. It doesn't make an image, at least not one I understand. Just, like spirals, sometimes, or grids or odd patterns."

"Grids?" I ask, taking the orb from her. There are three rings, each about as thick as my thumb, that spin around it. On one side is the double ring symbol, but with the rings around the orb cutting through it. But that's almost definitely where the images have to line up. I spin the rings, getting a look at the potential images, but Jean is right. They're all abstract. A few of them seem like maybe they'd complete the rings, but when I try it, they don't line up with the carving.

"Where did you see a grid?" I ask her.

She leans over and spins the rings. "The dots. There are a few of them on each ring. They can make a grid of three by five, or four by eight, or—"

"Six by six?" I ask, already spinning the rings. And yes, the top has a row of six dots, the middle ring has two by six, and the bottom has three by six. I push them all into place over the ring symbol, and it clicks.

"How did you know?" Jean asks.

"We've been seeing grids everywhere. Three by three on the Hydra heads; then here, there was a four-by-four grid and a five by five, so six by six . . ."

"Growing exponentially," Jean says, carefully lifting the top of the orb, which now comes away easily. "Like an army."

I hold my breath as the lid comes off. Inside, the orb is filled, flat, two solid pieces pressed together, aside from space carved away for rings. Two rings. Laying perfectly in their place.

My entire body shivers as I reach in and take one. I finally have them, I realize. They're real, and they're in my hand, and despite everything, every miserable thing, I found them. I'm touching my history, a part of it people have tried to deny exists forever and which I wasn't even sure was real. Imagine the people from the Village seeing this, or Gabe or the Good Upstanding Queers. Imagine how it would make them feel—like we all share something. Something important.

It's like something inside me uncoils. Like I've proven something, finally, after years, and can finally relax.

But that's all I feel. No magic.

I twist it in my hand. It's gold, hammered, with a large flat end. I've seen plenty of ancient Greek rings like this. They're not perfect circles, because they were hammered into shape, not molded. More like arcs on wide bases, where things were carved. On this one is carved a symbol I'm familiar with: wings. Well, one wing. For Eros, the god of love. I look over at the other ring, which Jean is holding. It has a wing going the other way. A matching set with the symbol of love. Definitely wedding rings. So unless Luke wants to claim that the Sacred Band was made up of men and women, definitely gay.

Luke, I suddenly remember. He wants these. We're alone on an island with a small military hunting us. Any joy I felt drops away again. The rings are just metal now.

I look up at Leo. He's filming. That's smart, I should have thought to do that. I can see his face is splotchy, though, like he cried talking to his sister. I turn to the camera. It calms me, strangely. The camera I'm used to. So I do what I usually do with the camera. I speak.

"They're real," I say. "But we're in danger. A private security force is after them, too, and they have my dad. We couldn't film them, but Jean has joined us. We're going to try putting on the rings and seeing if that can help us rescue Dad, but . . . I don't know. I don't feel anything magic. Do you, Jean?"

Jean stares at me, then the camera. "You're filming it?"

"If we get out of here, I want proof, even if we don't make it with the rings," I say. "I want the world to see that these rings"—I hold them up to the lens—"have wings on them. Matching wings. For Eros. They were love bands as much as commitment to the Sacred Band of Thebes. Maybe more love bands than military."

"Yes," Jean says. "They're definitely symbols of romantic commitment. Based on the Temple of Iolaus and the wing symbol, these are love bands." She holds the rings close to the light of her flashlight, casting a dark halo on the ceiling. "Amazing. These are going to be one of the biggest archaeological finds in centuries."

"If we can keep them away from Luke," Leo says, lowering the camera.

"Yeah," Jean says. "I hope they do what they're supposed to. Ten." She pauses, takes a deep breath. "You want to try them on?"

I swallow. "Am I allowed?" I ask, only half kidding.

"Normally, no," Jean says. "But the circumstances are special. Let's put them on and pray they do what they're supposed to."

I nod and lift the ring to my hand. "Which finger?"

"Ring finger," Jean almost laughs, holding the ring up over her own fingers. "Right hand."

"Okay," I say. I lift the ring and slide it on.

❧ SIXTEEN ❧

It slides on and almost immediately I feel it. What "it" is is impossible to explain: a sensation in my brain and body, and in the world, too. A connectedness. It's like that feeling walking through the Village with my pin on but stronger. Larger. It's like I'm connected to every queer person in the world.

I look at Jean, and I can tell she feels it, too. In fact, I can tell a lot of what she's feeling. She's worried about my dad, whom she loves, but not in a romantic way, more in a best friends way, and she's worried about me, and sad that I'm so angry at my dad, and she's angry, really angry at Luke, and angry at herself for involving Bulwark and feels guilty that that means Dad might be dying because of her and that we might be dying because of her, too, and she's scared and she's looking at me, and I know she can feel everything I'm feeling, too.

"I'm so sorry," she says.

"I know," I say. "It's okay. It's not your fault. You needed funding." She did, I know it. She hated going to them. But she needed to find the Temple of Iolaus, dig it up, give it the attention it was worth, prove to the world how important it was, same as I needed to find these rings.

"What are you talking about?" Leo asks. I can feel him, too. He's part of the web, but he's distant, not like Jean. She's bright and everything seems to be coming off her. Without even meaning to, simultaneously, Jean and I reach out and hug each other. I realize a moment later it was Jean who wanted to hug, and I felt that, and gave it to her, without even saying anything.

She didn't force me to hug her, she didn't control me, I just knew she wanted it and I wanted to give it to her all in one moment.

As we hug, I feel other people, too. Not just all the queer people in the world—there are so *many* of us!—humming, going about their lives, but the ones who went about their lives before, too. The Sacred Band. Those who have worn the rings before. I can feel them around us, almost curious. They're not ghosts, just experiences. Experience. I can feel what they can do, and know I can do it, too. I know how to fight, suddenly, how to use a spear, a shield, a bow and arrows. I'm . . . a member of the Sacred Band.

"What is going on?" Leo asks again. "Are they working? They're real?"

"Here," Jean says, slipping her ring off. She goes quiet suddenly. Still thrumming, still there, part of this web, but I can't read her thoughts anymore. We're not directly linked. She hands the ring to Leo, and I almost want to say no, but he takes it and slips it on and looks at me.

And I see it all. How sorry he is. How he really didn't know there was a tracker, he thought it was to call for help, like Jean said, and he was afraid to tell me because then I'd know he was afraid of coming with us, that he was excited but terrified, too, and he didn't want me to know because then I would think less of him, wouldn't bring him along, wouldn't contact him again. He didn't trust my dad to understand he was worried without firing him. And then he wouldn't have as much money to give to his sister. The money is for her, to thank her for raising him; for all the work she's done to provide for him. He'd never had the chance to pay her back before, and then suddenly, there it was. He couldn't lose that. But he couldn't risk being stranded with me and my dad, either. And now he is anyway. I know all that in the blink of an eye, and in the second blink, I forgive him, and he knows I forgive him.

"Oh," Leo says. I reach out and take his hand, and he holds mine.

"I'm glad that helped you two make up." Jean smiles. "They are something. A bit heady, honestly. But also spectacular to know how not alone we are. To feel all that family, all that history."

"Same thing," I say with a shrug. "And we can feel all this knowledge, too, from the previous Sacred Band members. We can fight."

"With spears and bows," Jean says. "Not quite the ace I was hoping they'd be if I'm being honest."

"We can make bows," Leo says. He looks confused. "I don't know how I know it, but I do. We can make bows. Spears, too, maybe, but they'll take longer. Arrows are easier."

"And probably better for taking the enemy HQ," I say. "I have strategy in my brain. War tactics."

"Here, give me a ring again," Jean says.

I take off mine and hand it to her. She's right, it is heady, a little like brain freeze, losing all that connection at once. I feel sort of cold. But she slips it on and uses her finger to start drawing in the dust on the desk.

"This is the island," she says. "Here's HQ. We brought about a dozen men, plus Luke and myself. Luke had six of them up with us before. We took out one, but we should assume he's been found by now."

"The traps could have taken care of more of them, too," Leo adds.

"Aye," Jean says. "But we should assume everyone is up and running, just to be safe. We need to take over the base camp; then, if your father's not there, we can head back up the mountain. Those are rough conditions to fight on, though."

"I think they're probably headed back already," Leo says. "They know we escaped. They can assume we have the rings. They're going to come back and start hunting us."

"It's nearly dark," Jean says. "And they have your dad, which will slow them down. If we're quick and quiet, we can take out a bunch of them on the edges before Luke is back. Here's where they'll be positioned, too." She makes some marks on the map. "Then we can wait and spring on the last four and Luke when they get back."

"We'll have to move fast, though," Leo says. "And I think it should be me and Ten who do it."

"Aye," Jean says. "More muscle in the arms, easier to choke them out. No time for bows and arrows, I'm afraid."

"So, let's go," Leo says.

Jean slips off the ring and hands it to me, laughing. "I sounded proper military, didn't I? So strange knowing all that, and then unknowing it."

I take the ring and put it on. The plan they've outlined suddenly becomes crystal clear. "Leo and I will take out the pairs as pairs," I say, nodding. "The guards stationed around HQ are two inside, and then one at each corner around the rectangular area. Leo and I will move to take out the two on the east, then the west, then the two inside the tent. We'll move as one. We can do that now. Don't even need to sing ABBA."

"Exactly," Leo says, grinning.

"Jean, you stay behind us, low to the ground."

"I'll do my best," Jean says, looking much more nervous than either Leo or me.

I hand her the camera. "Wear this, too. I know even if we make it out of here alive that Dad probably won't put it on the show, but if we don't . . . I want people to see. These rings."

She nods and slips the camera strap over her neck.

I don't feel nervous. Maybe I should, but I don't. The Sacred Band of Thebes did stealthy missions like this hundreds of times to weaken enemy forces. So I've done it hundreds of times, too. Except not really, I realize, a little nervousness creeping in.

Leo turns to me and puts his hand on my shoulder. "We can do this," he says. I nod. I know he's right.

We step out of the office. Between the rain and the sun going down, it's dark now. A blue-gray darkness that's turned all the bushes and plants on the island into shadows, and turned every shadow long and perfect for hiding. And I know how to hide in them now. So does Leo. We hike back up to the mainland and head for where Jean had said the base camp was.

"Hey," Leo whispers. "I just wanted to say, again—"

"Don't apologize," I say. "I know. And I was stupid to be so mad. I think just with my dad and everything . . . no, that's an excuse. I was mad. I wanted you to believe in me."

"I do!"

"I know. But you were also scared. And I get that, too."

"Yeah. Funny. We get everything now. It feels better than I thought. It's not like we're the same person."

"We just understand each other," I say, knowing he was about to say it. He smiles in the dark and I feel it without looking at him.

"Wait," he says, as we approach the camp. "Before we do this."

"What?" I turn to him, and he takes my face in his hands and kisses me. It feels electric. Not just filled with desire, but with faith, too, and comfort and a need for comfort. It feels like everything we both needed.

"For luck," he says.

I laugh softly. "All right, I'll take northeast, you take southeast?"

"Yeah," he says. "Click your tongue when you're in place." He takes my hand and squeezes it. We can't speak now and need to move separately so we don't draw too much attention. We're coming from southeast, so I turn north. I watch Leo keep heading west. He's practically invisible in the low light. I hope I am, too.

It's weird, letting instinct take over, knowing exactly what to do. There's no list of choices in my head because the Sacred Band knows what choice to make—they calculate faster than I could, use their experience. I see which shadows are big enough to hide me without even thinking, I spot loose pebbles that will make noise, even in the dark, and I know exactly how to move my body. And weirdly, it doesn't hurt, like my body is used to it, too. Because crouching this much and walking like this normally would have my legs aching by now.

HQ is a large camo tent, big enough for several beds, that they've put up at the edge of the woods. Inside is lit up, but the tent is dark enough it's not making the forest around it glow. I spot the two guards on the east side. They're about ten feet out from the corners of the tent. They can see each other, but only if they're looking—too many trees and shadows in the way, which is good for us. The northeastern guard, the one I'm going to take out, is easy to see because he's smoking a cigarette, something my ring-brain isn't sure what to do with. I only have the former wearers of the ring in my head, after all, and cigarettes weren't a big part of ancient Greek life. I can translate what they think into modern thought, but I can't get my understanding of the modern world back to them. So I wonder what will happen when I approach him from behind and put my arms around his throat. Will it fall and start a fire? Will it burn me? I don't know. It's an equation the band I'm wearing can't do.

I watch him a moment more. He tosses the cigarette into the dirt and steps it out.

I'm not worried anymore.

I creep around behind him, waiting for his eyes to turn left before I move at him from the right, or right before I move in front of him.

When I'm finally in place I click my tongue once. It sounds so loud, disturbingly loud to me, like he must know I'm there now, but he just turns briefly to me, and seeing nothing, turns back. It's just another sound of branches creaking, or a bird maybe.

After five seconds, which is the right number to wait, I know, I stand quickly and place my arms around his throat and pull him back toward me. He grunts but can't call out. He kicks behind him, but I knew he would do that and dodge. He pulls at my arms, but I keep them tight with a strength I didn't know I had. Or maybe didn't have.

It doesn't take long for him to go limp, passing out, but I keep my arm around him about a minute longer. If I release too soon, he'll come to in less than a minute.

Once I've let go, I check him. His gun is still slung around his back, where he couldn't reach it, and he has some zip ties, which I put around his wrists and ankles. I'm not super sure how they work, but they feel tight enough. Then I take his belt and hat off and stuff the hat in his mouth, tying it in place with the belt, to make a gag. When he comes to, he'll be immobile and silent.

I look up over at the other guard south of the tent. Leo is standing over him. I know he did everything I did. I know we did it in perfect unison.

I look down at the guard and suddenly realize exactly what I've just done. I choked a man into unconsciousness. I could have killed him. What if I did? I bend down and check he's breathing. He is. He's alive. Just . . . going to be in pain when he comes to. Like a bad hangover. And I did that. I pick up his gun and move quietly away from him, burying it, just in case. He might have killed me, I remind myself. Or Leo, or my dad. These aren't good people.

I sneak away from the tent, this time to the south, where I meet Leo again.

"You all right?" he asks.

I nod. "You?"

"Rattled. I've been in fights before but . . ."

"Yeah," I say. "But we have to, right? And we're not killing them."

"Did you bind your guy and gag him?"

"Yes. And I buried his gun a distance from him." I point a little.

"Me too. It was like . . . I didn't know how to use it, but I knew it was a weapon, so I wanted it hidden."

"Same with me. It's weird having all this in my head."

"But it makes me feel so . . ." He takes my hand.

"Yeah," I say.

"I feel like I know new things to do besides fight, too," he says, his mouth close to my ear.

I try not to laugh and turn and kiss him. "Let's get through this first," I say. "Then we can test out some ancient Greek sex positions."

"Deal," he says. "I'll take the north this time."

"Be careful. Click when you're in place."

He nods and we separate again. Maybe because we've done it once already it's easier this time. I just trust my body and get in position. Soon as I hear the click, I'm up, my arm over his throat again. Again he tries to fight back and I dodge his elbow and foot, knowing what he'll be doing. And again he's down in just a few seconds, and I hold it awhile longer before tying him up, gagging him with his own belt and sock (he didn't have a hat) and burying his gun.

Leo and I meet in the bushes on the far side of the tent. The flap is closed, but we can see the two figures inside. One is lying down, gesturing at the sky. The other is sitting.

"They don't look like they're facing away," Leo says. "This will be harder."

"They look unarmed, though," I say. "Or at least their guns are on the ground or something. We should tackle them. Pin them down fast, then choke them."

"I know."

I smile. "So we have to burst through at the same time."

"The flap doesn't look zippered at least."

"Enjoying the breeze," I say with a sigh. It is a nice breeze. This is not how I want to be spending the night. But then I think about Luke with these rings, with this power, and I think of Dad, bleeding, and how I still need to yell at him.

"You ready?" Leo asks. "Let's do this."

"You take the one lying down," I say.

"Are you sure? That'll be easier and I'm bigger than you." He pats his belly.

I kiss him lightly on the cheek. The one lying down is safer, and this is all my fault anyway. "I'm sure," I say.

We quietly approach the tent. The entrance flap is hanging half open. To the right is the standing man; to the left, the person lying down. They're talking. The one lying down is a woman.

"They'll be back soon," the man is saying. "You should put on your shoes."

"Yeah, yeah," she says back to him. "I haven't slept in almost forty hours. I was at the end of my guard shift when Luke told me to get on the plane. Just give me a second here."

I look over at Leo, who nods. I jump into the tent, charging at the man. He stares at me for a moment before throwing his hands up to block me, but I have enough momentum to topple him. I land on top, taking the wind out of him, but his hands are still up, wrestling me back. I grab at his wrists and block his punches, tightening my knees around his waist and using the ground as leverage to push him down. In one hand I grab his wrist and in the other I press my forearm down on his throat. Once it's there, I know I've won. His hands get free and try to shove me off but he's out quick as the rest of them. It's strange how easy it is. Maybe not psychologically. Knowing I could kill him is . . . unsettling, and I'm glad the band isn't making me feel like I have to. But just knowing how competent I am at something I haven't thought about before, just because of some jewelry—that's weird. It's like playing a video game. I just press a button for an action and then my body takes over and does it.

Leo is already tying the woman up. I start tying the man up, and I'm not even done when Jean comes in.

"It's easy to see why Luke wants the rings so badly," she says. "You are . . . machines, almost. I watched from a distance, and it was just like seeing shadows come up from the ground to take the guards outside down."

Leo and I are quiet. I know he feels as weird about our new abilities as I do.

"It's just the rings," I say, reassuring both of us.

"Yeah," Leo says. "Now we need to get ready for Luke."

"For me?"

I swallow and turn to the open tent flap. Because of the angle, all I can see outside are feet. But the voice was Luke's. I glance at Leo and Jean, then step outside.

Luke is holding Dad upright, a gun to his head, Dad wobbling on his one good leg. His men are on either side of us, guns aimed at the tent.

"People in the tent are pretty clear if you forget to turn out the light," Luke says. "We could see your whole little shadow play from quite a distance."

I glare as Leo and Jean step out behind me. Then I focus on Dad. He looks pale, like he's in a lot of pain. And the bandages around his leg are a dark red.

"Can you take them?" Jean whispers.

Luke shoves the barrel of his gun into Dad's temple. "I think not. Not without losing your father, at least. Plus anyone else who gets hit by a bullet." He looks at Jean. "Gun down," he says to her, and she takes the stolen rifle she'd had on her back off and lays it on the ground. "Disappointing, Jean. You promised us you'd find the rings, and now you're helping children escape with them."

"I thought they weren't real . . . ," Jean says.

"Clearly they are," Luke says, glancing at my hand. "I assume they work, too. That you're warriors now. That's how you took out six of my men?"

"Maybe we could do that before," I say.

"I'm shocked your father let you carry them. I guess you were a good mule to get them off the island. But they came back for you, Henry. Isn't that cute?"

Dad stares at me, sad. "Sorry, Tenny," he says. "But I'm glad you found them."

"So, hand them over," Luke says. He nods at one of his men, who steps forward, hand open. There are only six of them. Luke can't move his gun from Dad. I wonder how fast Leo and I can work. If we can kick and punch. I know we can take them out. It'll take a minute at most. But the guns . . . I don't know about the guns. How they'll work in this, how they'll factor into the fight. If they were spears or bows, I'd be able to figure it out, but guns . . .

1. Fight. Maybe Dad dies. Maybe we get hurt. Maybe we win.
2. Give them the rings. Maybe we get to live. Dad gets to live.

Why am I agonizing so much over Dad? Dad, who puts the artifacts first. Dad, who only asked me back because the producers made him. Dad, who is so addicted to the adventure and the fame that he views me as just an assistant . . . and Dad, who's taken me on these adventures. Who's made me a part of this thing he loves. I hate him and I love him, and I don't know how to save him without giving up these rings, which I'm sure now are mine. My history. The history of queer people. Not for Luke.

Which makes me realize something.

There is no choice. I can't let my dad die. No matter how much I hate him, I still love him. And maybe he loved the adventures more than he loves me . . . but he still loves me, too.

I look at Leo. He nods. I take off the ring, shaking my head as my brain empties again. I feel lighter, and weaker, and suddenly so much more scared. My mouth goes dry all at once, and I put the ring in the guard's hand.

"Now give us Henry back," Jean says.

Luke rolls his eyes and pushes my dad to the ground, but keeps his gun trained on him. I run over and drop to my knees, Jean close behind me.

"Shouldn't have done that," Dad says to me. "Those are yours."

"No, they're not," I say. "They're . . . all of ours. All queer people's."

"Not anymore," Dad says, looking up at Luke. I follow his gaze and watch as Luke holds the ring up to the dim light from the tent. It shines as he rotates it in his hand.

"Is that a wing?" Luke asks, sounding confused. "Well . . . what does it matter if it works?" He puts the ring on, and I swallow. It's not just about all the training he has now, all the experience along with his presumably evil intentions. It's the idea of him stepping into that mind-space that the ring showed me. That interconnectedness of queer people. He doesn't belong there. It's like someone stepping into someone else's sacred space. Our sacred space. I feel dirty thinking about it. I feel dirtier knowing I gave him the key.

"Well," he says, looking around. "This is . . . not quite what I expected, but . . ." He stares at Leo. "Don't even try it. I know what you're thinking and—"

Before he can finish the sentence, though, his face turns, like he's been slapped. He rubs his jaw, looking into the space in front of him.

"No," he says. "You work for me now—"

His face turns again. This time his lip is bloody. His men look around at each other, confused. He grunts, and curves forward like he's been punched in the stomach and then looks up, eyes filled with rage. He glares at me.

"What did you do?" he shouts, spittle and blood flying from his face. "Why won't they—"

Suddenly, his chest thrusts forward, his shoulders back, and he holds like that for a moment, his eyes wide with shock. A hole opens over his heart. It's a long, wicked slice, like something has gone through him. Blood spurts from the wound. The men look around, trying to spot the weapon. Some point their guns at us, but Jean holds out her hand, motions for them to lower them, and they do.

Luke falls to his knees and looks behind him. "No, stop," he says, his voice thick with blood.

He seems to be hit again, his arm suddenly with a gaping hole in it. He clutches it with his other hand as he starts to fall. I stand and pull back from him, carrying Dad, trying to keep him out of the way of whatever is happening. Jean stays, though, staring at Luke, her eyes wide. The camera around her neck glints in the dim light, capturing Luke crying out in pain as a new hole appears in his side. He falls to the ground, his eyes going glassy, and then his head splits down the middle. Everyone flinches back, even the soldiers.

"What is happening?" Dad asks.

"I don't know," I say. We're nearly behind the tent now and I look back. Everyone is staring at Luke—well, at his body—which is bleeding out on the ground. I don't look at it, though. It's gruesome.

"Some things just aren't for straight people," Jean says, a smile in her voice.

I nod. That's what I'd been hoping for. That the rings wouldn't work for him. But I didn't think they would kill him.

The guards turn to her, confused, but while everyone had been staring at Luke, Leo had been moving. I didn't even see it, but now he's behind all the guards and in a series of punches and kicks, he's taking them down. A fist to the head here, a foot to someone's back. No one even has time to draw their gun on him before he's sent it flying from their grip. He moves so fast he's almost blurry. Is that how I looked wearing the ring? It's scary, inhuman . . . and kind of hot.

When the soldiers are all down and staying down, he stands over them, breathing heavily. He and Jean start tying them up.

"Show me the body," Dad says, trying to stand. I help him over to Luke's body. What's left of it, anyway. It's been punctured more times than I can count. Viscera, organs, and blood spill out of the holes in him.

"I don't know what happened," I say.

"It was the Sacred Band," Leo says, walking over to us. "They killed him."

"Just for being straight?" Dad asks.

"I think more for . . . wanting to hurt queer people. For wanting to take the rings away. They sensed his every intention. He just wanted the power—not the connection. So they killed him."

I reach down and pull the ring off his severed finger, then wipe it off on my shirt. I show it to Dad. "It's amazing," I say.

Dad holds up his hand, pushing the ring back at me. "But not for me, I think," he says. "But I want you to tell me all about it."

❧ SEVENTEEN ❧

I tell Dad everything on the plane. The feeling we have wearing the rings. The community and connectedness and how it's not like reading someone's mind, but just knowing them so well that you know what they're thinking. About how wearing the ring makes me feel my history, know it, and feel my community, too—everything I'd hoped the rings would do! Just much more magical.

Jean had found Sonny and the plane hidden under some bushes, east of where we landed. He had apparently seen Bulwark pulling in, covered the plane with leaves and dirt to hide it, and then just waited inside.

"I knew you'd come to get me, little man," he'd said when we'd found him.

We'd charted a course for Alexandria, Egypt, because Dad knew a doctor there with her own clinic who wouldn't ask too many questions (he said he knew her from "exploring a tomb together," which I decided was literally what they did and not a metaphor, no matter how gross Dad's smirk was when he said it). I'd called Mom again on the plane and she'd just woken up to my message and was freaking out, so she was glad she just had to book a plane ticket to meet us there. When we landed she showered me with kisses and hugged me so I couldn't breathe before I got to tell her everything: the rings, Bulwark.

"That's . . . more adventure than I wish you'd had," she'd said as we'd waited outside the exam room where Dad was with the doctor. "But you're safe. That's what matters."

"And I have the rings," I said.

"How do you feel about that? Is it everything you wanted?"

"I don't know," I said, feeling them in my pocket. "Yes? Sort of? I want more, though, too."

Mom smiled. "I want that for you, too."

Jean and Mom handled the Greek authorities and let them know about Bulwark and the men still on the island. Jean didn't tell them more than that, or give her name. She wants to go back to the Temple of Iolaus and finish her dig without any more distractions. The money to finish was already in her account, and now she's technically fulfilled her end of the bargain—Luke had the rings. There's video proof. It's not her fault he couldn't hold on to them.

Leo and I wait in the clinic where Dad's doctor friend, Imaan, has bandaged him up and given him some painkillers. Mom and Jean are in the hall, talking to Imaan, while Leo and I sit, watching Dad get more and more stoned.

"It's so cool you have that," Dad says, staring at me.

"Have what, Dad?" I ask, looking at Leo.

"The rings. That—" He pauses, and I wonder if he's going to fall asleep. "That, like, place it takes you."

"Oh." I grin. "Yeah."

"I've always been jealous of that, I think, since you came out," he says. His words are sloshing around.

"Of magic rings?"

"No, of family," Dad says. "You have this whole family, you haven't even met all of them. My only family is you."

He reaches out a hand to me from his bed and paws at the air until I take it.

"I'm going to go call my sister again with the satellite phone," Leo says, standing and walking out of the room.

"You know, the first girl I took adventuring wasn't nearly as cool as he is," Dad says.

"Okay." I stop him before it gets any weirder. "Dad. Why didn't you tell me the producers wanted me back?"

Dad pulls his hand back and turns to look up at the ceiling. "I should have, maybe. They didn't insist on it, you know. They just said ratings were down and you coming back would be good. They wanted you back. And . . . I wanted you back, too. That's real, you know that, right?"

"You didn't talk to me for two years," I say. I can feel the emotions rising in me again, that knot adding new twists. My face shakes a little, tears brimming up, some mudslide about to roll down my cheeks. "Two years."

Dad lets out a long sigh. "I'm a bad father." He pauses like I'm supposed to disagree, but I don't know if I can. "I never thought I'd be one, you know? I thought it would just be me and exploring and adventures and, like, new friends."

"Women you met on your adventures," I correct.

"Yeah, well . . . you did the same thing, right?" I don't say anything. "The point is, I never imagined kids. I never imagined family. I mean, you know, my folks died when I was in my twenties. It had been over a decade of just me before your mom got pregnant. And then she wanted to keep you. And . . . I'm glad she did, but I was surprised, you know. I didn't want to give up the life I had. I liked it being so free. It was easy. Lonely, maybe . . . but not as much as you might think." He pauses and smiles.

"So you never wanted me?"

He turns to me. His eyes are foggy. "Your mom is one of the most amazing people I know, Tenny. I told her she'd have to raise you on her own, and she said sure. She was fine with that. But she always invited me back for the holidays, and when you were born, and—" He sighs. "It's hard to explain. It's not like I saw you and suddenly wanted to be a dad. But . . . you were cool. Even as a baby, you were curious and your mom would set up these little foam blocks like temples for you when I was there. I think that was because she wanted me to correct her and fix them and get you involved. We made this big pillow fort when you were like two, and you loved it. Oh man. So did your mom. After you went to bed, we—"

"Dad."

"Right, sorry. So . . . you were cool. And you liked my stories. And I liked it, being a sort-of sometimes dad. But it was weird, too, because I kept thinking of you while I was away. I was in this sunken fortress in Norway, and I remember thinking to myself, okay, how am I going to tell this story to Tenny? And I'd never worried about that before. I mean, I always knew how I'd tell the story to an audience, I know how to talk to the camera, but you—you're better than a camera or a crowd of people. Seeing your eyes light up . . ." He closes his eyes and doesn't open them for a few seconds. I take a breath. The emotions in me are lighter, somehow, like one of the knots has come loose, and I can pull it completely free, if I want to.

"Dad," I say.

His eyes flutter open. "Huh?"

"So why did you leave me for two years, then?" I ask. "If my eyes light up better than a crowd of people?"

"Oh." He frowns. "Because you hated me."

I shake my head. "What?"

"You yelled at me, Tenny. You called me names and said what I did was immoral and all the other things I get called by people all the time. But from you . . ." He stops, and for a moment I think he might cry, but he shakes his head. "It was a lot worse. So much worse."

I stare at him. My limbs suddenly feel like shooting out in all directions. I want to explode. My dad is a child. That's always been the issue here. He's a child who was having a tantrum.

"But you didn't even argue with me, Dad," I say. "You didn't explain, you just . . . walked away."

"Because I knew you were done with me."

"Done with you?"

He shrugs, a slow, rolling movement. "You were so angry, Tenny. And you were so righteous. So I decided we were done."

"I'm your son."

"Like I said, I'm a bad father."

I sigh, the tears coming now. This is what it was the whole time? He knew it was wounded pride, hurt feelings, and so he stayed away because of that. Because he didn't like that I'd made him feel bad. He closes his eyes and seems to nod off for a while and I watch him. He is a bad father. And a good father. Both, somehow. A knot pulls free in me. But there are still a lot left.

"Dad," I say again.

He blinks open his eyes and stares at me. "I should sleep."

"Not yet. You need to say you're sorry."

"What good would that do? C'mon, Tenny. After this . . . I'm surprised you even came back for me. You should have just run with the rings."

"Just . . . apologize."

"I—" He starts to cry. "I'm sorry, Tenny. I really am. I missed you those two years, you know. I called your mom more than ever just to check how you were. I kept hoping you'd want to be my son again, but I thought with the rings, you'd have to be."

"Dad," I sigh. "I am your son. I do want to be your son. But that doesn't mean I agree with everything you do. We can still love each other. It's not like you're trying to make me not gay, or saying that I can't get married. You just think that the relics we recover are yours."

"Not mine. The world's. I just want to make sure they'll be shown off. History has to be lived, Tenny. It can't be in the back of a closet or the third shelf down in exhibit hall H. It needs stories to be told, people to listen. That's why I give my artifacts to the people who can pay. Because then history can live."

"I know," I say. "I understand your perspective. I've been thinking about it since we got on the plane."

"Yeah?" Dad asks, hopeful. "So you forgive me?"

"I think you should have talked to Mrs. Misumune. You should have let her see the katana, told her in person how you found it, what you wanted to do with it. I think she would have let you. Might have come to the exhibition."

"And if she didn't? If she wanted to put it in a closet?"

I shake my head. "I don't know. After that, I really don't know. I understand why you do what you do, I just think there's always got to be a good answer. History belongs to all of us, but it also belongs to the people whose history it is. The rings belong to me, as a queer person. They belong to Leo, as a queer Greek person. But if I give them to the Greek government, you're right, they won't get to live."

"So what are you going to do?" Dad asks.

"I'm working on it," I say, crossing my arms and putting my hand on my chin. "I have an idea. But—you're actually going to let me decide?"

"Of course. That was the deal."

"No regrets?"

"Why would I have regrets?" Dad says, wiping his tears away.

"Because I could give them to some tiny museum that doesn't let them live. That doesn't have an exhibition for you."

Dad shrugs. "I have the show. I can do some talk shows if I want to talk to people."

I narrow my eyes. "So it's really not about that?"

"What?"

I uncross my arms, wave them wide, trying to capture what I mean. "Fame," I say finally.

Dad laughs. "I told you, Tenny. I figured out years ago that telling you these stories is more important than telling them to anyone else."

I smile, crying again at that. "Okay. Then I forgive you, but I have some rules."

"Rules?"

"Yeah. First, you can't just leave anymore. You can't just go silent because we had a fight. Even if I call you names, even if I disagree with you. That's not what good dads do, and you're going to be a good dad now."

"Tenny . . ."

"Promise. You're going to try."

Dad swallows. "Okay, I promise."

"And second, we will both decide what to do with what we find next season."

Dad sits up slightly in bed, his eyes glowing. "Next season? For real, Tenny?"

"I need something to do this summer," I say with a shrug.

"So you're forgiving me, for being a thief?"

"That's number three. You're going to apologize. To Mrs. Misumune. To everyone. A statement at the end of the season about everything you just said, about history needing to live, about trying to find the right place for everything you find. And then, like I said, we're going to figure it out together."

Dad's frown fades. "But if I do that"—he pauses, swallowing—"we can keep doing this? Adventuring? Together?"

"Yeah," I say. "I'd like that."

"Then yes, that's easy. Yes."

I stand and go over to his bed to hug him. "Thank you, Dad."

"I love you, Tenny," Dad says. "I should have just . . . talked to you, I guess. Apologized. Years ago."

"Yeah, you should have," I say, holding him tightly. He smells like sand and the antiseptic cleanness of his hospital gown. "You're the dad."

"Yeah," he says, his arms around me going slack. I let go of him and he smiles at me for a moment. "Your eyes," he says, and then falls asleep. I'll probably have to remind him of those rules when he's awake and not on painkillers, but at least I feel like he was too stoned to lie. He loves me. He loves adventuring with me. He hated that I hated him, and instead of just dealing with it like an adult he walked away. Like I did after I heard about the producers, I guess. But I'm allowed, right? I'm the kid.

I stick my head out into the hall to look for Leo, but he's leaning against the door, just out of sight. I quickly wipe my face and smile at him.

"You heard all that?" I ask.

"Yeah," he says. "I'm glad you made up."

"I feel like I need to make up with you, too," I say. "I'm sorry I rushed you into the adventure. And made you feel like you couldn't tell me you were scared."

"You didn't do that," he says, putting his arms around my waist and pulling me in. "That was the show. It's a scary show."

He grins and I grin back. "Still, I say. I'm sorry. And I'm sorry I was so angry and . . ."

"I know all this. We wore the rings, remember? I know all of it. I forgive you. You forgive me."

"Yeah? That easy?"

"Easy?" He looks shocked. "How many times did we almost die getting those rings?"

I laugh. "Okay, not easy. It just feels easy."

"I think it's good when it feels easy," he says, pulling me close and kissing me. He tastes like mouthwash. He must have found some in the clinic bathroom.

"Wait," I say, pulling back after the kiss. "Are you calling me easy?"

"Want to find someplace quiet and find out?"

I laugh and look up and down the hall. "I do still have the rings," I say. "I bet there's more they can teach us."

Later, on the roof of the clinic, lying on Leo's open jacket and staring up at the stars, I put my head on his chest and weave my fingers with his. "I guess you'll be going home soon," he says.

"Yeah. Sorry."

"Don't be."

"I mean, sorry to be leaving you," I say, kissing his chest.

He laughs. "Me? Or my body?"

"Can't it be both?" I ask, moving up his neck to kiss him gently on the lips.

"Well, me you'll be able to keep in touch with. We can email and FaceTime and all of that."

"I know. And maybe we'll be back, or you can come to the opening for the rings."

"You decide where that's going to be, then?"

"I have an idea," I say, shifting so I'm staring up again.

"Going to tell me?"

"Not yet," I say. "I need to make sure I can make it happen."

My phone vibrates and rings and I reach for it in my pocket, which is above me. I pull out the phone. It's Gabe. Leo laughs. "Put him on speaker."

I answer the call. "What time is it there?" I ask.

"You called me late last time," Gabe says. "Fair's fair. You have those rings yet?"

"Yeah," I say. "It's a long story."

FIVE MONTHS LATER

I look around the gallery. It's packed. Part of that is because of me and Gabe. We'd gone around to every queer person we knew and a lot we didn't know and handed out flyers for the opening of Anika's show. I'd given them to everyone who I recognized but didn't know from the Village—the grumpy drag queen, the butches, the college students. I'd even invited everyone from the "good" queer table. Yes, even David. He didn't come, coward, but Daniela did. She's smiling politely in the back of the room, next to a camera crew.

Gabe takes my hand in his and squeezes. "You nervous?" he asks.

I shake my head. "Nah. This is easy."

"Oh, tough guy, took down men with guns, dodged spear traps, so big, so strong, can't be scared of public speaking, because it's so related to combat and physical trials."

I smirk. Since I got back, Gabe has been my best friend. Sometimes, physically, more, too, but Gabe doesn't do monogamy and I don't know if I want to for a while, either. I love him, but *in* love is something else, and since I realized I was never really in love with David, it's not something I need. I don't need to be a good queer. I don't need to practice monogamy and scale back my dramatic impulses. I'm queer. I'm part of that family. No matter how I behave.

Leo is still in Athens. He has school but he's going to join us when we go to Germany next month for the tour part. We try to talk at least once a week. He's very nervous about the public speaking. And Jean sold her book on the Temple of Iolaus. A history book! Not just a textbook, but something that'll be sold in bookstores, she thinks. Or so she told me in an email. She's going to meet us in Germany, too. She's helping Anika curate the exhibit for the rings there before going back to Greece.

In the end, the choices for what to do with the rings were all bad:

1. Give them to the Greeks, where they'd be celebrated for their Greek history but not their queer history.

2. Give them to the Schwules Museum in Germany, where they'd be celebrated for their queer history but wouldn't be in Greece.

3. Give them to the Athens Museum of Queer History and Culture, who couldn't afford to insure them and didn't have enough security, so they'd be stolen within a month.

None of those were what I wanted. I wanted them safe, and shown off, and I wanted their queer history celebrated, and their Greek history. So I came up with an idea. It took a lot of work on Anika's part, and Leo had to do a lot of convincing with his boss, but in the end I got the compromise I wanted: Technically, I gifted the rings to the Athens Museum of Queer History and Culture. But, as they can't afford to display them yet, they'll be on loan to the Schwules Museum in Berlin, who also generously paid me and Dad for our time finding them. Schwules is going to create an entire display around them, and send the rings—and me, Dad, and Leo—on tour with them. But part of the money they make off the rings will go back to the Athens Museum, where they'll put it toward creating a secure and permanent display. It might take a while before that happens, but the Athens Museum can ask for them back and lend them out to someone else at any time, if they want.

And people have been clamoring over the rings since we revealed them. They were on the cover of magazines! So was I! Just archaeological magazines, but it was still kind of cool. Me and Dad, standing there, next to the rings, which are being hailed as one of the biggest archaeological discoveries in years. Even mainstream news is reporting on them, and people are excited about this season of the show, which started airing a few weeks ago. The reviews are great.

"So did you decide where you're going to go with your dad after the tour?" Gabe asks.

"Not yet. But did you know that there was a bisexual cult leader who practiced sex magic involved with the dedication of Oscar Wilde's tomb?"

"What?" Gabe barks out a laugh. He laughs like that, in short bursts. I love it. "You're making that up."

"Nope. It's real. I'm not saying that means the tomb is somehow connected to a lost magical temple or anything, but . . ."

"But?"

"But maybe it's worth doing some research on."

"So you're turning your dad's show into just a gay history show?"

"I mean . . ." I hadn't thought of it that way. Dad is excited to let me help plan the next expedition. The next adventure. He's happy to let me lead, almost. Like all he wants is an adventure, with me, and a lost tomb and magic artifact to make him happy. I don't know whether the adventure or me on our own would make him happier, but I'm okay with the fact that it's both that makes his heart sing. And he promises our next big find—if we find anything—will go to the right people. He was impressed by how I worked out the deal with the two museums and still managed to get us paid a decent amount and a tour set up besides.

I stare at the podium in front of the crowd. Behind it is a glass case covered by a bit of pretty fabric. And behind that are a few UN Special Forces guards. Dad told them about the rings, but apparently they can't find any volunteers to try them on.

On the show, Dad kept it vague, like he always does, though I almost told him not to—to show the magic of queer community—but then no one could really see it. Us slinking through the woods, suddenly working in tandem. A lot of it wasn't even on camera, because by then we were fighting for our lives. And what we did get on film just looks like two people being very in sync. Which we were. It doesn't really look magic. The only thing really supernatural was how Luke died. Dad didn't show that—just Luke putting on the ring and then bleeding from the mouth. Then he cut to himself saying it was too graphic and disrespectful to show more.

Poison needle in the rings, most people think. Leo and I are young, our hands are small; or we knew how to put them on safely or were just lucky. But Luke was poisoned by the rings, or maybe a parasite he picked up in the temple. Or it was all faked.

But even if people knew the truth, like the UN does, I doubt anyone would want to mess with the rings. Except maybe queer people. Which is probably what the UN is most worried about. The guards are there to prevent a new queer army from rising up. As if they could stop us.

"So what are you going to say?" Gabe asks.

"I'm about to say it—you'll just have to listen," I tell him. "Oh, and make sure you get a video for Leo."

"Yes, you and Leo have both reminded me, like, twenty times today."

I roll my eyes and grin. The rings aren't technically having their own show until next month, in Germany, but when I was working out the deal with Schwules, I asked if they could be on display here, for Anika's show, for a month. If she was okay with it—which she was. It got a lot more attention for the exhibit. Right now, they're in a glass case in the center of the room, under a sheet, waiting to be seen.

Anika steps up to the podium and the murmurs in the audience die down. Gabe raises his phone to start recording. Mom, who's been wandering the room talking to colleagues, quietly finds her place on the other side of me and rests a hand on my shoulder.

"You're going to do great," she whispers.

"I am so thrilled to see everyone today," Anika says to the audience. She looks down at the little stack of cards she's holding, then back up. "I know that normally, this sort of exhibition wouldn't attract so much attention. Queer history is notable in how it's constantly erased, in how people don't know about it, how even an exhibition like this is something people turn away from. How many times have we seen historians declare two people of the same sex to be 'just friends' or that a man was really just 'a woman who masqueraded as a man'? Our history is taken from us, and then we emerge into life, queer, and feeling as though we have no history to bind us. Because history is what makes a people. And make no mistake—queer people, the queer community, we are a people. So, while I know a lot of you are here because of a particular TV show, and a particular young man over there"—she nods at me, and I grin, awkward—"I hope you'll stick around and look at everything else we've put together here as well. The pieces I've chosen reflect the huge breadth of queerness across the world, from as long ago as ancient Greece to as recent as the 1960s.

"Queerness has always been part of history, always been explored, discussed, and present, no matter how many times people have tried to cover it up or hide it away. Because we as queer people aren't born into our queer family but instead have to find and assemble it ourselves, that history is often abandoned, forgotten, or dies with us. But even when that happens, it's our job as queer people to find what's left and reassemble the pieces. Few people remember Magnus Hirschfeld and Arthur Kronfeld's Institut für Sexualwissenschaft—the Institute of Sex Research in pre-Nazi Berlin. It was founded in 1919 and became the largest library in the world for books about queerness. Hirschfeld was the first to use the word *transsexual*, which, though it may be outdated today, was a revelation at the time. He even worked with the Berlin police to create transvestite passes, which let people who wanted to wear clothing that didn't match the sex on their IDs avoid arrest." She smiles and shakes her head. "I know, not a perfect system. But a major step forward, which few people, even queer people, know about. That's because the Nazis burned the entire institute to the ground when they took over. Records of it were just wiped out. And that's the cycle we queer people face when looking for our own history. We need to sift through ashes to find the community of our past, the family of our past, and then we need to reconnect it to the community we have now. So I hope you'll spend some time here, finding those connections to our shared history and tying yourselves to them. The art in this gallery is our stories, and we should be so lucky as to know them and be able to go out into the world and tell the rest of our family, too."

She pauses and I start applauding, Mom and the rest of the crowd joining me a minute later. Anika smiles and signals me to come over. I take a deep breath and approach the podium.

"And now, to reveal to the public for the first time the rings of the Sacred Band of Thebes, here's one of the men who tracked them down, to tell us about the experience, Tennessee Russo."

The audience starts to clap again and I blush. It's silly, me being the focus of all this attention. It should be the rings. It should be the history.

"Hi," I say to the crowd, and smile. Dad is standing right in the middle of the crowd, pointing a camera at me. I'd asked him if he wanted to talk first, but he said no, I should be the one to do it. He smiles at me now, and his eyes are so bright I look away for a moment, scanning the rest of the crowd. "I know a lot of you. Not personally, maybe, but I know you. We've seen each other, recognized each other. You're family." I turn and take the fabric off the glass case, revealing the rings. "And now I'm going to tell you a little family history."

DISCUSSION QUESTIONS

1. In the opening scene, Tennessee's quick thinking saves his dad, Henry, and the katana. Even though Tennessee doesn't have time to explain his plan, his dad unquestioningly follows his instructions. What does this tell us about their relationship?

2. Tennessee and Henry only air footage that exists "at the edge of believable"—seemingly impossible footage but which can be explained away with special effects or other tricks. Why might their audience prefer "edited" video over being confronted with magical, inexplicable footage? Would it be too overwhelming to have proof that the impossible exists?

3. Why might Tennessee make a distinction between the Good Upstanding Queers at his school and other queer kids?

4. Why might Tennessee's pride pins mean so much to him? What does it mean for him to always wear them? Why do you think he notices that Anika doesn't wear hers?

5. Tennessee explains that people are always shocked his mother allows him to go on adventures with his dad. What might this say about parental gender roles that Tennessee is never asked why his dad lets him come along?

6. In what ways does his love for the New York queer community manifest in his passion for finding the Sacred Bands of Thebes?

7. How does Tennessee's involvement with the show and fame as a young child relate to the experiences of child stars and celebrities today? What can be said about his dad and the producers using him to get higher ratings?

8. Throughout *Lion's Legacy*, Tennessee frequently encounters artifacts depicting the hydra, a symbol he associates with homophobia. These moments understandably evoke powerful emotions. Are there symbols or imagery you encounter daily that induce a strong response? Why?

9. Tennessee and his dad disagree over who their found artifacts "belong" to. While Tennessee believes that, no matter what, they should be returned to their country of origin, his dad thinks they should go wherever they will be cared for best. Who do you agree with? Why?

10. Do you think Tennessee will have his own show one day? What kind of show would you want to start?

11. Even though Tennessee is confident and secure in his queer identity, how does finding and wearing the sacred rings change the way he thinks about queerness, his own and others?

12. What does finding these rings mean to Tennessee? How does the magic in the Sacred Bands relate to the bonds within the present-day queer community?

AUTHOR'S NOTE

The Sacred Band of Thebes was real. While most archaeologists and historians agree that the band was queer and composed of one-hundred-and-fifty pairs of lovers, there are still those who insist that such an army could never have existed—that it was legends, or that they weren't queer but bonded as brothers, or that they were a patchwork of other stories and only one story was about queer people, and so on. Queer history is always being erased. For more information on the Sacred Band, I recommend reading James Romm's *The Sacred Band: Three Hundred Theban Lovers Fighting to Save Greek Freedom.* What little history I have covered in this book barely scratches the surface, and I've taken fictional liberties in service to the sort of story I was telling.

And on that note, I'm sorry to tell you, the actual rings are completely fictional. Although by some accounts the Sacred Band did have commitment ceremonies of some kind at the Tomb or Temple of Iolaus, I don't know if they exchanged rings, and if they did, they probably didn't lend the Sacred Band any powers. Because the power they had—as Plato said—came from their own Eros—their own queer love. We don't need rings to be magical: in so many mythologies and ancient histories, queer people are mystical and powerful. I chose the Sacred Band for the start of this series because they weren't just a powerful queer army, they were powerful because of their queerness. They fought so mightily because of their queerness. So even without rings, we are all warriors and we are all sacred. Don't ever forget that.

Now, as with all books, I have many people to thank. This idea I had, of melding adventure, romance, and queer history into what I hope is an empowering adventure, would not be what it is without the help of so many people.

First and foremost so many thanks to my editor, Suzy, who has been my biggest cheerleader on this for ages. She's helped me with my bigger worldbuilding concerns and made sure I never lost sight of what was important—the characters and the empowerment. She's listened to me voice all my anxieties and wishes with real empathy and helped me out where she could, which with all the stuff I wanted, was probably very difficult. So thank you, Suzy, for seeing the potential in this story and making sure it got told in its best form.

As always, infinite thanks to Joy, my agent, one of my oldest and dearest friends and my staunchest defender and closest thing I have to a shrink, the poor woman. The venting I've done to you is a historical treatise all on its own, and I'm so thankful every day for getting to work with you and talk to you and just go down this absurd career road with you. I would have jumped off a cliff or lit a building on fire ages ago if you weren't there.

And my amazing film agent, Lucy, who is not only quick-witted and honest, but has been so encouraging about this project, which I was worried was cinematic without being cinema-worthy. Thank you.

And so many thanks to the team at Union Square for not just making this book happen but pushing it out there with pride: Stefanie, Shannon, Tracey, Emily, Stefanie, Scott, Marcie, Daniel, and Jenny. I'm so thrilled you're part of my team!

So many thanks to Anne, a real-life archaeologist who was willing to talk to me about real-life archaeology and tell me stories from digs and discuss the ethics of famous archaeologists who have the same name as states. I learned about very specific tech from you and you let me ramble and ask all kinds of weird questions. I probably got most of it wrong in this book, so I'm sorry about that. But it was just so helpful to talk and to know what a dig would look like and to know also what inspires an archaeologist and how history can be alive even when you're just slowly brushing away dirt in a pit for hours. And thank you so much to Justine for introducing us.

Thank you to my oldest, dearest friend Lauren, a professional ethicist, who talked through with me the ethics of treasure-hunting, and how to best balance multiple histories when deciding which to tell.

Thank you to George, my Greek sensitivity reader. I think ancient Greece, being "the cradle of modern Western civilization," is distantly my history, but I know that modern Greece, which the book takes place in, is not the same, and I'm grateful for your perspective on the way queerness is seen there, as well as your descriptions of the food I got wrong. And thank you to Bradley for introducing us.

Thank you to my amazing readers: Gus, Cory, and Adam! Your thoughts really helped me shape the book, and your encouragement really helped me when I thought this was the worst thing I'd ever written.

As always thank you to my boys: Adam, Sandy, Tom, Cale, Julian, Caleb, and Adib. Couldn't do any of this without your moral (mental) support, and to Dahlia, my best publishing gossip pal and venting buddy. Though I don't think they ever saw this book, forever thanks to my writing group: Robin, Laura, Dan, and Jesse, for keeping me on track and thinking about words. And thank you to my family for the years of unending support.

And always thank you to Chris, for being Chris.

ABOUT THE AUTHOR

L. C. ROSEN writes books for people of all ages, most recently *Lavender House*, which the *New York Times* says "movingly explores the strain of trying to pass as straight at a time when living an authentic life could be deadly" and was a best book of the year from Buzzfeed, *Library Journal*, Amazon, and Bookpage, among others. His prior novel, *Camp*, was also a best book of the year from places such as *Forbes*, *Elle*, and the *Today* show. He lives in NYC with his husband and a very small cat. You can find him online at LevACRosen.com and @LevACRosen.

COMING IN SPRING 2024!

KING'S LEGACY

BY
L. C. ROSEN

It's summer break, college applications are in, and it's time for Tennessee Russo's next adventure!

The lyre Jonathan gave King David. It was one of the things I'd found in all my research, something I'd shown Dad. It was just mentioned in a few records. A gift Jonathan gave David, a lyre he hand-carved and strung, and which David then played only for Jonathan. Jonathan his lover. A lot of people disagree on that point. After all, these are ancient figures in the Torah, the Bible. No way they were queer, right? Except they were. And not just because of their solemn promise to be *best friends*—as it's been interpreted—or because Jonathan stripped naked when giving up his throne to David—that's all just symbolic, according to straight people.

No, the thing that proved it to me was the word for love. Jonathan and David loved each other. There are a lot of words for love in ancient Hebrew. Love between parents and children, between a king and his people, between siblings. But the word used for them was only used in two other places—the love people have for god and the love between husbands and wives. Jonathan and David may have had wives, but they were lovers too. They were queer. I'm sure of it. And it's just the centuries of straight people rewriting history that's erased that.

"Okay," I tell Dad, my eyes wide. "We're going to find the lyre!" My voice goes up a little at the end and I blush.

"I'll make sure Gabe has tickets too. I'll meet you in Rome. Go pack."

"Okay," I say again. Dad hangs up and I look up at Gabe.

"What's going on?" Gabe asks. "Can I come?"

"Yes," I say, grinning. "But we're not going to Paris. We're going to Rome. To find King David's lyre."

"Who?"

"King David. From the Bible."

"Like David and Goliath?"

I nod.

"He was queer?"

"Yeah, I mean . . . people say no, but there's evidence he was. It's in the text."

"Okay, well . . . I'm still coming though?"

"Yes. Dad is getting you a plane ticket right now. He's going to email them to me. But . . . we gotta leave tomorrow."

"Tomorrow? I guess that means I have to pack now. No time for old movies."

"Sorry to cut your birthday short. I should probably head home soon."

"Yeah." He nods, then grins, wicked. "Though if you wanted to try that thing with the helmet . . ." he wiggles his eyebrows.

"Well, I guess it is your birthday."

The next morning, I meet Gabe at the gate for our flight to Rome. He's reading about King David and Jonathan on his phone.

"It says they wrote each other poetry," he says when I sit down next to him. "Why don't I know any of this?"

"Queer history, especially of Biblical figures, isn't usually taught in school. Too controversial. People get really angry."

"Yeah, I know, sometimes your mean commenters migrate over to my page."

"Sorry about that."

"Hey, I don't mind it. Price of fame, right?"

I shrug, and sip from the overpriced bottle of water I just bought. "Not my favorite part."

"You get it a lot worse."

"Well, get ready." I pull my backpack onto my lap. "After this season, you'll be even more famous."

"Whatever. I'll just go private. You should do that."

"Maybe," I say, hugging my bag. "But, like, there are so many queer kids out there who follow me and say nice things, too. I don't want to close them out. Just the assholes."

"Yeah," Gabe says.

"Oh my god, you two are so cute," says a woman suddenly standing in front of us. She takes out her phone and snaps a photo without asking permission. "Adorable."

"Hey," I say, "could you not? I didn't give permission to have my photo taken."

"Oh, like that matters," she says, rolling her eyes. "But actually, you did. In your contract. We have permission to use your image for promotional purposes for the show, and that means I get to take your photo!"

"What?" I ask. "We?"

"Oh riiiiight." She shakes her head like she's a funny dizzy sitcom character. "Sorry, sorry. I've talked with your dad so many times, and

I follow you on all the socials, and I've watched last season like three times, so I forgot you don't know me, even if I know you. I'm Sterling! Your new producer and camerawoman extraordinaire!" she grins wide and fake. I look her over. She's white, older than me, but not as old as Dad, maybe in her thirties, and her blonde hair falls to her shoulders, where it's curled a little, and the ends are pink. She's got black cat-eyed glasses, a black leather moto jacket, skinny jeans, and a white tee. Her roller bag is bright purple. I frown. Roller bags aren't great for adventuring. To get to the hotel, sure, but you want a backpack for running around.

"Camera equipment," she says, catching my stare. "Special case, foam inserts. Not trusting it to luggage handlers, though."

"Okay," I say. "I'm going to check this with my Dad though."

"She sounds like who I talked to," Gabe says as I call my Dad.

"Hey! You at the airport?" Dad asks. "I think a bunch of people are going to be looking for this harp."

"Yeah," I say, "and there's a woman here saying she's our new camerawoman and producer?"

"Oh, right, Sterling," Dad says. "Sorry, forgot to tell you. They insisted we bring someone along so the camera isn't as shaky. We've FaceTimed once or twice. She seems all right. Knows her stuff. Wanted me to wear foundation, though. So maybe she doesn't realize what she's in for."

"Thirties or forties?" I ask, looking Sterling over, who crosses her arms when I say "forties." "Pink hair tips?"

"Yeah, that's her."

"All right," I say. "I'll see you soon."

"Meet you at the airport. Try to sleep on the plane, we're going to head out right away."

"Okay."

I hang up and look at Sterling, whose eyebrows are raised, waiting.

"Nice to meet you," I say.

"You too!" She sits down next to me and a I catch a whiff of peppermint. "I'm so excited to be on this show. I think since you came back last season we have a real angle to work with. Like your dad is great for the academics and the Gen X crowd, but a younger audience, millennial, Gen Z, they are SO into this LGBTQ plus stuff, it makes the archaeology thing new. Like, this isn't just some guy in temples with old stuff. This is the history of people that's been erased."

"You could do that with people of color, too," Gabe says.

"Right," Sterling says, still smiling. "But honestly, then we'd lose some advertisers. Love is Love is a great brand, but BLM is more . . . controversial."

Gabe stares at me and I stare back, our eyes wide.

"Wow, really saying the quiet part out loud," Gabe says. "What if we were going after the history of trans folks?"

"Yeah, that wouldn't be great for us, either. Cis white gays are what sells." She shrugs, but doesn't look apologetic. "Look, it's not like I like it. But my job is to manage the brand and make sure our sponsors are happy."

"Well, I don't think of it as a brand, exactly," I say carefully. "This is history. And I like researching queer history because it's mine. Dad wanted me back, and he said I get to pick what we go after. This is what

I'm interested in and feel like I should be bringing to light. I'd love to get into the history of queer cultures of color, or trans history, but I think then I would want a queer person of color or trans person to be part of—"

"Right, sure." Sterling waves me off. "I get it. You love it. But it is a brand, whether you want it to be or not. A brand is what gets advertisers, and advertisers pay for marketing, and that means more people who watch and more people who learn about this history and stuff. Which you want, right? So let me handle the branding. In fact, let's go over your socials. I saw you don't have a Twitter, and we need to get you one, stat."

"I have my Instagram," I say, but she keeps talking.

"And what about a TikTok? You two can do all those couple challenges."

"We're not a couple," Gabe says.

"What? Yes you are. You're so cute together."

"We're best friends," I say. I don't add that sure, sometimes we have sex. But Gabe doesn't want to be tied into something and honestly, with the show, neither do I. I love Gabe, but I'm not in love with him. When we make out or sleep together, that's not romantic. It's fun.

"What? No." She takes out her phone, her smile dropping for the first time, and starts scrolling through Instagram. "See?" She holds up a photo I posted a while ago, Gabe kissing me on the cheek, close to the lips, as I laugh because he was also surprise tickling me at the time. "Did you break up?"

"I kiss my friends," Gabe says. "Do you not kiss your friends?"

"Not like that," she says, making it sound dirty, somehow.

"So you're straight, then," Gabe says, smiling.

"I feel like that's supposed to be a dig, but yes, I'm straight," she says tucking her hair behind her ears. But I love you queers so much, that's why I wanted on this show. And because you two are so cute. C'mon, snuggle up." She leans back holding her phone like a camera.

Gabe and I don't move.

She sighs. "Fine." She puts the phone away. "But really, your cuteness and coupledom is part of the appeal right now, so don't go, like, announcing the breakup on socials, okay?"

"We didn't break up because we were never together," I say. "Am I in a cartoon? You feel like a cartoon."

"Huh?" she looks at me confused, and I shake my head. I don't like this at all.

"Okay, well, we're going to go over more research on the lyre now," I say, taking my own phone out. "I can talk about that for the camera, if you want."

"Yeah . . ." she tilts her head. "Yeah, sure, okay, that's part of the formula. And I don't know anything about it, honestly. Your dad just texted last night and was like 'new plan!' but I just go with it, you know? Follow adventure."

"Sure," I say. I look around for a seat and find one with just the window behind it, no people, and sit down in it. Gabe comes over but stands with Sterling, looking at me. He grins.

"I get to see this happen!" he says.

Sterling opens her wheelie bag up and gets out her camera. It's a nice one, but too unwieldy for running around, and heavy too. I hope she has others. If she doesn't, I do, at least. Small waterproof ones.

The kind that have always worked fine before. She points the camera at me and when I see the little green light go off, I smile, and turn on the charm.

"So we're going for the Lyre that Jonathan gave King David," I say. "You might not think that's queer history, but it is. People always try to act like queer people weren't in the Torah or Bible, but—"

"Wait." Sterling lets the camera slump. "The Bible? You're making the Bible gay now?"

"I'm not making anything gay," I say. "It always was. I'm just not participating in erasing that queerness. I'm not making it straight. That's what most people do."

She blinks a few times. "Okay, look, I agree with you, but I just want to say that this could be a little . . . controversial. Like, ancient Greeks, sure, everyone knows they were kinda gay. And Oscar Wilde? Yes, no problem. But the Bible?"

"Not the *whole* Bible," Gabe says. I smirk.

"Still," she says. "People aren't going to like this. This isn't good for advertising. Maybe we can change our flights?"

"We get to choose the artifact," I say. "I read the contract."

She frowns. "I guess you do, but is there anything I can say to convince you this is a bad idea? I mean . . . surely you can't really prove they were gay, right? We'd know about it, then."

"No, we wouldn't," I say. "That's the point. Hold up your camera and I'll tell you the queer history though."

She sighs and puts the camera back up. The green light goes back on, and while we wait for our flight, I talk; about the word for Love, and how Jonathan's Dad was so keen to get David married, and hated

David, too. I go through the books, starting with Tom Horner, and explain how people have thought this since Stonewall, and probably way before. I bring up art on my phone depicting them, art that shows them looking like romantic partners in love; a French illuminated manuscript from 1290, a Goez illustration from the 1700s, a Victorian stained-glass window from Edinburgh. This idea has been present for centuries. Everyone keeps seeing it even as everyone tries to deny it. David and Jonathan is a love story. And when I'm done explaining all that to the camera, I smile, and say "and that's why it's queer history. This lyre was a love token. A gay one. And we're going to find it."

I wait for the little green light to turn off. I'm done. But instead she keeps filming.

"So what would you say to devout Christians who think what you're saying is a lie?" She asks.

"I'd tell them to do the research themselves. And that if they want to keep believing Jonathan and David were just close friends who got naked and wrote each other romantic poetry, then I'm not going to stop them from thinking it. But this is my history, no matter how much they want to deny it."